ESCAPE FROM ATLANTIS

ALSO BY
KATE O'HEARN

THE PEGASUS SERIES
The Flame of Olympus
Olympus at War
The New Olympians
Origins of Olympus
Rise of the Titans
The End of Olympus

THE VALKYRIE SERIES
Valkyrie
The Runaway
War of the Realms

THE TITANS SERIES
Titans
The Missing
The Fallen Queen

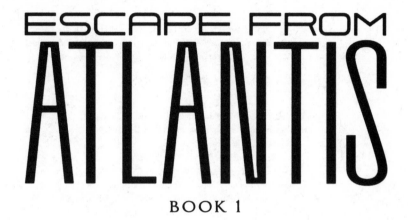

ESCAPE FROM ATLANTIS

BOOK 1

KATE O'HEARN

ALADDIN

NEW YORK   LONDON   TORONTO   SYDNEY   NEW DELHI

ALADDIN

An imprint of Simon & Schuster Children's Publishing Division
1230 Avenue of the Americas, New York, New York 10020
First Aladdin hardcover edition December 2021
Text copyright © 2021 by Kate O'Hearn
Jacket illustration copyright © 2021 by Devin Elle Kurtz
Wave illustration by Pannawish Jarusilawong/iStock
All rights reserved, including the right of reproduction in whole or in part in any form.
ALADDIN and related logo are registered trademarks of Simon & Schuster, Inc.
For information about special discounts for bulk purchases, please contact Simon & Schuster
Special Sales at 1-866-506-1949 or business@simonandschuster.com.
The Simon & Schuster Speakers Bureau can bring authors to your live event.
For more information or to book an event contact the Simon & Schuster Speakers Bureau
at 1-866-248-3049 or visit our website at www.simonspeakers.com.
Jacket designed by Karin Paprocki
Interior designed by Mike Rosamilia
The text of this book was set in Adobe Garamond.
Manufactured in the United States of America 1121 FFG
2 4 6 8 10 9 7 5 3 1
Library of Congress Cataloging-in-Publication Data
Names: O'Hearn, Kate, author.
Title: Escape from Atlantis / Kate O'Hearn.
Description: First Aladdin hardcover edition. | New York : Aladdin, 2021. |
Series: Atlantis ; 1 | Audience: Ages 8 to 12 | Summary: "When Riley and her family are stranded
on the mythical island of Atlantis, they'll have to uncover its secrets in order to
find a way home." —Provided by publisher.
Identifiers: LCCN 2021021978 (print) | LCCN 2021021979 (ebook) |
ISBN 9781534456914 (hardcover) | ISBN 9781534456938 (ebook)
Subjects: CYAC: Atlantis (Legendary place)—Fiction. |
Fantasy. | LCGFT: Fantasy fiction.
Classification: LCC PZ7.O4137 Es 2021 (print) | LCC PZ7.O4137 (ebook) |
DDC [Fic]—dc23
LC record available at https://lccn.loc.gov/2021021978
LC ebook record available at https://lccn.loc.gov/2021021979

For my two brothers
who always have my back

ESCAPE FROM
ATLANTIS

1

RILEY GAZED OUT OVER THE SEEMINGLY endless ocean. The water was calm as their sailboat, the *Event Horizon*, cut smoothly across the surface. Above them the sky was cloudless and the kind of blue she never saw at home. She inhaled the clean, salty air and felt a sense of peace wash over her. This was the start of their second week out on the boat with one more week facing them.

"Lunch!" Her father appeared at the hatch that led down to the lower deck.

"Coming." Riley walked confidently along the smooth deck and made it to the hatch. She paused long enough to call to her aunt, who was at the helm. "Aunt Mary, I'll eat quickly and then take over, if you like."

"Thanks, Riley. Go enjoy yourself."

When she reached the small galley, her father said, "I don't know where your cousin is."

"He's probably in his cupboard."

"Cabin," her father corrected. "Go get him before the food gets cold."

Riley nodded and walked toward the back of the boat where the cabins were. She liked to tease her father and call them cupboards because that was about the size of them. She knocked on Alfie's door but heard no response. "Alfie, it's lunch."

Riley walked down to her own cabin and opened the door. There she saw her cousin sitting on her bunk, reading her diary.

"What are you doing in here, Creep? Give that back!"

Riley rushed at her cousin as he held her diary aloft. His teasing smile broadened farther as he climbed on her bunk and held the book high above her head.

"Alfie, give it back!"

"Oh, poor little Shorty isn't having any fun. . . ." He opened the diary to her last entry and started to read aloud. *"I hate my life. I hate this boat and I hate the ocean. I just want to go home and be with my friends. . . ."*

Riley snatched at her diary, but Alfie kept pulling it away and taunting her with it. Finally, her frustrations got the better of her, and she hauled back and punched her cousin in the stomach as hard as she could.

Alfie dropped the diary, collapsing onto the bunk, gasping for breath.

Just as Riley picked the book up, her father burst into her cabin. "What's going on in here?" When he saw Alfie lying on Riley's bunk, he rushed over. "What happened? Alfie, what's wrong?"

Her cousin's face was red as he tried to regain his breath. He pointed a shaking finger at Riley. "Sh-she p-punched me in the stomach."

Her father's eyes flashed to her. "Is that true?"

"He started it!" Riley cried. "Dad, he came in here and stole my diary. He was reading it and everything!"

Her father helped Alfie sit up on the bunk and lower his head between his knees to ease the pain. Then his ice-blue eyes landed on her. "We don't hit people—ever. Do you hear me?"

"But, Dad . . . ," Riley cried.

"No buts," he spat. "Your mother and I raised you better than that. Now, I want you to apologize to your cousin."

"What? That's not fair! He snuck in here and went through my stuff. Why should I apologize?"

"It doesn't matter what he did. You don't hit people! Apologize to Alfie."

Riley looked from her father to her despicable cousin and back to her father again. The expression on her dad's face said he wasn't going to back down.

Riley gritted her teeth. "Okay, I'm sorry. . . ." She turned and ran out of her cabin and up the small steps to the upper deck, muttering, "I'm sorry I didn't push you off the boat . . . !"

Bitter tears of frustration were stinging her eyes as she sat down at the pointed front end of the boat with her legs dangling over the side. This was as far away from the others as she could get, but it wasn't far enough.

"You okay up there, Riley?" Mary called.

Riley had her back to her aunt and didn't want to answer. She didn't want Mary to see her tears.

"Riley?" Mary called.

"I'm fine!" Riley snapped. But she wasn't fine. She wanted to go home. Instead she was trapped on the boat for another two weeks with her father, aunt, and cousin.

This was meant to be a family-bonding trip, since she hadn't seen her relatives in over a year. She loved her aunt Mary very much but hated Alfie. He was twelve, making him just a year younger than her. But he was already taller and stronger and took every opportunity to prove it.

When the trip was first announced, Riley thought her mother and brother, Danny, would be going. But her mother couldn't leave her job at the hospital. She was a doctor with a lot of patients that needed her. Danny didn't want to go. At sixteen, he was given the choice. Riley wasn't. So instead of spending her spring break at home with her friends, she had to go on this stupid trip.

Aunt Mary was recently divorced and going through a hard time with Alfie. The five-week voyage around the Bahamas was meant to clear things up between them. Maybe it was working for Mary, but being stuck on the sailboat with Alfie was ruining Riley's life.

From the moment they left their home in Denver, Colorado, Riley had a bad feeling about the trip. By the time they'd flown to Miami, Florida, and made it to the port and their sailboat, her premonition came true.

The first thing Alfie did when he saw her was pat her on the head and call her *Shorty*. Since then, the teasing had been nonstop—but only when her father or aunt weren't around.

Gazing into crystal clear ocean, Riley wondered how things could get any worse. As tears trickled down her cheeks, she saw the sunlight glinting off something reflective in the water. It was there, and then it wasn't. She watched the spot, and again the sun caught the silvery sparkle of fish scales. It was a tail. A long one. As the fish moved, Riley gasped. The silver tail trailed up to what looked like a torso with stubby arms and a round head covered in shaggy dark hair. As she watched, the head turned. The face was gray like the body, with two holes where a nose should be and large deep-set eyes that were as black as night. When it opened its mouth, it revealed a row of sharp, pointed teeth.

Riley was too stunned to scream. She pulled her

legs in and moved back from the edge. A moment later, the creature darted down into the depth.

"Riley?"

Riley jumped at her father's voice. Her heart was pounding ferociously in her chest, and she opened her mouth to tell him what had just happened. But then she looked back at the water and saw only the ocean. Had the creature been real? What was it? Some kind of mermaid? If it was a mermaid, it wasn't anything like the ones she'd read about in books. This was a terrifying monster. Or worse, maybe it wasn't there at all.

Riley was still shaking as she looked from the water to her father and back to the water again. Would he believe her if she told him? Considering he spent most of his life in water as a marine biologist, she doubted it.

"If you're thinking about going for a swim before lunch, forget it. That water looks pretty, but don't be fooled, it's cold and deep."

Did her father think she would actually go into the water with that sharp-toothed monster swimming around? "I—I wasn't going to," she stammered.

He sat down on the deck beside her and scooted

up to the edge until his legs were dangling over the side.

"Bring your legs in, Dad," Riley warned. She may have been angry with him, but there was no way she'd let him endanger himself if that creature was still around.

"It's fine," he said. "I won't fall in."

"What about being pulled in?" Riley said.

He smiled at her and shook his head. "I doubt anything out there would be interested in me."

"Don't be too sure," Riley warned.

He gazed into the water and sighed heavily, but then said nothing. After what seemed an eternity of silence, he said, "Did I ever tell you that humpbacks are the only whales that sing a long, complicated song that they change as they move around the world? And a male's song can be heard for hundreds of miles?"

Riley did know that because her father had told her a million times before. And when he wasn't telling her, he was listening to whale songs at full volume in his study. That's when he was home and not on some expedition. As a marine biologist, his specialty was cetaceans and he was especially obsessed with humpbacks. She figured that was why he wanted to go on this trip. Yes, for Mary and Alfie, but also to study the humpbacks during their spring migration from the Caribbean to far up north. What she really resented was her father dragging her along with him. Whales were his thing, not hers.

He continued, "Also, humpbacks are—"

"Dad, enough about the stupid whales," Riley said. "I know you love them and the ocean and all that, but I don't. To me, they're just big stinky fish."

Her father gasped. "Whales are not fish!"

"I know," Riley sighed tiredly. "They're mammals, just like us." She turned and saw the hurt her comments had caused shining in his eyes. "Dad, I'm sorry. I just don't understand why you like them so much. They're kinda pretty if you're into barnacles and stuff like that. But you spend more time on the ocean with your whales than at home with us."

He looked away and stared into the deep blue waters. Finally, he said, "You're right. I'm sorry. It was unfair of me to bring you on this research trip. But since I spend so much time away from home, I just thought it would be extra special for you and me to spend some time together."

"But we're not spending time together," Riley said. "You're always on deck with your binoculars looking for whales or you're photographing them or writing notes about them. Aunt Mary is always busy steering the boat—that leaves me stuck with Alfie. Dad, he hates me and he's doing everything he can to annoy me. You don't see it because he stops when you're around. Even today, you only noticed when I hit him and not before when it was him tormenting me."

He was still staring into the water but nodding his head. "I'll talk to him."

"Why bother? He's not going to stop no matter what you say. He's a spoiled brat, and Mary is letting him get away with everything."

"I know," he agreed. "That's why Mary asked to go on this trip. She's hoping I might be a good influence on him. . . ." He chuckled softly. "But you're right. I haven't been much of a role model for him." He turned and looked at her. "Or you."

It was Riley's turn to gaze into the ocean.

"So when did you start keeping a diary?"

Riley shrugged. "Mom gave it to me for this trip. She said writing things down on paper is different than putting them on my phone or laptop. She said a diary should be about experiences and my personal feelings—just for me to write and read."

"Is that what it is?"

Riley nodded. "Yeah, I guess it kinda is. I write down where we've been, what I've seen, and what I'm feeling—even if what I am feeling is anger at Alfie."

"So when you caught him reading it . . ."

"I lost it and hit him—just as hard as I could."

"How did that make you feel?" he asked.

Riley shrugged. "I guess it was good at first because he felt just as bad as I did. But then I started to feel guilty because I'd really hurt him."

"So no more hitting?"

"No more hitting . . . ," Riley agreed. "But I won't make any promises about kicking or maybe biting!"

He smiled at her. "Good enough."

There was another long period of silence, but this time it was a good silence. It was the silence of being comfortable and not angry anymore. Riley pulled out her cell phone from her pocket, but there was still no signal.

"We're too far out," her dad said.

"I know, I just keep checking anyway."

He laughed. "Your mom said it'd be a nightmare getting you off that thing."

"I'm not on it all the time," Riley said defensively.

"No, just most of it," he teased. "Even when there isn't a signal."

"Well, I like to stay current."

"Current?" he laughed. "You mean keeping track of what your friends are saying on that Facie . . . thingy?"

"Facebook," Riley said. "I don't use it. I was hoping to look up more about the Bermuda Triangle and the creatures that live in it. You know, like . . . mermaids?"

"Mermaids?"

Riley nodded. "My friend Lisa says that when boats or planes go into the Bermuda Triangle, they see really weird things and sometimes they even disappear completely. She says aliens live in there and destroy ships.

"When I told her where we were going, she said to be careful and not go into the Bermuda Triangle. I wanted to look it up to see how far away from it we are."

He chuckled again and shook his head. "Well, honey, I hate to tell you this, but technically speaking, we've been in the Bermuda Triangle for most of this trip." He pointed out over the water. "It spans from Miami down to Puerto Rico and over to Bermuda. But you don't have to worry. In all the times I've been in here, I haven't seen anything unusual at all—including mermaids or aliens."

Riley's eyes went big and she gasped. "We're in the Bermuda Triangle? Really?"

"Uh-huh."

"That explains it."

"Explains what?"

"Just before you came on deck, I saw something weird in the water, right here off the bow. It might have been a mermaid, but not a nice-looking one."

Her father started to laugh. "Oh, so you only like nice mermaids?"

"Dad, I'm serious. I swear I saw something in the water right before you arrived. It had a long silver tail, a gray body, and a head with big black eyes and two slits for a nose. Its mouth was full of sharp teeth. It looked right at me."

He frowned. "From what you describe, it could have been a barracuda. They have a nasty mouth full of teeth and can look very threatening. Though there aren't many cases of attacks on human. Believe me, we are more dangerous to them than they are to us."

"No Dad, it wasn't a fish. It was a—a . . ."

Her father shook his head. "Riley, you're too old to believe in mermaids. If they existed, with all the time I've spent in water, I'm sure I would have seen one by now. Trust me, there are a lot of strange creatures out there, but mermaids aren't one of them."

Riley looked back at the water. She had seen something there and it *had* seen her.

Her father tapped her on the end of her nose. "Now, how about you and I go into the galley and have some lunch?" He winked. "Though I don't think Alfie will be hungry for a while."

Riley started to get up. "I guess I should go say sorry again."

"Maybe," he agreed. "But not for a while yet—let him think about what he's done and your response to it. I've sent him to his cabin for the rest of the day as punishment for going through your things. So the rest of the day is for you and me."

"And the humpbacks," Riley added.

He rose up beside her. "Well, maybe a few humpbacks—or mermaids, if we're lucky."

2

RIGHT BEFORE BED, RILEY PULLED OUT her diary and wrote about her day, going into great detail about hitting Alfie and then seeing the mermaid. Her father may not have believed her, but she knew she'd seen something.

When she finished, she closed her diary, sealed it in the watertight bag they used for precious things on board, and put it in the small sliding cupboard mounted above her bunk. Turning off the light, she rolled onto her side and thought about the mermaid as she drifted off to sleep.

* * *

The acrid smell of burning toast woke Riley. She dressed quickly and left her cabin to find the passage filled with gray smoke.

"Dad, you've burned the toast again. . . ." She was shaking her head and walking toward the galley. "I wish he wouldn't cook; he burns everything!"

Riley was surprised to find it empty. The table was set for four, and orange juice had been poured in four glasses. On the stove was a frying pan filled with burning scrambled eggs. Turning off the heat, Riley reached for the toaster and popped out the charcoaled slices of bread.

"Dad?" she called as she opened one of the portholes to clear the smoke. "Aunt Mary?"

Receiving no answer, Riley left the galley and climbed up the wooden steps onto the deck. The wind was up and whipping back her hair. Looking around, she saw her father was at the helm and her aunt was standing beside him. They were both gazing forward with fear on their faces.

"Andrew, turn us around now!" Mary called. "Get us out of here."

Her father was already spinning the big wheel to bring the boat around. "Mary, pull in the sails.

I'm starting the engine. We've got to move."

"Dad, what's happening?" Riley called. "The toast was burned, and you left the eggs on—they've burned too."

"Not now, Riley. Go help your aunt with the sails."

"What's wrong?"

Her aunt pointed toward the front of the boat. "Look at that sky."

Riley turned and gasped. The distant horizon was filled with black-and-red scudding clouds. "What is that?"

"We don't know," Mary said.

"It's some kind of storm," her father called. "But not one I've ever seen before."

"It's like it's following us!" her aunt cried. "No matter what course change Andrew makes, it's always there."

"That's impossible!" Riley called above the howling winds. "Storms can't chase people."

"Tell that to the storm!" her father replied.

Riley had been taught how to work the sails by her father. But it was hard as they had to fight the growing winds that kept filling them. From the mainsail they moved to the foresail and kept looking over at the approaching storm.

"It's not on any of the weather charts!" her father called. "And we've lost radio contact."

Riley heard fear edging his voice. She was already feeling it in her stomach.

"Riley," Mary said. "Go below and get Alfie up. I want you both to put on your life vests."

"Are we in trouble?"

Her aunt didn't reply. But her silence said enough.

3

RILEY RAN FOR THE STAIRS AND JUMPED down to below deck. "Alfie," she shouted as she raced down the passage. She stopped before her cousin's door and pounded loudly. "Alfie, get up. There's a big storm approaching."

She heard mumbling from behind the door. Breaking ship's rules, Riley shoved open the door and ran into her cousin's cabin. Alfie was just a lump in his bed with his head beneath the covers.

"Alfie, wake up!"

Alfie pulled down the covers and shouted, "Get out of my room!" Then he pulled the covers up again.

Riley found his clothes in a heap and threw them

on the bed. "Get up, you jerk. We're in trouble from a storm."

"What storm?"

In that instant, the boat lurched to the side and Riley was thrown on top of her cousin. "That storm," she said, righting herself. "Aunt Mary says we have to put on our vests. . . ." She dropped her voice. "Alfie, I think we're in danger. That thing is huge; it's taking up half the sky."

"Where's Mom?"

"She's on deck with my dad. We've lowered the sails, and Dad is using the engines to try to outrun the storm."

Alfie threw back the covers and climbed from the bed. He was wearing the same shorts from yesterday. "Get out. I wanna get dressed."

Riley made it to the door. "Just hurry. I'm getting the life vests."

Back in the corridor, Riley struggled to reach the storage cupboard against the rocking of the boat. Her father made sure there were extra life vests stored all over the boat. But the specially named and fitted ones were here in the emergency cupboard.

Pulling out the vests, Riley also reached for the

waterproof emergency packs. Each one contained flares, a lighter, bottled water, energy bars, a small fishing kit, a mobile phone with an extra battery, and a whistle. They might not need the packs, but she felt safer having them with her.

Riley pulled on her life vest just as Alfie emerged from his cabin. She threw his to him. "Here, put this on!"

By the time she and Alfie made it on deck, the wind was even wilder. Waves were slamming into the *Event Horizon* and breaking over the railing, soaking them to the skin. The dark storm clouds were now encircling the boat, and the water had lost its calm green color and was now almost black with high-peaking waves.

"Wow!" Alfie cried, looking around. "You weren't kidding."

Riley's father and aunt were already in life vests and standing together, struggling to hold the wheel steady. Her father had to shout to be heard over the roaring winds. "Kids, get below. The waves are rising—it's too dangerous up here."

"I want to help," Alfie called.

"You help by staying below," Mary shouted. "Go now!"

Riley caught hold of her cousin's arm. "C'mon, it's getting too rough up here."

For the first time in their lives, Alfie didn't pull his arm away from her. Instead he followed Riley back to the stairs and climbed down the slippery steps. Below deck, Riley handed her cousin one of the emergency packs.

"Tie this around your waist just in case. . . ."

While she was securing her own pack, Alfie said fearfully, "In case of what?"

Just then they heard the thunderous sound of something smacking the side of the boat before everything turned sideways. Riley and Alfie were thrown to the floor as the boat rolled heavily and then righted itself again.

"What was that?" Riley cried.

"I think we hit something!" Alfie climbed unsteadily to his feet and rubbed his elbow. "Ow, I hurt my arm."

"This is bad," Riley said. "Really, really bad."

The boat was struck again, knocking it on its side. Riley and Alfie were once again thrown violently over. This time, the sailboat didn't right itself and water poured down the steps from above.

"We're sinking!" Alfie cried.

"We'll be fine," Riley said, not feeling anywhere near as confident as she forced herself to sound. "Just stay with me."

"Riley, Alfie, are you okay? Can you hear me?"

"Dad!" Riley cried. She looked back to the steps and saw her father's arm reaching down. "What's happening?"

"Something big just hit us and we're capsizing. Get out of there!"

"Andrew, it's coming back!" Mary screamed from above. "Hold on!"

Another violent strike knocked the boat, followed by a rush of water that nearly washed her father away.

"Move it!" he shouted.

Riley helped Alfie crawl on hands and knees along the flooded passage. They could no longer stand up, as the side wall of the passage was now the floor beneath them. They crawled over the emergency cupboard to the stairs.

"Is it a whale?" Riley cried.

"I don't think so; it's too big." Her father was leaning down and reaching for them. "Hold on to me to climb out."

Just as Riley was reaching for his arm, Mary screamed, "Hang on!"

The boat was struck again. This time from the other side. The blow was so powerful, the *Event Horizon* righted again.

Tossed around like rag dolls, Riley and Alfie made it to their feet and ran toward the steps just as another scream came from above. This was followed by an explosive crash.

Climbing up into the ferocious storm, Riley gasped. The sky was black, and rain blew in all directions as the wind howled like an enraged animal. The tallest mast was broken and lying along the deck. Her father moved away from the steps and started edging along it. Moments later he struggled back. "Come on, we have to abandon ship."

"Why?" Alfie called. "The boat is still floating."

Riley's father shook his head. "Not for long. The mast damaged the bow. We're taking on a lot of water."

"We're sinking?" Riley cried.

"Yes, now come on, we have to inflate the life raft and get off here before it's too late."

"But—but what about that thing in the water?" Riley asked.

The words were just out of her mouth when Mary screamed and pointed toward the front of the boat.

Riley added her own scream when she saw the dark head of some kind of massive snakelike sea serpent rising out of the water and smashing against the front end of the boat. Its long, scaled body coiled completely around the boat like a snake constricting around its prey. The *Event Horizon* cracked and broke like an eggshell as the sea serpent tightened its grip and crushed their sailboat.

"What is that?" Riley shouted.

"It's a sea monster!" Alfie yelled.

"Whatever it is, it's sinking us," Riley's father cried. "We have to get to the life raft!"

They huddled closely together and moved toward the stern of the ship. With each passing moment, the *Event Horizon* groaned and creaked as the monster crushed it.

Riley looked back and saw more of the dark creature climbing onto the bow and pulling it down as the rear of the boat rose out of the water.

They reached the inflatable life raft, and Riley's father and aunt struggled to free it from its cradle and toss it into the water. As the two of them pulled the line on the inflation handle, the six-person raft burst to life. But just as they were preparing to climb in, Alfie screamed, "Look!"

Everyone looked up and gasped. The sea monster was raising itself farther out of the water and climbing high above the ship. It roared once, and then opened its mouth even wider and struck like a viper, biting off the front end of the boat.

4

THERE WAS NO TIME TO REACT OR MOVE as the creature tore through the *Event Horizon* with enough force to push the sailboat beneath the surface of the water. Everyone was washed overboard and thrown into the cold waters of the North Atlantic.

Riley swallowed a mouthful of salty water as she was dragged beneath the surface. But just as quickly as she went down, she sprang up again as her life vest did its job. Coughing and spewing salt water, she looked around in the tall waves, searching for the others. She could hear Alfie calling, but she couldn't see him.

She thought she heard her aunt's voice, but it sounded several waves away. Riley couldn't be sure if it was Mary or just the ferocious wind. Panic struck as she called for her family. That monster was still in the water. Had it eaten them? What about that terrifying mermaid with the teeth? Was she still around? Were they about to eat her? The more she thought about it, the more terrified she became. "Dad! Daddy, where are you? Mary, are you out there?"

"Riley!" her father called. "Where are you?"

"Dad, I'm here!" Riley struggled to swim in the rough water. But the tall waves seemed to always be against her. The more she tried to swim, the harder they pushed back.

"Dad! Dad, can you hear me?"

Riley could no longer hear her father or Mary. She could hear Alfie calling, but even that was growing faint as the waves separated them.

"Dad, please . . . ," she cried.

Spinning in the water, she searched for her family or the creature that had sunk the boat. She thought she saw shadows moving in the waves around her, but she couldn't be sure as the light had faded to near dark. This caused her to panic even more. "Dad, please, where are you?"

With each moment, the waves rose higher and

crashed over her. It took all her strength just to stay at the surface. Suddenly something sharp stung her left leg and she screamed. "Dad! Help me, please!"

"Hush, child," a soft voice called from behind her. "Do not fear; you are safe with us. . . ."

"Who said that?" Riley cried.

"Hush now and sleep, sleep . . . sleep . . ."

Riley spun in the water, and for a brief moment she saw the mermaid she'd seen earlier. The mermaid's eyes were black as night with no white whatsoever. There was no nose, just two slits where her nose should be. In the strange light, her skin was slate gray, and her hair was shaggy and long.

"Who are you . . . ," Riley managed before her eyes became too heavy to keep open. "Daddy . . . ," she called out softly as she drifted off to sleep.

5

THE SOUND OF SEABIRDS ROUSED RILEY from a deep sleep. She was lying on a warm, sandy beach with gentle waves lapping at her feet. Opening her eyes, she lifted her head and saw Alfie lying just a few feet away.

The sun was bright overhead, and all traces of the storm were gone. A soft, warm, salty breeze was blowing lightly and mixing with the hushing sounds of the water.

Riley checked the opposite direction, but all she saw was a long, empty stretch of beach. Looking back at Alfie, she raised her head higher and searched for her father or aunt, but there was no sign of them. It was then that she noticed strange marks in the sand. She knew they weren't from a sea turtle, as her father had shown her those many times before. These were wide like a seal's tracks or something big like that. And like those trails, they headed into the water.

"Alfie . . . ," she rasped. Her throat was sore and burned from the salt water she'd swallowed. "Alfie," she repeated. "Are you alive?"

"No," Alfie moaned as he raised his head and turned to her. "No, I'm dead. Leave me alone."

"What happened?" Riley sat up and gazed around. Behind them the beach continued up to a dense line of trees. After that, all she could see was jungle. In front of her were the beautiful, calm, blue-green waters of the ocean. There was no sign of her father, Aunt Mary, or the *Event Horizon*.

"The sea monster sank us, that's what happened," Alfie said. He sat up and looked around. "Where's Mom?"

"I—I don't know. I can't see my dad either."

Fear filled Alfie's eyes. "You don't think the sea monster ate them, do you?"

"No!" Riley snapped. "They're fine. They've probably washed ashore in a different place, that's all."

"What place? Where are we?"

"I dunno. Somewhere in the Bahamas, I guess." Riley could hardly believe what was happening. A real sea serpent had attacked their boat. The *Event Horizon*, her father's pride and joy, was gone. Things like that only ever happened in movies. But this was no movie. The sand beneath her fingers was real. Her wet feet were real. Somehow, she and Alfie had survived a shipwreck.

When Riley pulled up her legs to stand, she felt a sore on her left calf and remembered the sting. Then she remembered the face. . . .

She looked down and saw a tiny red pinprick in the center of a dark bruise. She turned to her cousin. "Alfie, you're not going to believe this, but I saw something in the water right before I blacked out."

"Yeah, dummy, we saw that sea monster. It ate the boat, remember?"

"No, I mean something else. It was like a woman, but not. I saw her before in the water and told Dad, but he didn't believe me. She was really scary-looking with sharp, pointed teeth and no nose and these freaky black eyes. I saw her again right after she stung me. She told me to go to sleep."

Alfie gasped. "I heard a voice telling me not to be afraid and to go to sleep too!" He looked down at his leg and saw a red dot in the middle of a bruise. "Look, I was stung too. You can still see it."

Riley looked at Alfie's leg and saw it was the same mark she had. "What happened to us?"

"I can't remember." Alfie climbed to his feet and cupped his hands over his mouth. "Mom!" he shouted. "Mom, where are you?"

"Dad!" Riley joined in. "Dad, can you hear me?" She took a few steps down the beach and then stopped. She turned in a tight circle, staring at the sand.

"What are you looking at?" Alfie demanded.

"The sand."

"Duh, I know that. Why?"

"Alfie, look at it. The only footprints here are ours."

"So?"

"So where is everybody? You know how crowded the other islands are with tourists. But, look, there are no footprints here, no coffee cups or candy-bar wrappers or anything. It's like we're the first people on this beach."

"Don't be so stupid," Alfie snapped. "It was the

storm. The wind was blowing all over the place. It wiped away all the footprints. Or maybe it was the tide smoothing down the sand. Whatever island this is, it'll be jammed with people."

"Yeah, that must be it," Riley agreed. She started to walk along the shoreline.

"Hey, Shorty, where're you going?"

"I'm going to look for Dad and Aunt Mary. If we made it to shore, they must have too."

"I think we should stay here and wait for someone to find us. That's what happens in the movies.

"Fine, you can stay here and wait. But I'm going to find Dad."

"Shorty," Alfie called as she walked away. "Shorty . . . Riley, wait for me."

Riley turned back and watched her cousin running after her. His face was flushed, and he looked frightened. The truth was, she was frightened too. Very frightened. They were on a beach with no sign of anyone or anything around them. She glanced back out at the calm blue waters and saw only the light waves. She could hardly believe what had just happened to them. They had been sunk by a monster. But where was the debris from the

Event Horizon, or even the life raft? Surely some of the wreckage should have made it to shore.

Alfie didn't say anything as he took his place beside her. "Now what? If we leave the area, what happens if Mom or Uncle Andrew come? They'll never know we were here."

Riley considered for a moment, then nodded. "Stay here. I'll be right back." She ran up the beach to where the dense jungle started. Without entering, she looked down until she found what she was searching for. She picked up a long stick and carried it back.

"What's that for?" Alfie asked.

Riley broke the stick into three pieces. A long one and two shorter ones. Then she laid them down on the sand to form an arrow. After that, she pulled off her life vest and laid it down beside the arrow with her name clearly showing. "Okay, so if Dad or Aunt Mary sees this, they'll know I was here and what direction I went."

Alfie took his vest off and placed it down beside hers. "This way they know we're together."

"Good idea," Riley agreed.

With the message left in the sand, Riley and Alfie started to walk along the shoreline, looking for any signs of their parents or the wreckage. But after what felt like hours, they didn't see anything.

"What time is it?" Alfie asked. "How long have we been walking?"

Riley reached into her pocket for her cell phone, but it was gone. Then she realized the emergency pack she'd tied around her waist was gone too. She looked over at Alfie and saw that he didn't have his pack either.

"Alfie, did you untie your emergency pack when we were in the water?"

Alfie shook his head. "No way. I knew we'd need it."

"I didn't undo mine, either, but they're both gone. So's my cell phone."

Alfie frowned. "But I tied mine really tight."

"Me too," Riley agreed. "So how come they're gone?" She looked back out at the water as the terrible memory of the disaster flooded back to her. "She did it. I don't know how or why, but I'm sure that woman took our stuff."

"That's wacko, Shorty. There couldn't have been a woman. I mean, yes, there was that thing that wrecked the boat. But a woman? Like a mermaid or something?"

"I don't know what she was. But she was there. Who else could have spoken to us in the water or taken our packs?" She looked around at the empty beach. "I know how it sounds, Alfie, but I swear I saw her."

"I dunno," Alfie said. "This whole thing is really freaky."

They continued walking in silence. Riley kept replaying the final moments of the disaster in her head. Reaching the deck, going back to the life raft with her family, then the sea serpent rising out of the water and crushing the boat . . . the cold water and the stinging in her leg . . . the woman.

She stopped again and looked down at her calf. The bruise was still there, and a scab had formed over the center sting. Then she looked at Alfie's calf and the exact same mark.

"So a sea serpent sank our boat," she said, trying to make sense of the impossible. "Then we were both stung and heard voices telling us to go to sleep." She looked at the water again. "That's unbelievable, right?"

"But it happened." Alfie was inspecting his own injury. "You know, this almost looks like the mark I got when they had to do a blood test on me when

I was going to have my appendix out last year. Only that was on my arm. But that's too weird. We were in the water—who would want to take our blood?"

"Not take, give," Riley suggested. "What if that woman gave us a shot that made us go to sleep?"

Alfie was shaking his head. "Why?"

"I don't know," Riley said. "But someone had to bring us to this island. We weren't near one when the ship went down."

"If it's true, do you think they could have gotten Mom and Uncle Andrew?"

"That's what I'm hoping."

They started walking again, but after a few more minutes, Alfie stopped. "I'm thirsty." He sat down in the sand. "I need a break."

Riley took a seat beside him. She was thirsty too. But more than that, she was scared. Genuinely scared that something terrible had happened to her father and aunt. She looked back at the jungle behind them. "Alfie, you don't think we're alone here, do you?"

"Don't be such an idiot, Shorty. We have satellites and airplanes and stuff like that. There are no more deserted islands. I think we're just on the wrong side of this one."

Riley shrugged. "I don't know. We've been walking and walking and haven't seen anybody."

"Yeah, 'cause it's a really big island." He stood up and looked toward the jungle. "I bet there are hotels and stuff in there. I'm gonna check."

Riley stood up as well. "There could also be dangerous animals. What about snakes and poisonous bugs?"

"Or what about quicksand?" Alfie teased, making scary noises. "You're just a chicken."

"No, I'm not," Riley said. "I'm being cautious."

The sound of a barking dog stopped their argument. Riley looked down the beach. "Is that a . . . ?"

"It's a dog!" Alfie cried.

Riley watched the large, thin dog bounding down the beach from the direction they'd been walking. But as the animal got closer, it didn't look like any kind of dog she'd seen before.

"That can't be a dog, it's too big."

"Sure it is," Alfie said.

"Since when are dogs the size of a small pony? C'mon, let's get out of here before it attacks us!" She caught hold of Alfie's arm and they started to run.

But the large animal was moving too fast. It soon

caught up with them and leaped up on Alfie, knocking him down into the sand.

Alfie and Riley both screamed as the dog pounced, but instead of going for Alfie's throat, the enormous animal started to lick his face excitedly.

"Get it off me," Alfie cried. "Get off!"

Riley tried to shove the dog away, but then it turned its affections on her and tackled her to the ground. Pinning her down, the dog thoroughly licked her face.

"Miss Pigglesworth!" a voice called. "Miss Pigglesworth, stop that! Let them up!"

Riley couldn't see where the voice was coming from. All she could see was a dark, furry head and a long pink tongue.

"Miss Pigglesworth," the voice called again. This time it was much closer. "Get off her and leave them alone!"

The huge animal climbed off Riley and bounded back to the boy who'd called it. He ran over and knelt beside Riley. "I'm so sorry about that. Miss Pigglesworth can be a handful at times, but she's really sweet. She'd never hurt you."

"No, she'd drown us," Alfie complained as he

stood up and wiped dog slobber off his face. "What is that thing?"

The boy helped Riley to her feet. It was hard to tell, but he looked to be around her age, or maybe a bit older. He had dark blue eyes and shaggy black hair and was taller than Alfie but much leaner. He was wearing white pants and a striped shirt in a style that seemed old-fashioned.

The animal came over to Riley and licked her arm. It almost looked like an Irish wolfhound with the same dark coloring, but it was so much bigger.

"That's Miss Pigglesworth," the boy said. "And I'm Sebastian, but everyone just calls me Bastian."

"What kind of dog is that?" Riley asked. "I've never seen one so big."

"I know," Bastian agreed. "That's what makes her special. What's your name?"

"I'm Riley," Riley said. "And this is Alfie."

"Alfie," Bastian said. He offered to shake Alfie's hand.

Alfie swatted it away. "So, like, is your family here on vacation or something? 'Cause we need to talk to someone quick. We've been shipwrecked and can't find my mom or Riley's dad. We need to send out a search party immediately."

Bastian frowned. "Your mom and her dad? You aren't brother and sister?"

Riley shook her head. "Alfie's my cousin. His mom is my dad's sister. We were on our sailboat, the *Event Horizon*, when this big storm hit. Then an enormous sea monster attacked our boat and sank it. Can you help us find them?"

Riley noticed how Bastian didn't react to the news of a sea monster. Instead he smiled and said, "Of course I'll help. So will Miss Pigglesworth." He looked down at the dog. "Can you smell anyone else?"

The strange dog raised her head and sniffed the air. She ran farther down the beach, sniffing all the way. After a moment, she turned and bounded back.

"Well?" Bastian asked.

Miss Pigglesworth shook her head and gave a soft woof.

"I'm sorry," Bastian said. "She can't smell them. Perhaps they landed on the other side of the island."

"You're listening to your dog?" Alfie said.

"Of course. Miss Pigglesworth never lies."

"No, he means your dog can understand you and you can understand her?" Riley asked.

"Well, yes. Miss Pigglesworth has been with me

my whole life. We understand each other perfectly."

The dog whined and barked again. Bastian nodded. "They might have." He looked at Riley. "Perhaps your family has gone into the Community ahead of you."

"Community?" Riley said."

"Do you mean like a city or town?" Alfie asked.

"No, it's the Community," Bastian said. He pointed toward the jungle. "Come, I'll take you there."

Riley looked at the dense jungle. "We were worried this was a deserted island."

"Deserted?" Bastian laughed. "Oh no, far from it. But not many people like to venture down to the water's edge. The Leviathan hunts these waters and sometimes comes ashore. It can be a bit dangerous without protection."

Riley looked around nervously. "What's the Leviathan?"

"The Leviathan is the Leviathan," Bastian said. "Everyone knows what it is."

"I don't," Alfie said.

"Well," Bastian continued, "it's really long and dark and has large scales. It's like an eel, but different. And it's got a huge head, big eyes, and a mouth full of teeth. If you're walking on the shore and not paying attention, the Leviathan can beach itself to get you."

Riley looked at her cousin. "That's what attacked our boat!"

"The Leviathan sank your boat and you're still alive?" Bastian said. He whistled. "You really were lucky."

"Lucky?" Alfie said. "That thing nearly killed us. Now my mom and uncle are missing. You call that lucky?"

"Surviving the Leviathan is *very* lucky. It eats anything."

Miss Pigglesworth started barking again.

"Of course," Bastian answered. "We must tell the others what's happened." He gave the dog a pat on the head and turned up toward the jungle. "Come, everyone is expecting you."

Riley looked over to Alfie. None of this made any sense. They had washed up on what looked like an empty island, but Bastian said everyone was expecting them. Who was everyone? And what about the Leviathan?

"How can anyone be expecting us," Alfie said, "when we weren't expecting to be shipwrecked?"

"Oh, we always know when there are new arrivals coming," Bastian said casually. "But it's been a very long time."

"How do you know?"

Bastian stopped. "The older ones tell us. Come, it's this way."

Riley followed Bastian toward the jungle. Yesterday she was irritated when her father didn't believe her about seeing the mermaid. Today she was irritated by Bastian's casual response to the news that a sea monster attacked their sailboat. The more she thought about it, the less she believed any of it was real.

At the edge of the jungle, Alfie stopped. "Nope. I'm not going anywhere until you tell me what's happening. This is getting too weird."

Bastian frowned, looking confused. "Why would you want to stay here when you could be in the Community? Aren't you hungry or thirsty? We have food and everything you need."

"What I need," Alfie said slowly, "is to find my mom. I don't care about any Community and I don't care about Leviathans—I just want to find her."

"There is no need to be rude," Bastian said. "Rudeness leads to strife, and none of us want that."

"Strife? What are you talking about?" Alfie said. He looked at Riley. "I don't like this moron and I don't trust him. I'm not going to any Community. Come on, we don't need his help."

"But you can't go much farther down the beach. It's not allowed."

"Why not?" Riley asked.

"Because," Bastian said. "Farther along is the start of the Red Cloak territory, and beyond that belongs to the others. Please, just come back to the Community. We can help find your family."

Riley shrugged. "Let's just go to the Community. We haven't seen anyone else on the beach or debris from the boat. Dad and Mary might be there already."

Alfie looked at her for a moment and then nodded. "Okay, we'll go with him. But if this is some kind of trick . . ."

Riley nodded. "I know."

"So you will come?" Bastian asked.

"Yes," Riley said. "But only if you promise that they'll help us find our family."

Bastian grinned. "I promise. Now, it's this way."

Riley and Alfie followed Bastian into the jungle. Almost immediately they felt a change. The temperature was a bit cooler out of the sun, and whereas the beach was mostly silent except for a few seabirds and the gentle washing of waves on the shore, the jungle was teeming with sounds. Birds chirped and unseen animals rustled in the undergrowth.

All around them, impossibly large leaves grew on vines that wrapped around tall trees with trunks wider than a car.

"Shorty, look at the size of this tree! It's bigger than a redwood."

"And those vine leaves are almost as big as me!"

Bastian appeared surprised at her comment. "These trees? They're small because they're still young. There are others that are much larger."

"Please tell me you're kidding," Alfie said. "Trees that are bigger than these?"

Bastian nodded.

Riley looked at her cousin but said nothing. Everything about this island was strange. Including Bastian.

"Riley, why did Alfie call you 'Shorty'?" Bastian asked.

Riley sighed. "Because I'm older than him, but he's taller than me. He does it to annoy me."

"But that isn't nice," Bastian said. "It could hurt your feelings." He turned to Alfie. "Why would you want to hurt Riley?"

Alfie shrugged. "Because she calls me 'Creep.'"

"You do?" Bastian asked Riley.

"Well, yeah, sometimes."

"I don't understand. Why would you use hurtful names for each other?"

"Don't you ever tease anyone?" Riley asked.

Bastian shook his head. "No, we all get along here. Using names to hurt someone would be wrong."

Riley looked over at her cousin and raised her eyebrows.

"Wow," Alfie muttered. His expression showed he was just as shocked as she was. "How much farther is this Community?"

"It's just ahead," Bastian said.

They pressed on through the dense jungle for a short while longer. Then the trees thinned, giving way to neatly groomed grass and shrubs. Just beyond that were strange structures.

Riley gasped. She had never seen anything like it before in her entire life. "What is this place?"

Bastian grinned and swept his arm wide to invite them forward. "Welcome to Atlantis!"

6

"WHERE ARE WE?" ALFIE ASKED.

"Atlantis," Bastian repeated.

"But it's . . . it's . . ."

"It's unbelievable," Riley said. She took several steps closer and looked around. There were houses that looked like boats and short buildings made of multicolored stones of red, white, yellow, and black. In the far distance they saw the tip of a spire, rising tall above the trees, that looked to be made of white crystals. "What is that sparkly thing way over there?"

"That's the Crucible," Bastian explained. "It's on the other side of the island. We're not allowed to go there."

"Why?" Alfie asked.

"It's part of the area that I told you about on the beach. Others live there that can't come here, and we don't go there."

"Why?" Riley asked.

Bastian shrugged. "Those are just the rules."

Riley could hardly believe what she was seeing. The multicolored buildings in the area also glinted in the light and looked like they were decorated with precious stones. In the blazing sun, the whole area appeared to sparkle and glow.

Alfie looked up into the sky and frowned. "How?"

"How what?" Bastian asked.

"How do you not blind airplanes flying overhead with all that glow?"

Bastian frowned as though he didn't understand. "Airplanes?"

"Yeah, airplanes," Alfie said. "You know, those big things that fly."

"You mean birds?" Bastian said.

"Not birds, dummy, airplanes. People fly around in them."

"Really?" Bastian said. "People can fly?"

Alfie looked at Riley and rolled his eyes.

When Bastian led them closer to the village, Riley

realized the houses that looked like boats really *were* boats. They'd been set deep in the ground to keep them upright, and long wooden planks went from the ground to the deck. A woman was walking down one of the planks to get off the boat.

The stone buildings mixed among them didn't look like anything that she'd seen on any of the other Bahamian islands. Some didn't even have doors on them.

From what Riley could see, there were no paved roads and no cars, buses, trucks, or even bicycles. She did see a large group of people walking toward them. They were wearing an odd assortment of mismatched clothing, but everyone had a beaming smile on their face.

A woman approached Riley and hugged her. "Aren't you a pretty one? Everyone, look how pretty she is. I would be honored if you would work with me."

"Um—thanks?" Riley said. "But I'm not here to work."

Everyone laughed.

"Look how young and strong this one is," a man said, grabbing Alfie by the arm. "He will be a wonderful addition."

"Addition to what?" Alfie said, yanking his arm back. "The only addition I'm gonna be is to the search party looking for my mom."

"Yes," Riley agreed. "Please, we really need your help. Something sank our boat and now we can't find our family. Will you help us?"

There were hushed mutters, and the word "Leviathan" was repeated several times from the gathering.

"Of course," the woman beside Riley finally said. "But first you must join us for the celebration."

"What celebration?" Riley asked.

"Why, you, child," the woman said. "We are celebrating your arrival."

A man who looked like he was in his forties arrived, and everyone parted to let him through. Riley had never seen such a tall man. His dark eyes sparkled. "Everyone, please, I know we're excited to have these young people join us, but stand back, let them breathe."

His dark skin and soft, lilting accent were the same as the people from the Bahamas. Riley realized she and Alfie must have washed up on one of the smaller islands. But she couldn't remember her father ever talking about an island or village called Atlantis.

"Are you in charge here?" Riley asked.

The man smiled brightly. "You might say that. I am Beresford."

"We need to call the police or something," Riley started. "Our boat was attacked by a sea serpent, and now we can't find my father and aunt. We're really scared something has happened to them. We have to start searching."

"Of course, we will." He looked over the crowd. "Shane, come forward."

A younger man approached. He wasn't as tall as Beresford and had short-cropped hair and blue-green eyes.

"Shane, I want you to take a search party and go looking for . . ." He looked back at Riley. "I don't know your names yet."

"I'm Riley, and this is my cousin Alfie."

"It's a pleasure to meet you, Riley and Alfie." He turned back to Shane. "Take out a team and start searching for their family."

Shane nodded and started to walk away. Riley frowned at how casual he was. He didn't even bother to ask what their family looked like or what their names were. "I'll come with you," she called as she started to run after him.

Beresford caught her arm. "No, child, you must stay here. You've been through an ordeal and need time to recover."

"But I'm fine," Riley said. "We just need to find my father and aunt."

"Not just yet," Beresford said. "Shane needs to arrange his team. In the meantime, why don't you let Bastian show you around? There is a lot to see and do in Atlantis."

"Are you serious?" Alfie cried. "You want us to take a tour? Don't you get it? Our boat was attacked by a monster and we were shipwrecked. I don't want a stupid tour; I want to find my mom!"

Beresford smiled, and so did everyone else in the gathering, as though Alfie had just told an amusing story.

"Of course," Beresford said. "And when Shane and his team have searched the area, we will tell you what he finds. But for now, you must stay with Bastian. He will instruct you on the ways of Atlantis and its boundaries. It is a wonderful place, but not without its dangers. You have much to learn."

"But—but—" Riley started.

"All in good time," Beresford said as he turned and walked away.

7

RILEY LOOKED AT HER COUSIN IN complete disbelief. Were these people real? Didn't they get it? Two people were missing and all they did was stand there smiling at them.

Their lack of concern for her father and aunt was making Riley uncomfortable. She moved closer to her cousin. Alfie might be a jerk, but he was loads better than these strangers.

The woman who wanted Riley to work with her clapped her hands. "All right, everyone, back to work. Let's give these newcomers a chance to settle in."

The crowds dispersed slowly but continued to smile and greet them. When most were gone, the woman said, "I am Lisette, and I'm in charge of job assignments. There is plenty of work for you to do here. But take today to settle in. Tomorrow we shall discuss your duties." She smiled again and walked away.

Alfie leaned closer to Riley and whispered, "Duties? What is she talking about? Look at them, they don't care what happened to us or that Mom and Uncle Andrew are missing. It's like it doesn't matter. That guy Beresford is a real freak and I don't trust him."

"Beresford is not a freak," Bastian said. "He is our leader and keeps us safe."

"From what?" Riley asked.

"The North Side, Red Cloak territory, the Forbidden Zone and its monsters, the Red Moon—everything."

Alfie raised his eyebrows. "Forbidden Zone? Monsters? Where are we, the Horror Channel?"

Bastian said innocently, "No, Atlantis."

Alfie shook his head. "He's been on this island way too long. We'd better get outta here soon or we'll end up like them too."

Miss Pigglesworth barked, whined, and pushed Bastian in the backside.

"Yes, I was going to," Bastian said to the dog. He looked back at Riley. "Miss Pigglesworth says we should get moving and then you can join us at the banquet."

"She said that, did she?" Riley looked at the odd tall dog. When she did, Miss Pigglesworth tilted her head to the side and stared at her with an intensity that made Riley uncomfortable. "Okay, we can look around, but only until the search party is ready. We really need to find our family."

"Of course," Bastian said. "Come, let's go this way."

They started walking through the neatly groomed gardens. There were people working on the grounds and others planting flowers. In the distance to her left, Riley could see large patches of cleared ground where vegetables were growing, and beyond that were orchards with fruit trees.

"How many people live here?" she asked distractedly.

"A few," Bastian said.

"Oh, that's helpful," Alfie snapped.

Bastian stopped and looked at him. "Why are you always so angry?"

"Why?" Alfie cried. "Oh, I dunno, maybe because we've just been shipwrecked, and no one cares that our family is missing!"

"Of course we care," Bastian said. "But in Atlantis, things happen in their own time. Beresford said he will find your family, and he will. But until then, why not enjoy yourself?"

Alfie charged at Bastian and shoved him back. "I don't want to look around. I don't want to enjoy myself! I want to find my mom and then I want to leave this stupid island with your diamond buildings no one can go into and all these strange pod people."

"Leave?" Bastian said. "You can't leave. No one ever leaves."

"What do you mean no one leaves?" Riley demanded. "We have to. I live in Colorado and Alfie lives in Idaho. We have homes, families, and friends. We aren't going to stay here."

"But—but no one leaves, at least not until . . ."

Miss Pigglesworth barked, and Bastian stopped speaking. Finally, he said, "I mean, we all stay here."

Riley could hardly believe what she was hearing. "Are you saying we're trapped here?"

"'Trapped' is a harsh word," Bastian said. "But, actually, yes. You're trapped here. We all are."

8

ALFIE SHOVED BASTIAN ASIDE AND started to walk. "No way. You can stay trapped here if you like. But I'm going to find my mom, and then we're outta here!"

"Alfie, wait, I'm coming with you," Riley called after him.

They pushed through the jungle with Bastian and Miss Pigglesworth trailing behind. When they reached the beach, they headed down to the water's edge and walked in the same direction they did when they first awoke.

Behind them, Miss Pigglesworth barked, and Bastian shook his head in frustration. "Please stop.

We are about to cross the boundary into Red Cloak territory and we mustn't go there, especially today. Just come back with me to the Community."

Alfie charged up to Bastian and poked him in the chest. "The only place I'm going is home after I find my mom."

Riley watched her cousin go and then turned back to Bastian. "I'm sorry, but he's right. We can't stay." She started to run after Alfie. "Hey, Alfie, wait up!"

When she caught up to her cousin, Alfie turned on her. "They're so stupid. Like we don't know the truth."

"What are you talking about?"

Alfie pointed to Bastian. "Him and all of them. They've done this to us."

Riley looked back at Bastian and saw the confusion on his face. "Alfie, you don't really think they caused our boat to sink, do you? It was the sea serpent!"

"No, they're part of it!"

"That doesn't make sense!" Riley insisted. "You make it sound like they made the storm."

"Prove that they didn't."

Riley put her hands on her hips. "No, you prove that they did!"

Alfie shook his head. "You're so stupid. . . ." He turned and stormed down the beach.

Riley stood, watching him go. This was the cousin she hated. He was mean and spiteful. Even now when they were in trouble, he was still being nasty.

"Your cousin is a very angry person," Bastian said, coming up to her.

Riley nodded. "Now do you see why I call him 'Creep'? My dad says he has anger management problems. He's always been so mean, even when we were young. His family would visit us at Christmas, and it would be a nightmare. He'd break my new toys and bother my brother. Maybe because he doesn't have any brothers or sisters of his own—I don't know. His dad was always angry too. But when his dad left and his parents divorced, Alfie became even worse. My mom and dad hoped this trip would help him. But it hasn't. And now that he's scared . . ."

"You think he's scared?"

"Of course he's scared. So am I."

"Riley, there is nothing to fear. If you follow the rules, Atlantis can be a wonderful place to live. But, really, we must go back. It is dangerous to be here on the beach."

"Bastian, I already have a home. I just want to find my family and go back there."

She ran after Alfie. He might be the most annoying person in the world, but they were family and had to stick together. Falling in line with her cousin, they continued walking. Riley would occasionally look back to see Bastian and Miss Pigglesworth trailing farther behind. Bastian was talking to the dog and she was barking back at him. Their behavior alone was enough to make Riley really weirded out.

After a while, they reached a curve in the island where the beach veered sharply to the left. Rounding the bend, they stopped. Riley stared in disbelief.

"Do you see what I see?"

"Uh-huh," Alfie said.

A small group of people were emerging from the trees. They were all wearing red cloaks with the hoods drawn up and walking in two straight lines while carrying something on their shoulders. That something—or someone—was also in a red cloak and appeared to be struggling to get down.

Directly behind them was a line of four magnificent black horses. Each horse had a golden horn on its head that sparkled in the sunlight.

Riley gasped. "They've put horns on those horses to make them look like unicorns!" She continued to walk forward toward the beautiful horses.

"Riley, Alfie, stop!" Bastian cried tightly. He caught up to them and hauled them over to a large piece of driftwood and pushed them down to their knees. "Get down. I told you, this is Red Cloak territory. It is forbidden for us to be here and witness this."

"Witness what?" Alfie said.

"Yeah," Riley agreed. "That you guys have glued horns on those poor horses? I sure hope they come off easily or I swear I'll report you for animal cruelty."

"We haven't glued the horns on. They are real," Bastian said nervously. "The unicorns are the guardians of the island. They are ensuring that the Red Cloaks carry the one on their shoulders to the water. It is time for her release into the ocean."

Riley was about to ask what that meant when they heard a ferocious roar. Then another Red Cloak appeared out of the jungle. His cloak was filthy and torn as he ran toward the unicorns. "Wait, no, you can't do this! I love her. She belongs with me! It's not her time. Please, stop!"

The last unicorn in the line turned on the red-cloaked figure and whinnied loudly.

"No!" the voice from under the hood howled. "Please, she's my life. . . ." He collapsed to the sand, and his shoulders rose and fell with tearful grief. Then he threw back his head and roared mournfully, "Susan, no . . ."

"What's happening?" Riley asked.

"We shouldn't be here," Bastian whispered tightly. "If Mada sees us, he'll be furious."

"So what?" Alfie said. "What is this freak show?"

Bastian's voice was becoming frantic. "Please, we have to go before Mada . . ."

The person in the red cloak was still on the ground, sobbing. But then he glanced their way and released another ferocious roar. He leaped forward and down to all fours as he charged at them.

"Run!" Bastian cried.

Riley was too stunned to move. She stayed kneeling in the sand, watching the Red Cloak coming right at her.

Behind them, Miss Pigglesworth growled, barked, and then leaped over Riley and Alfie and ran straight at the Red Cloak.

"No! Miss Pigglesworth, stop!" Bastian cried.

The sights and sounds were sickening as the

immense dog and Red Cloak met in a vicious fight. They started rolling in the sand. Riley saw flashes of orange, white, and black, and as she watched, she could have sworn she saw a long striped tail from beneath the cloak.

As the fight intensified, Mada rolled over and rose above Miss Pigglesworth. His red-cloaked arm moved incredibly fast as he swiped the dog and knocked her several feet away. Miss Pigglesworth yelped and howled as she hit the sand and tried to get up.

"Miss Pigglesworth!" Bastian shouted.

Mada's cloaked head shot back to Riley and Alfie. With the dog out of the way, he growled and roared in rage. He charged again and then jumped in the air, shooting straight at them.

All Riley could do was watch as Mada crossed a great distance in the single leap. Right before he landed, two of the unicorns galloped forward. Their golden horns glowed brightly as one of the unicorns lowered its head and grazed the length of the red cloak with the tip of its horn.

Mada roared once and then collapsed to the sand, unconscious.

Riley could hardly believe what she had seen. But

it wasn't over yet. The other unicorn galloped over to Alfie and her and reared up as it let out a shrill scream. Once again its golden horn started to glow.

"We're sorry. Please forgive us!" Bastian threw himself down in the sand in front of the rearing unicorn and held up his hands in surrender. "Please . . . Riley and Alfie just arrived here; they don't know the rules yet. Please don't punish us."

The unicorn went back down to the sand but snorted furiously. It took a step closer with its horn still glowing. The other unicorns also trotted forward with glowing horns.

Bastian rose and ran back to Riley and Alfie. Catching them by the arms, he forced them to run. "We have to get out of here!"

Riley didn't resist as Bastian pulled her and Alfie away from the furious unicorns and farther down the beach.

Moments later, Miss Pigglesworth appeared alongside them. She was limping badly, and blood from deep scratches was matting her fur.

They kept moving until they were back where they started. Just before they reached the Community, Alfie stopped and turned on Bastian.

"Okay, now you're gonna tell us what just happened back there. Who were those guys in the red cloaks? What were they carrying? And what was Mada? Don't try to tell me that he was a man because I know he wasn't. He had a tail!"

Bastian backed up. "I—I can't tell you—not yet."

Alfie caught Bastian by the arm and poked his finger in his chest. "You're gonna tell us or else . . ." As he leaned in close to Bastian, Miss Pigglesworth started to growl.

"Alfie, stop!" Riley cried. "Look at the dog!"

Alfie looked at Miss Pigglesworth. Her hackles were raised, and her teeth were bared as she took a step closer.

"Call off your dog," Alfie warned.

"I can't," Bastian said. "You saw her. Miss Pigglesworth is very protective of me. If she attacked Mada, I promise you, she'll attack you too."

Alfie looked at the dog and backed away from Bastian. He raised his hands. "Okay, okay, I'm not going to touch him."

Miss Pigglesworth stopped growling. Then she whined again as she gazed back at her injured side.

"Please," Bastian said. "I have to help her. Just

come back to the Community. Beresford can tell you everything."

"Fine," Alfie said. "But he'd better or there's gonna be big trouble."

9

THEY ARRIVED BACK AT THE EDGE OF the settlement. Once again they saw the people working in the vegetable fields. As they got closer, Lisette and the workers paused and waved.

Alfie stopped. "All right, Bastian, if you won't tell us what happened back there, will you at least tell me why everyone here is so calm when there are monsters like Mada out there?"

Riley was looking at the happy people smiling and waving at them and wondered the same thing. "Yes, they don't seem to care."

Bastian sighed. "Everyone is perfectly safe if you follow the rules. I told you we weren't allowed to see that. Especially as Mada was crying over losing Susan. He's never going to forgive us for seeing him weak like that and is going to be even more dangerous now."

"More dangerous!" Riley cried. "He would have killed us if Miss Pigglesworth and that unicorn hadn't stopped him. What is Mada?"

"Mada is, well, Mada. You'll understand soon. But you must trust me when I tell you to do something, otherwise something very bad could happen."

"Oh, so you're saying that nearly getting killed back there was our fault?" Alfie demanded.

"Well, yes," Bastian said. "I warned you that we were entering Red Cloak territory, but you wouldn't listen. You are going to have to learn that Atlantis does have some dangers if you don't follow the rules."

"Hey, I don't have to follow any—"

A loud gong sounded and reverberated through the area, cutting off Alfie's comment. The people working on the grounds and vegetables put down their tools and started to walk toward the buildings. Others came out of the orchards and followed the same path.

"Now what?" Alfie said.

"It is time to eat," Bastian said softly without looking up. "That gong is calling us together. They will be expecting us."

"I'm not hungry," Riley said. "I just want to find my dad."

"Me too," Alfie agreed. "We need to find Shane and see what they've found."

"He will be with the others at the banquet."

Riley frowned. "But I thought he was going to get a search party together."

"Maybe he has," Bastian responded. "I have been with you two, so I don't know what they've been doing."

"Well, they'd better have been looking!" Alfie said.

"Stop it, Alfie," Riley said. "You're not helping."

As they made their way forward, Riley got a better look at the buildings and boat homes. They were all neatly kept without a spot of dirt or trash around them.

Making it around a two-story stone building, Riley gasped, unable to believe her eyes. Just ahead was a half-buried cruise ship sitting in the middle of a clearing. Grass grew up the sides, and there were floral planters all around it.

She turned sharply and looked back at Bastian. "How did that big cruise ship get here?"

"That's not a cruise ship," Alfie said. "They've just made it look like one."

The events of the morning were temporarily forgotten as Riley focused fully on the cruise ship. Somehow it had been buried in the ground almost halfway up the hull. There was a ramp leading up to a large loading door on the side, from which people were emerging.

Above the wide door, four rows of portholes ran the length of the ship. Above them were the first-class cabins that had larger windows and their own balconies. High at the top near the deck was a long line of white-and-red lifeboats.

Three tall red-and-black smokestacks climbed up into the sky. A name was painted on the side—the *Queen of Bermuda*.

"It *is* a cruise ship," Riley insisted. "It kinda looks like the ones we saw at the port of Miami. But those were much bigger. This one looks older."

"So now you're an expert on cruise ships?" Alfie snapped.

"Okay, smarty, you tell me what it is, then."

They walked around a stone bell tower where the loud gonging was coming from. As they got closer,

Alfie jogged forward and stared up at the large, white ship. "Well, it's a—it's a . . . Okay, it's a cruise ship." He turned to Bastian. "How did it get here?"

Bastian paused and frowned. "I—I don't really remember. It was a long time ago. I do remember others digging a big hole and then somehow it was here. But it's been here so long now, we don't even think about it. I live in there. There are cabins for each of you."

"So it's a hotel?" Riley asked.

Bastian frowned. "I don't know what that is."

"You don't know what a hotel is?" Alfie gasped. "Seriously?"

Bastian nodded. "I will take you to your cabins later. Right now, it's time to eat."

Riley was too stunned to do anything other than follow Bastian. They walked around the huge ship and saw how deeply it had been set in the ground.

Alfie approached the hull and peered up the side. From this close, they couldn't see the top deck. He pounded on the side, and each strike made a dull thud as though the metal was very thick. "This place is unbelievable. Where are we?"

"I told you," Bastian said. "We are in Atlantis."

"No, I mean *where are we*?" Alfie repeated. "Are we still on Earth? 'Cause this place ain't like anywhere I've ever seen before."

Riley stopped as a cold shiver ran down her spine. She crossed her arms over her chest to keep from trembling. "I know where we are."

"Where?" Alfie demanded.

Riley turned and looked at her cousin. "We're in the middle of the Bermuda Triangle."

"No way," Alfie spat.

Riley nodded. "Yes. When I told my best friend, Lisa, where we were going, she told me about it, saying that boats and planes disappear in the triangle and are never seen again. So yesterday I asked Dad, and he said we were already in it, but that he'd been in it many times before and nothing ever happened."

"Well, it happened this time," Alfie said. He looked at Bastian. "That's it, isn't it? We've been shipwrecked in the Bermuda Triangle. That could explain some of the freaky things we've been seeing."

Bastian frowned. "I don't know. All I do know is that this is Atlantis."

As they talked, people were arriving from all around them. They were smiling warmly and saying hello. Some even shook Riley's and Alfie's hands.

As Riley looked at all the people, she started to realize there was something else that was very odd. There were no children and no elderly people. Everyone looked to be in their early thirties or forties and maybe a couple in their fifties. But there was no one with gray hair and definitely no children or babies.

"Where are the kids?" Riley asked.

"What kids?" Bastian said.

"Any kids," Riley said. "Everywhere I look I see adults. Where are the children?"

"We have a few. They are always served first, so they're already at the banquet to ensure that they eat. That's why it's important for us to go now."

"Kids eat first here?" Alfie said.

Bastian nodded. "Always. So, please, can we go now? It's very rude to make the others wait for us."

Riley was left speechless. Atlantis was the strangest place she'd ever been. Why would everyone wait for them? Even the best tourist resorts their family went to weren't like that.

Walking with the crowds, they moved around more multicolored stone buildings and entered a public square. The ground was tiled with a smooth white marble and encircled by flowing trees. In the center of the square were three long lines of trestle tables. There was also a single table at the front. Riley counted seven kids sitting there. Four girls and three boys, all ranging in age from about eight to fifteen. It really was a kids-only table, as none of the adults sat with them. She also saw three empty place settings and realized they were for her, Alfie, and Bastian. The kids at the table were looking at them and smiling. The youngest among them was a girl who was barely able to contain herself and clapped her hands excitedly.

All the tables had neatly laid, formal place settings using what looked like the best china. Linen napkins were set on the plates, and the silverware looked like real silver. What really put it at the top of the weird-o-meter was the fact that everything was set up outside like strange, public picnic. Soft sail-like fabric on a framework sheltered the area. The gentle breeze caused the silken fabric to billow softly.

Riley looked at the gathering, guessing there had to be at least two hundred people. "Is this everyone from the resort?"

Bastian frowned. "If you mean if this is everyone

from the Community, then, mostly, but not all. Some of the others eat elsewhere. Like the Cloaks. I don't know where they eat or what."

"Cloaks?" Riley questioned.

Bastian paused. "You saw the Red Cloaks earlier today—Mada, Susan, and the others. But there are also Yellow and Blue Cloaks. I'm sure you'll see them soon."

As they approached, everyone stood up and started to applaud. Riley turned around, expecting to see someone famous standing behind them, but there was no one. They were applauding *them*.

"What?" Alfie said, looking around. "Did we win the lottery or something?"

Bastian laughed. "They're just glad to see you and letting you know that you are welcome here."

Alfie pointed to one of the tables. "Shorty, there's Shane—but he's supposed to be out looking for Mom and Uncle Andrew." He ran over to Shane.

Riley looked at Bastian. "Why isn't he looking for our family?"

Bastian opened his mouth to speak, but Alfie's loud shout silenced him.

"What do you mean you couldn't find them? Did you even look?"

Riley trotted over to her cousin just as Shane stood. "Of course we did. We searched everywhere within our boundaries."

"It couldn't have been much of a search if you're back here already," Riley said. "What about taking a boat out to look for them? They could be floating in the ocean right now. We all had our life vests on. They're out there somewhere, waiting for us to rescue them!"

"We can't take boats out," Shane said.

"Why not?" Riley demanded.

"Because of the Leviathan."

"You know about the sea monster that sank our sailboat?" Riley asked.

Shane nodded. "Of course. The Leviathan will try to sink anything that is near Atlantis."

"Lemme get this straight," Alfie cried. "Our family is missing, and you won't look for them because you're scared of a giant eel?"

"The Leviathan isn't an eel," Shane said.

"What's going on here?" Beresford approached the table. "I will have peace at mealtime!"

Riley turned to him. "Shane says he looked for my dad and Aunt Mary on land, but he won't take any boats out."

"He's correct," Beresford said. "We must remain on land at all times."

"What?" Alfie cried. "What kind of place is this? If you won't find my mom, I want to use a phone to call someone who will."

"I am sorry, there are no phones here."

"That's impossible!" Riley said. "How can there not be phones? How do you talk to the other islands? What about getting supplies in? Where's the airport?"

Beresford shook his head. "I don't think you quite grasp where you are. We are alone here and with no way to leave. But why would anyone want to when it is paradise? Atlantis provides us with everything we need and asks only that we follow a few simple rules and don't abuse the land."

Riley's mouth hung open as she looked at her cousin. "Are these people for real?"

"I assure you, we are very real," Beresford said. He looked back at Bastian. "Please escort Riley and Alfie to your table. Everyone is waiting to start."

Bastian bowed his head. "Of course, Beresford."

"No!" Alfie shouted. "I need to find my mom and Riley needs her dad!"

Beresford shook his head. "We will discuss this after the meal."

"No," Riley said. "We'll discuss it now. I want to know why you won't help us find our family."

Beresford sighed heavily. "All right. I didn't want to tell you this so soon after your ordeal. But as you are so insistent, I have no choice. We have already found your parents. In fact, we found them before we found you. They were both washed ashore on the other side of the island. We tried our best to save them, but they were already gone."

"What do you mean gone?" Alfie asked softly.

"I am sorry, children. But your parents are dead."

10

RILEY COULDN'T BREATHE. SHE COULDN'T even stand as her legs buckled and she collapsed to the ground. It was impossible. How could her father be dead? Fathers didn't die. They stayed and played baseball after school, they told stupid jokes and talked about humpback whales all the time. They didn't drown and wash up on an island in the middle of nowhere.

Alfie screamed, "You're lying to me. My mom's not dead!" He turned and ran, vanishing into the trees.

Bastian knelt beside Riley and put his arm around her. "I am so sorry, Riley. I promise I didn't know."

Riley looked up at him but couldn't speak. Finally,

she looked over to Beresford. "Are—are you sure?"

"I'm so sorry, my child, but yes, I am. But don't you worry, we will take good care of you and Alfie."

Riley started to shake. "How is this possible? My dad is a great swimmer. He—he spends more time in the water than on land researching whales, and—and—and we all had our life vests on. He couldn't have drowned."

"The waters around here are treacherous. Storms appear out of nowhere. Waves come at you in all directions and there are dangerous predators that will eat anything. You and Alfie were lucky to survive."

The words seemed to swirl in the air around her. They were words she understood, yet they didn't make sense. "They—they can't be dead."

Beresford looked back at the gathering. "Everyone, please start your meal. Don't wait for us. Go on, now."

Servers appeared and started to distribute food. The sounds of expensive cutlery clinking on fine china and the soft murmur of discussion filled the area. Everyone seemed so casual and lighthearted, as though they didn't care that her world had just been destroyed.

"I need to see him," Riley said. "I need to know for sure."

Beresford knelt beside Bastian and laid his hand on Riley's shoulders. "I am sorry, child, but you can't. He's already been buried with his sister. With this tropical heat, there is no time to waste. But we can show you where they lie."

He looked at Bastian. "Would you please take Riley to the place of resting? We will hold your meal for you."

Bastian nodded. "Of course, Beresford." He reached for Riley's arm to help her up. "Come, Riley. Let me show you."

Riley moved as if in a dream. As though her legs were working without her permission. She felt them lift her up and then start to walk beside Bastian. They moved past the rows of tables with all the people eating. Past the table with the island's only children. Past the whole area and into the jungle.

If there were birds singing, Riley didn't hear them. If branches hit her in the face, she didn't feel them. She was walking in a dream—no, a nightmare.

"I really am so very sorry," Bastian said gently.

Miss Pigglesworth was walking beside her and licked Riley's hand, which hung limply at her side. She looked down into the eyes of the dog and thought she saw tears there.

"Shouldn't she be at the vet?" Riley asked. "Her side is still bleeding. . . ."

Miss Pigglesworth whined lightly.

"She says she's fine," Bastian said. "This is more important."

The three walked toward a clearing. On the opposite side of the open area were two mounds of freshly dug earth. Riley tried to stop. She didn't want to get closer to the mounds. To see them meant it was true. But once again, her legs betrayed her and kept her moving zombielike until finally she stopped at the base of the mounds.

"I don't remember my family," Bastian said. "But I lost them too." He pointed to a spot not far from them. "They are buried there."

Lost. What a horrible word. Lost meant missing. Lost meant gone. But her father wasn't missing or gone. He was right here. Buried under the dirt.

"They should have waited," Riley said softly.

"Waited?" Bastian asked.

Riley nodded slowly. "They should have waited before they buried him. I never got to say goodbye. . . ."

"You can say it now. He's right here."

Finally, all the shock, hurt, and pain swelled in Riley until she could no longer contain it. She collapsed on the mound and started to howl.

Riley lost all track of time as she lay on her father's grave. Heaving sobs came from deep within. Her eyes were stinging, and her nose was plugged shut from crying. She'd never lost anyone before, and the pain was unimaginable.

Bastian stayed at her side, and Miss Pigglesworth lay in the mound beside her, whining.

After a long time, her tears dried, and the hiccups arrived. It always happened when she cried, and she hated it. Soon she became aware of movement behind her. Looking up, she saw her cousin walking with a very tiny someone in a royal-blue cloak. The hood was pulled up over the person's head, but she could hear a high-pitched voice saying, "There she is, young Alfie."

Riley didn't know if the cloaked figure was talking about her or Alfie's mother, buried beside her father. Alfie screamed and ran over to the mound. He threw himself down and lay there as he called for his mother and started to cry.

Alfie's tears made her cry again. Riley crawled over to her cousin and reached for him. For as much as they didn't get along, right now Alfie was the only one who understood how she was feeling.

Alfie raised his head and threw his arms around her as the two cousins grieved the loss of a parent.

"We'll be okay," Riley wept as she clung to her cousin.

Alfie shook his head as he held her even tighter. "No, we won't."

"Yes, you will, in time . . . ," said the high-pitched voice from beneath the hood of the cloak. A strange-looking hand reached out and patted Alfie on the back. "You will see. In time you will be very happy here."

Despite her blurry eyes, Riley saw that the hand patting her cousin was small and covered in soft gray fur. There were sharp black claws at the end of the short furry fingers.

Riley sniffed and released her cousin. She sat up and reached for the hood on the cloak and pulled it back. She gasped when she saw the face beneath it.

11

"RILEY!" BASTIAN CRIED. "I KNOW YOU ARE grieving, but what you just did was unforgivable! I told you not to stare at those in cloaks. Instead you actually pulled the hood off one!"

Riley stared at the furry creature. He looked just like a cuddly koala, with a large black nose and round ears on the top of his head. But he was bigger and had golden eyes.

"It is all right, Bastian," the koala said gently. He pulled off his cloak and laid it aside. "They are unused to our ways and are suffering."

Alfie looked at the koala and his eyes went huge. "You're a—you're a—you're a talking teddy bear."

The koala chuckled softly. "No, Alfie, I am Pea."
He looked at Riley. "It is a pleasure to meet you, even
if the circumstances are so terribly, terribly sad."

At any other time in her life, Riley would have
been thrilled to meet a talking koala. Pea was the
most adorable thing she could ever imagine, with
his warm eyes, furry face, and stubby round body.
He had white tufts of fur on his small chin that
moved when he spoke, and his accent suggested he
was English. But the pain over her father and aunt
shredded any other feelings she had.

"Don't stare, Riley," Bastian chastised.

"Truly, it is all right, Bastian," Pea said gently. "I
don't mind at all. If it helps her, then she is welcome
to stare all she wants." Pea leaned closer to Riley.
"You may touch me to prove I am real, if it helps."

Pea leaned his face closer to Riley. Unable to stop
herself, she reached out and stroked the top of his
warm head between his furry round ears. Pea closed
his eyes and sighed as she scratched behind his ears.

"See? Very real," Pea finally said. His eyes opened.
"I truly am sorry about your father."

When he said that, Riley's tears started again. Pea
opened his tiny arms and wrapped them around her.

Riley collapsed into his furry embrace and cried into his shoulder. When her tears finally slowed, she sat up again. Sniffing, she said, "I'm sorry I pulled off your hood."

"I'm not." Pea kicked his cloak. "I hate wearing it. It's very hot and makes me itch."

"Then why do you wear it?" Alfie asked. He wiped his runny nose on his sleeve and sniffed back his tears.

Pea sighed, and for Riley, even that was adorable.

"I must," Pea said. "The others don't want to be reminded."

"Reminded of what?"

Pea started to speak, but then Miss Pigglesworth barked and whined, and he stopped. Finally, he looked at her and nodded. "They don't want to be reminded that there are others out there who look different from them. But in case Bastian hasn't warned you, you must never approach or speak to those in red cloaks. They wear red because it is a warning to stay back. Whereas I am harmless, so I wear blue."

Riley sniffed and nodded. "We've already seen some Red Cloaks."

"You have?" Pea gasped.

Bastian nodded. "Yes, it was a water ceremony—they

were releasing Susan to the ocean. Mada was there and he was crying."

"Oh my," Pea said. "Did he see you?"

Bastian nodded. "He tried to attack us, but the unicorns stopped him."

"Oh dear, oh dear, oh dear," Pea said. "Mada will not be best pleased, especially if you saw him crying over Susan. To him, tears are a sign of weakness. For you to witness that weakness will make him especially vicious." He reached forward and touched Riley's hand. "You must be very careful. Mada is the most ferocious of all the Red Cloaks. The only one in the world he cared about was Susan. Now that she's gone, he will be even more dangerous. I fear you might have made an enemy. He might even try to take his fury at the unicorns out on you."

"I tried to warn them, but they didn't understand," Bastian said.

"I still don't," Riley sniffed. "I don't understand anything here. Red Cloaks, sea monster, and even you . . ."

Pea giggled, and it was adorable coming out of his furry face. "I am only as I am. But you need never fear me. If you like, we could be friends."

Riley sniffed again. "I would like that. But I don't understand. What is Mada? He—he spoke like a man, but then roared like a lion and it looked like he had a tail."

Bastian answered, "I don't know. I've never seen him without his cloak. I've never seen any Red Cloaks without them. All I do know is that they're danger-ous."

"Indeed, they are," Pea agreed. "Promise me you'll stay away from them."

Riley lowered her head. "I want to stay away from everyone and just go home."

Pea patted her arm with his soft paw. "This is your home now, Riley. There is no way for you to go back to the life you had. But don't be afraid. We'll help you adjust to your new life. Won't we, Bastian and Miss Pigglesworth?"

Bastian nodded and Miss Pigglesworth barked.

"See? You aren't alone," Pea said.

"Now, I'm sure the others will be expecting you back," Pea continued. "And Miss Pigglesworth needs seeing to. Why don't we go show them that you're both all right?"

"But I'm not all right," Alfie snapped. "I'll never

be all right again. Just leave me alone!" Once again he got up and stormed off.

Riley watched him go and felt the same. This was the worst nightmare imaginable. Her father and aunt were dead, and all she wanted to do was go home to her mother and Danny. But that was impossible.

"Pea, do you know where my father and aunt washed ashore?"

"I was not there," Pea said. "But I heard Shane talking, so I think I know where it is."

"Will you take me there, please?"

"I mustn't. It is past the boundary line of the Community and in Red Cloak territory. It is very dangerous."

"Please," Riley begged. "I need to see it."

"Would it truly help to settle your mind?" Pea asked.

Riley nodded.

"Then all right."

"Pea, no!" Bastian cried. "Mada's already mad at us. If we go back across the boundary, he'll kill us."

"I do not think so, Bastian," Pea said. "You said the unicorns touched him. Their touch lasts a long time. I am sure we will be fine." The small koala reached for his cloak and pulled it back on again. Then he drew up his hood and offered Riley his paw.

Riley rose to her feet, took Pea's paw, and walked with the strange talking koala into the jungle with Bastian and Miss Pigglesworth following behind.

12

RILEY, PEA, BASTIAN, AND MISS PIGGLES-
worth made their way through the trees. With each
step, Riley's head was clearing. The pain was still
fresh and raw as tears trickled down her cheeks. But
at least she was aware of what she was doing.

It seemed to take ages to cross the jungle. When
they reached a split rail fence cutting through the
trees, Bastian paused. "Pea, really, we can't go in
there. This is the boundary line where the Community ends. We'll have no protection if we do."

"True," Pea said. He looked up at Riley. "After
today, you must never, ever, cross this fence. This is the
start of the Red Cloak territory. And past that is . . ."

Miss Pigglesworth barked, and Pea nodded. "You're right, it's too soon."

"Too soon for what?" Riley asked softly.

"Too soon for you to have to learn all the ways of Atlantis," Pea said. "For now, just know that if you see this fence surrounding the Community, you must never cross over it. However, today is an exception."

Pea slipped under one of the rails in the fence.

Riley climbed over the top. She turned back and saw Bastian hesitating. "You don't have to come if you don't want to."

Bastian glanced down at Miss Pigglesworth and then shrugged. "Mada is unconscious, and I'm sure the others are still with him. It should be all right." He also climbed over the fence.

Riley looked around and saw no difference between either side of the plain wooden fence. Trees were trees. She kept following Pea for some time until they walked clear of the jungle. Riley gasped. Up ahead was another golden beach and then water. But it was more like a channel, as just across from the water was another island. It looked much wilder than Atlantis. There was almost no beach, as the strange, immense trees came right up to the water's edge with their thick, gnarled roots reaching into the salty water. The biggest birds she'd ever seen soared above the trees but didn't cross over the water.

Riley looked up and could see the top of a rugged, rocky mountain with a rough, sharp peak. As she stared at it, she realized by the shape of it that it wasn't a mountain at all. It was an old volcano.

Bastian was shuffling his feet beside her, and Miss Pigglesworth was whining. "We shouldn't be here, Pea," he warned. "We're too close."

Riley sniffed through her tear-clogged nose. "Too close to what?"

Bastian nodded to the other island. "That, the Forbidden Zone."

"That's the Forbidden Zone?" Riley asked. "That island?"

Bastian nodded. "It's the most dangerous place there is. None of us can go there. It's filled with monsters."

"From what I've seen of Atlantis, there are monsters here too."

"Not like the Forbidden Zone," Pea said. "That is where some of the Red Cloaks go when they become too wild to stay in Atlantis. I would imagine Mada will be banished there soon."

Miss Pigglesworth barked again, and Pea looked back at her. "Why? She is going to find out eventually. Why wait?"

Perhaps it was the blinding grief, but none of what they were saying made any sense to Riley. Her eyes moved from the Forbidden Zone down to the beach before them. She saw something orange lying on the sand.

She started to walk to it, but Bastian caught her arm. "Don't go too close to the water, Riley—it's dangerous. Remember, the Leviathan patrols all these waters."

Riley looked at him and pulled her arm free. "I don't care if something eats me."

"But I do," Pea said gently.

"Me too," Bastian agreed.

Riley pointed to the item on the beach. "Do you see that orange thing by the water? I need to see it."

Pea's hood bowed. "Then allow me to fetch it for you. I am smaller and less likely to be seen by the Leviathan." He pulled off his cloak and waddled out of the trees and onto the sand.

Watching him move on his stubby, furry legs, Riley was again struck by how much he looked like a large koala. "What is he?" she asked Bastian. "How can he talk?"

"He is Pea," Bastian answered. "He's always talked."

"No, I mean, what species? He looks so much like a koala, but he's bigger."

"I don't know what a koala is," Bastian said. "So I don't know what Pea is, apart from being what he's meant to be."

Riley looked at Bastian and realized just how sheltered he was. Being stranded on Atlantis meant that he had no knowledge of the outside world. How could anyone live like that? No television, no cell phones, no internet. It would be terrible. Then she realized this was now going to be her life as well.

Pea returned carrying two orange life vests. He handed them up to Riley. She checked the names on them, and her breath caught when she read *Andrew*. There was also a small humpback whale pin on it that her father always kept there for luck. As her sobs started again, she realized the small pin hadn't been lucky at all.

She didn't need to read the name on the other life vest to know it was her aunt's. The silly daisies painted in Mary's blue nail polish proved it was hers. Riley remembered the night her aunt painted them. They had just had an emergency disaster rehearsal. Afterward she teased Riley's father about being paranoid. When he complained, she pulled out her blue nail polish and started to paint the large daisies— which irritated him even more.

Riley brushed her fingers over the flowers as the pain of loss rose to the surface again. She sat down on the warm sand, wondering how she was going to go on.

Bastian took a seat on her left, and Pea on her right. They said nothing as they sat beside her while her tears flowed unchecked.

Finally the tears slowed to hiccups again and trailed off completely. Riley looked up and over the water to the wild island across from them. "What am I supposed to do now?"

Pea put his paw on her hand. "You get up, go back to the Community, and you make a new life for yourself in Atlantis. It won't be the life you've known, but it is a good life. You will be happy here."

"Yes, you will," Bastian agreed. "We are."

Riley sniffed. "That's because you don't know what you're missing. All you know is here."

"It's all I want to know," Bastian said.

Riley said nothing more. There was no way they could understand what she'd lost. Her father, her mother and brother, and the life she had back home. It was all gone, wiped away by a vicious sea monster they called the Leviathan.

The roar of a large animal rose from deep in the jungle. Pea stood up quickly. "We must go. It is likely that isn't Mada, but it could be another Red Cloak. We must get you back to the *Queen*."

"Queen?" Riley repeated. "There is a queen here?"

Bastian nodded. "Yes, the *Queen of Bermuda*. I mentioned earlier that we have cabins on it. Around here, we just call it the *Queen*."

"Oh, the ship," Riley said as Pea drew her up. When the koala tried to take the life vests away, Riley refused to release them. "This is all I have left of my father and aunt. I'm keeping them."

"Of course," Pea said. "And so you should."

As they made their way back and climbed over the fence again, Pea pulled on his cloak. When they reached the outskirts of the Community, he stopped and bowed to her. "Forgive me, Riley, but this is where I must leave you. Bastian will take you the rest of the way. Please remember I am always around if you need me."

"Thank you, Pea," Riley said softly. She watched him waddle away, wishing that her father and aunt could have met him. They would have been so amazed.

Before going to the cruise ship, Bastian made a detour to what he called the doctor's office. They walked over to one of the smaller buildings made of colorful stones. The door was open, and Riley saw two people inside.

When they entered, a squat man of around thirty was wrapping a worker's hand in leaves and then a white fabric bandage on top. "That should do it," he said. "Just keep it dry for a day and you'll be fine."

Riley looked around the room. The walls were lined with shelves stacked full of jars. Each jar was filled with some kind of plant material or leaves. There were no instruments to be seen and no drugs. Not even aspirin. What was really missing was the doctor's-office smell made up of a mix of antiseptic and cleaners.

"This can't be a doctor's office," she whispered.

"It is," Bastian said.

When the patient left, the doctor came forward. His sympathetic eyes landed on Riley. "I am so sorry about your father, Riley. I wish there was something I could have done for him. But it was too late."

Riley felt her throat constrict. "I'll be outside," she managed before the sobs started.

Standing near the door, Riley took several deep breaths, trying to stop the tears. She and Alfie were in a terrible situation, and crying all the time wasn't helping. But each time someone walked past, they nodded to her and offered her their condolences, and the floodgates opened again.

Finally Bastian and Miss Pigglesworth appeared. The dog's side was wrapped in a bandage and Riley could see leaves poking out from the top of the bandage. From appearances, the doctor hadn't even shaved the dog's hair away from the wounds.

"Leaves?" Riley said. "He treated your dog with leaves?"

Bastian nodded. "I have to take off the bandage tomorrow."

"What kind of doctor is he?" Riley asked.

"A good one. We're very lucky to have him."

"My mother is a doctor, and she'd go ballistic if

she saw it in there. I mean, if he's the only medical person on Atlantis, and if he's going to treat people and animals, he should at least clean the area between patients!"

"Why? We're all the same here."

"No, you're not! You are a person, and Miss Pigglesworth is a dog. You have different germs and bacteria."

Her words seemed to go right over Bastian's head. "But he's everyone's doctor."

"He's not mine, that's for sure," Riley said.

Leaving the medical hut, they made their way back to the cruise ship. Again, more people smiled at her along the way.

"See?" Bastian said softly. "Everyone here cares for each other. It's how we live. I know you don't feel it now, but in time you will understand."

Riley looked up at him. She doubted it but didn't say anything. Instead she followed him toward the ramp leading up to the loading bay on the *Queen*. Once they were inside, Riley was shocked by how big it was.

"I'm told this is where they loaded the luggage when it was still sailing," Bastian explained. "The passengers never came down here—this deck was for staff only. But now anyone can go anywhere."

Riley was only half listening as she looked around the loading bay of the big cruise ship. "Are there elevators?"

Bastian grinned. "I know what you're talking about. Yes, there are, but they don't work anymore. So we walk up the stairs. Come, they're this way."

Bastian and Miss Pigglesworth led her to metal stairs. "Our cabins are four levels up. It's a bit of a climb, I'm afraid."

Riley followed Bastian through the maze that was the cruise ship. From the drab gray-and-white decks where the staff used to work, they moved down a passage and through a door that led to an open area that would have been for paying passengers.

Everything was beautiful. The furnishings were lush, and the decorations on the wall were stunning. If there wasn't dark wood paneling, there were paintings and tile mosaics. Everywhere she looked were marble statues on plinths and carved wooden railings. The carpeting was worn but clean and hinted at what it must have once looked like. Everything around Riley reminded her of her mother's favorite movie, *Titanic*.

As they climbed several flights of stairs, Riley imagined that when the *Queen of Bermuda* was cruising the ocean, it would have been a luxury liner and very expensive to sail on. It didn't look anything like the other big ships she'd been on. There were no arcade machines and none of the shops that she saw on the three-day cruise her family took last year when they went to Florida.

Pain stabbed through Riley as she thought of her family again. Suddenly the beauty of the old ship was forgotten.

"This is our deck," Bastian said. They walked along the passage to the very end.

Bastian stopped before a door. "Here you are. Alfie's is right next to you, and my cabin is across from his. I'm sure you'll be happy here."

Riley knew he was trying to be kind, but his words were lost on her. She needed to be left alone. "Thank you, Bastian. I guess I'll see you later."

"Of course you will," he said brightly. "If you need anything, just ask and it will be brought to you."

Riley almost said *I need my family* . . . but there was no point.

She opened the door and was once again struck

by the beauty of everything on the ship. Her cabin was bigger than she imagined on a boat. There was a double bed with an ornately carved headboard near an actual window. She was surprised they weren't just portholes but large square windows with flower curtains hanging down.

The room had a writing desk with a chair and a sofa with two side chairs. Everything looked antique. But they were in good condition without a tear or mark on the fabric. There also wasn't a spot of dust to be found.

Putting down the life vests, she noticed another door near the cabin door. Riley figured it would be a closet, but when she opened it, she found it was a bathroom with a toilet, sink, vanity, large mirror, and small shower. She approached the sink and turned on the faucet. There wasn't any water. She wondered how the toilet was supposed to flush without it. Then she spied a bucket of water beside it.

Standing at the sink, Riley saw her face in the mirror. It was red and puffy from crying. Her hair was a tangled mess and her clothing was filthy. But she didn't care. She didn't care about anything anymore. Not the pretty room, not the beautiful jungle. Everything she cared about was gone.

Leaving the bathroom, she walked back into the cabin that was to be her new home. The silence of the room brought all her thoughts to the surface. Did her mother and Danny know they were missing yet? Were they frantic? Had the wreck of the *Event Horizon* been found?

Riley walked over to the desk. There was stationery in a holder and a pen set. There was also a small supply of postcards showing the cruise ship. She turned one over and read the back. *Queen of Bermuda, 1951.*

"1951?" Riley said aloud. She looked around the room again. Everything did look old-fashioned. But could it really be that old? How long had the cruise ship been on the island? Were all the people of Atlantis from it? What about the unicorns? Pea? And the vicious Red Cloaks? Where did they all come from?

These questions swirled around Riley's head, and she would ask Bastian later. But now that she was alone, the grief took hold again. Walking over to the bed, she lay down as the sobs returned.

The soft knocking on her door roused Riley from a dreamless sleep. She awoke feeling disoriented and frightened. This wasn't the *Event Horizon.* Suddenly it all rushed back to her and she felt sick with grief.

The knocking continued. "Riley, it's me," Alfie said quietly. "Can I come in?"

"Yeah," Riley called as she sat up.

Her cousin entered her room. His face looked as bad as hers. "They said you were here."

"Bastian brought me a while ago. He says your room is next door."

"I've seen it and I hate it," he said. "I hate everything here."

In all her life, she'd never seen her cousin looking so lost and alone. She realized all they had now was each other.

"Riley, what are we gonna do?" His voice was small and trembling like a child.

Riley got up and walked over to her cousin. "We're going to find our way off this island and go home."

Alfie sniffed. "You think we can?"

Riley nodded. "I don't care what they say, we're going home."

Alfie's eyes landed on the orange life vests. "When did you get our stuff from the beach?"

"That's not ours," Riley said. "I asked Pea and Bastian to take me where Dad and Aunt Mary washed up. It's on the other side of the island, and these were still there."

Riley picked up the orange life vest covered in blue daisies and handed it to her cousin. Then she picked up her father's and pulled the whale pin off it and put it on her top. "Alfie, we gotta work together if we hope to get off this island. No more fighting, no more teasing. Dad and Aunt Mary would want that. What do you say? Truce?"

Alfie was on the verge of tears again as he held on to his mother's life vest. "Truce."

Riley sat down in one of the plush chairs. "I—I don't know what to do next. Everything here is so weird."

"No kidding," Alfie agreed as he sat opposite her. "I still don't know what's up with those guys in red. And what about Pea? What is he, some kind of talking animal? But that's impossible. And those unicorns, do you think they're for real?"

"I don't know," Riley said. "The Leviathan and mermaids were. Pea is. But none of it makes any sense." She paused and stared down at her father's life vest. "Mada really scares me. Pea said where Dad and Mary washed up was where he and the Red Cloaks live. You don't think . . ."

"Don't be stupid," Alfie shot. "If one of the Red Cloaks got them, there'd be blood on these. . . ."

"I guess," Riley agreed. She sighed heavily. "Maybe we should look for debris from the *Event Horizon*. If we washed ashore, the life raft might have too. We could take it back out."

"What about the sea monster, the Leviathan, or those mermaids?"

Riley shrugged. "Good question. But they can't be everywhere all the time. Maybe we should try to learn more about them."

Alfie nodded. "I guess I could start asking around."

"Me too. This place is full of questions and we need some answers."

13

WHEN ALFIE RETURNED TO HIS CABIN, Riley lay down again. She didn't think she would sleep but dropped right off. It was another loud gong that finally woke her up.

Gazing out the window, she saw the pink colors of sunset. Not long after, there was a knock on the cabin door. "Riley, it's me," Bastian called. "It is time for our evening meal. You haven't eaten anything today. Beresford told me to bring you and Alfie."

Riley went to the door and opened it. Bastian was standing there with Alfie beside him. Miss Pigglesworth was also there and wagging her tail excitedly.

"How are you feeling?"

"The same," Riley said. "Bastian, there's no running water. How do you wash your face and stuff? Or do we use the bucket of water for that and the toilet?"

Color rose in Bastian's face. He nodded, then looked at Alfie. "Filling the buckets every day is my job. Lisette says you are to help me."

"I have a job?" Alfie said.

Bastian nodded. "We all do. It is how we live."

"Yeah, get real," Alfie said. "I'm not working here."

"But you must," Bastian said. "We all have to do our share."

"No way . . ."

"Alfie," Riley said. "I think it would be good for you. You and Bastian can get to know each other better—you know, *talk* and stuff."

"Yes, it will be fun," Bastian said.

Riley gave her cousin an expression she hoped he would understand, relating to their earlier conversation.

"Oh yeah," Alfie finally said. "We can talk. Maybe you can tell me more about the Leviathan and Atlantis."

"Of course," Bastian said.

"Will I have a job?" Riley asked.

"Yes," Bastian answered. "But I don't know what yours will be yet. Lisette hasn't told me. She may wish to speak to you first to learn what you can do. But don't worry about it. Right now, you must come to eat."

Riley looked over at Alfie. "I can't remember the last time I ate."

"It was yesterday," Alfie said.

Bastian beamed with relief. "Wonderful. Let's go."

They followed Bastian along the same route they'd used earlier, but Riley doubted she'd remember it. If the ship looked big on the outside, it was even bigger inside, with miles of corridors where it would be easy to get lost.

"You'll get used to it," Bastian promised when Riley voiced her concerns.

Riley looked at Alfie and he nodded carefully. They both knew what it meant. There would be no getting used to it because they weren't going to be here long enough to learn.

When they reached outside, they joined the stream of people heading to the square to eat. Just like earlier, the tables were dressed in their formal wear of linen cloths and fine china and silver.

As they approached the dining area, everyone stopped what they were doing and looked at them. Their sympathetic stares were making Riley uncomfortable. This was the longest she'd managed to go without crying. If they weren't careful, their expressions would start the waterworks all over again.

"Welcome, children," Beresford said as he jogged over. "I am so pleased to see you joining us for the evening meal."

"Yeah, whatever," Alfie said.

"I'm sorry?" Beresford said.

"He means thank you for inviting us," Riley said. If they were going to start spying on the Atlanteans, now was the time to start. "I'm sorry about earlier. . . ."

"Please don't fret about it," Beresford said. "It has been a shock and you are grieving. But you are settling in now, and that's good." His eyes went to Bastian. "Would you escort them to your table? And then we can begin."

Riley and Alfie followed Bastian to the table. Once again all the children there appeared excited to see them.

Bastian held up his hands to calm everyone. "I

know we're all happy to welcome Riley and Alfie to our table, but they have had some very sad news, so please let them be for now."

Riley took a seat beside the young girl. She looked to be no more than eight or nine.

"I'm Soraya," she said as her face beamed with joy.

"I'm Riley."

The young girl giggled. "I know." She started to point to the others at the table. "That's Kerry there," she said, pointing to a girl a bit older than Riley. "And there's Elizabeth and Victoria. They're twins."

Riley looked at the twins. Soraya wasn't kidding. There was no telling Elizabeth and Victoria apart. Same red hair cut in the same style. They had the same green eyes and were completely identical. They might have been eleven or twelve.

Soraya continued. "Over there is Ellis, John, and that's Vadin."

"Vader?" Alfie repeated as he took a seat opposite Riley. "Like *Darth Vader*?"

"Who?" Bastian said.

"Darth Vader," Alfie said. "You know, from *Star Wars*."

Riley watched everyone at the table look at Alfie

in confusion. "Alfie, they don't have movies here, remember?"

"Oh yeah, right." Alfie lowered his head and Riley heard him say "losers" softly.

Even the kids' table was as strange as everything else in Atlantis. There were people of different ages and races seated with her, but they all had one thing in common: they were unusually polite, just like Bastian. She wondered if they had any bad habits at all.

Soon the servers arrived with a large cauldron. They set it beside a table that was filled with large soup bowls. As the bowls were filled, they were delivered to Riley first, then Alfie, and finally everyone else at the table. After that, the others on the long trestle tables were served.

The savory aroma of the soup made Riley's mouth water. Despite the heaviness in her chest from grief, she realized her stomach didn't get the message and was rumbling from hunger. She reached for her glass of water when Bastian cleared his throat. "Um, Riley, we have to wait until Beresford speaks."

Riley turned back and sought Beresford out at his table. Once everyone was served, he rose and held up his glass.

"This evening we celebrate a very special arrival. Riley and Alfie were drawn up from the depths of the ocean, and despite the danger from the Leviathan, they were delivered safely to our shores. Though they have suffered great losses and we suffer with them, we welcome them to Atlantis and know that they will be very happy here."

Beresford turned to Riley and Alfie and tipped his head. "To Riley and Alfie, welcome to Atlantis!"

Everyone raised their glasses and repeated softly, "Riley and Alfie, welcome to Atlantis."

Riley hated the attention and saw that Alfie was even more uncomfortable.

Finally, when Beresford sat again, Riley could breathe.

Kerry spoke for the first time. "You must feel very honored to be in Atlantis."

"You gotta be joking!" Alfie snorted.

"Alfie, please," Riley said. She shot him a look that warned him from saying more. She turned back to Kerry. "Excuse me, but we've both had the worst day of our lives, so we don't feel honored."

Alfie looked up at her sharply but held his tongue.

"So where do you all come from?" Riley asked.

Kerry snorted. "That's a really stupid question. We're from Atlantis."

"Kerry, be nice," Bastian said.

Kerry looked like Bastian had struck her. Her lower lip went out in a pout, and she looked like she might cry.

Riley ignored Kerry and looked at Ellis. "If you were born here, why aren't you sitting with your parents?"

Ellis frowned in confusion. "I don't understand."

"I mean . . . ," Riley started.

Bastian tapped her arm and leaned closer. "Some of the younger ones don't remember their families. Atlantis is our home and our parents. It is all we need. Now it is your family too."

None of this made any sense. How could Ellis not know his parents? They had to be sitting among the adults. Or perhaps like her father, Ellis's parents had died when they arrived. Saying nothing more, she picked up her spoon and started to eat the soup.

As they ate, Alfie looked up to Bastian. "So what's with all the freaky creatures here?"

Bastian frowned. "I don't know what you mean by 'freaky.'"

"You know," Alfie said. "Pea and the Red Cloaks and the unicorns. Freaky."

"They are not freaky," Bastian said. "They are normal."

"No way," Alfie said. "There is nothing normal about this place!"

"You will get used to it," Vadin offered. "Soon you will love Atlantis as we do."

"Don't count on it," Alfie scoffed.

"Alfie," Riley warned softly.

Alfie glared at her. "What?"

"Just stop it," Riley said.

Alfie had a retort on his lips but held it in and focused on eating.

After dinner, Bastian invited Riley and Alfie to attend the bonfire with him. When Riley tried to say no, Bastian insisted that everyone would be there, and it would be rude to miss it.

Riley surrendered and they walked to a clearing in the jungle where rows of logs were set up for people to sit on before a roaring fire.

When she sat down, Bastian took a seat beside her and Miss Pigglesworth took a place beside him. Kerry glared at her with an expression that could freeze boiling water.

Riley hadn't been on Atlantis a full day and already

she'd made an enemy. Despite everyone's good manners, Kerry was behaving like a jealous, spoiled child. It was obvious she was interested in Bastian and saw Riley as competition. Part of Riley wanted to say she didn't have to worry, that they wouldn't be here long. But she remained silent.

First there was storytelling as Beresford came forward and stood before the fire. He told tales of brave feats by Atlantean heroes who had "moved ahead." There were stories about the Leviathan and how it had hauled the *Queen of Bermuda* high into the jungle and settled the cruise ship where it now lay.

Throughout the telling, Riley would look at her cousin and see that he was thinking the same. That the stories sounded more like campfire tall tales than retellings of historic events.

After Beresford sat down, everyone started to sing. Despite the otherworldliness of the whole day, Riley found peace in the melodies. Each tune carried her away from the overwhelming grief of losing her father and home. But when the songs ended, once again she was crushed under the weight of loss.

After a time, Riley stood up. "I'm sorry, Bastian,

but I need to be alone right now. Would you take me back to the *Queen*?"

"Me too," Alfie agreed.

Bastian stood. "Of course. Let me walk you back to your cabins."

As they made their way through the jungle toward the *Queen*, Riley had the strangest feeling they were being followed. A soft, low growl sounded from the trees beside them that sent shivers down her spine. When she looked, she saw a flash of movement, but then it was gone. But the growl had been the same she'd heard on the beach. She glanced at Bastian and he was staring into the trees as well.

"It's him, isn't it?" Riley said. "Mada is stalking us."

"It can't be," Bastian said. "None of the Red Cloaks are allowed in the Community."

"Yeah, well, did anyone bother to tell him?" Alfie said as his wide eyes searched the darkness. "I mean, what is Mada? Does he really have a tail?"

"I don't know," Bastian said. "But I will tell Beresford. If Mada has broken the boundary rules, he will be punished."

"That's if we live long enough to tell him." Alfie

backed away from the sounds in the trees. The growling was getting closer.

"Bastian . . . ," Riley said. She looked at the cruise ship and saw that it was too far to reach even if they ran.

Miss Pigglesworth started to bark.

"Yes, Mada, we know it's you!" Bastian called. "Go away. You're not allowed here!"

The growl stopped, and then there was a nerve-chilling roar and the sound of snapping branches. Moments later, it was silent.

Miss Pigglesworth stopped and looked up at Bastian and whined.

Bastian looked deeper into the trees and then down to the dog. "Maybe."

"Has he gone?" Alfie whispered.

"I sure hope so," Riley said. She was shaking uncontrollably as she scanned the trees.

"What's going on here?"

Everyone jumped as Shane approached them from the direction of the gathering. "Bastian, I thought you were taking Riley and Alfie back to the *Queen*."

"I was," Bastian said. "But—but we heard growling. Shane, I think Mada is after us."

"Mada?" Shane laughed. "I hardly think so. It had to be something else."

"No, I'm sure it was Mada," Riley insisted. "We heard him growl earlier and it sounded the same."

Shane turned on her. "Riley, I know you are new here, but you cannot go around accusing people without good cause. It can lead to strife. Mada and the Red Cloaks are banned from this area. There is no way it could have been him. It was probably a wild animal."

"Lead to strife!" Riley cried. "What about us? If Mada had attacked us, would you consider that *strife*?"

Shane inhaled deeply and let it out slowly. "I will escort you to the *Queen*. You will each go to your cabins and stay there until the morning gong. Is that understood?"

Bastian lowered his head. "Yes, Shane."

"No!" Alfie said. "It was Mada! He's after us because we saw him cry."

"Enough!" Shane shouted.

They said nothing further as they followed Shane back to the grounded cruise ship. He stood at the base of the ramp and watched them climb up on board. "Straight to your cabins," he said firmly.

Bastian led them to the stairs and up to their deck. They reached their cabins in silence.

"I'll see you tomorrow," Bastian said glumly.

Riley lowered her head. "Good night, Bastian." She nodded to her cousin and then opened the door and slipped inside.

It was dark in her room except for a single oil lantern burning on the desk that had been lit by someone coming in. The glow was enough for her to get around, but also made the room look even eerier than it had earlier. Long, flickering shadows danced on the walls and curtains, making the cabin look somehow alive.

Before long, there was a light knock on her door. She didn't need to ask to know who it was.

"Come in, Alfie," she called.

Her cousin entered, carrying a blanket and pillow from his cabin. He nodded to the lantern. "They've been in your room too."

"I don't like it here," Riley said softly. "And I don't like Shane."

"Me neither," Alfie said.

Alfie appeared even more lost as he moved his

weight from one foot to the other. Finally he said, "Riley, can I sleep in here tonight? I'll be quiet and I'll stay on the sofa. I just don't want to be alone. I feel . . ."

His eyes were puffy, and the lantern light flickered on the fresh tears in his eyes. Which brought out the tears in Riley.

She nodded and sniffed. "Sure."

Nothing else was said as Alfie made up the sofa and settled down. They had both been provided with bed-clothes, but Riley couldn't bear the thought of changing out of the clothes she was wearing. They were the last link she had to the life that was now gone.

Climbing into bed fully dressed, her tears returned and trailed down her cheek as she drifted off to a dreamless sleep.

14

AFTER A NIGHT OF TOSSING AND TURNING, Riley lay in bed and wished the previous day had just been a bad dream. But it wasn't. She was in a cabin on an upper deck of a cruise ship sitting in the middle of a strange island. Her father and aunt were dead, some kind of monster seemed to have it in for her, and she was trapped in Atlantis with Alfie.

Unable to sleep, Riley rose. Alfie was snoring softly on the sofa across the cabin, so she moved silently to the window. The sun was just starting to rise over the ocean, giving the sky that strange bluish-gray look of predawn.

Down on the ground, no one was moving around.

Over the treetops in the distance she could see the top of the Crucible. The tall crystal tower glowed strangely in the rising light. With the sun behind it, she thought the light would shine right through it. But it just reflected and seemed to sparkle.

Feeling more lost and alone than she imagined possible, Riley crossed to the desk and pulled out one of the postcards and a pencil.

Can't sleep. Going for a walk. Back later.

Placing the note in Alfie's shoe, she tiptoed to the door and slipped out. The passage was empty and there were no sounds of movement anywhere.

Following the same route they took the previous evening, Riley went down to the loading doors and saw two people she didn't know opening them.

"Good morning, Riley," a middle-aged man said. "You're up early."

Riley nodded. "I couldn't sleep. Do you close these doors at night?"

"Always," the other worker said. "We can't have Red Cloaks creeping on board while we're sleeping."

Riley gasped. "But I thought Red Cloaks weren't allowed in the Community."

Both men laughed. "I'm just fooling with you.

Red Cloaks aren't around here. But we don't want any other wildlife making it inside, so we close things up sometime after the bonfire."

When the doors were opened fully, one of the men bowed elegantly. "There you go. It's a beautiful day. Please enjoy yourself."

Riley nodded and descended the ramp. The fresh morning air was ocean washed, and birdsong was just starting.

She gazed back up at the *Queen*, remembering the story Beresford had told the previous evening about how the Leviathan had dragged it up to its final resting place. Looking at the ship, she thought that the Leviathan was either much bigger than it seemed when it capsized their sailboat or Beresford was telling a very tall tale.

Glancing around, Riley didn't know where she wanted to go. Just that she had to keep moving. It was the only way she could stay ahead of the pain that was lingering just below the surface.

She recalled the encounter with Mada the previous evening and realized that whatever Mada was, he was still out there. But as she walked between the neat stone buildings and boat houses, she found she didn't care. If something were to eat her, then at least she could be back with her father again.

Wandering through the jungle without a plan, Riley arrived at an area that ended with a slope that went down several feet to the water's edge. There was no beach, just a bit of mud and bushes and then the water. The ocean was smooth, calm, and crystal clear. Across the way rose the imposing Forbidden Zone. Looking at the massive island, it appeared to sit alongside Atlantis for as far as her eyes could see. It might even be bigger than Atlantis with that volcano rising high in the air.

As noisy as the jungle around her was becoming as the sun rose, there were sounds coming from the volcanic island that were giving her chills. Roaring, louder than Mada's was, filled the air, as well as growling and the sounds of big animals tearing through the bushes. Just on the shore across the way, she saw movement in the trees close to the water. This was followed by a terrible cry, and then the movement and sounds stopped.

In the water below, Riley watched shoals of small fish darting past. Not far offshore, several dolphins surfaced and blew out air from their blowholes. This was perhaps the prettiest place she'd ever been, with the trees all around her, the wild island across from her, and the stunning, clear water before her. It was paradise.

But this paradise had killed her father and aunt.

As she sat down on the edge, the tears that were now always so close came back. Riley drew up her knees and hugged them tightly to herself as heaving sobs tore through her.

After a time, the sobs passed, and the hiccups started. Riley got up to leave. Just as she started to walk away, she heard the sound of a woman screaming, followed by loud shouting and the word "No!" coming from the Forbidden Zone. It was faint and far away, but it sounded a lot like her aunt.

Riley grasped a branch and leaned out over the water as far as she dared, straining to hear the sounds again, but they didn't repeat. "Aunt Mary, are you over there? Can you hear me? Aunt Mary, answer me!"

"Riley, get back!"

Riley jumped and turned around. Pea in his blue cloak was coming up behind her.

Riley looked back at the Forbidden Zone but didn't hear the shouting again. "Pea, did you hear that?"

"Oh, child," Pea said, clutching his heart with a furry gray paw. "You nearly gave me a heart attack.

Leaning out over the water like that is very dangerous. The Leviathan . . ."

"Yes, but did you hear that?"

"Hear what? I hear many things, including my poor heart pounding!"

"It sounded like a woman screaming and shouting. It was coming from the Forbidden Zone. It could have been my aunt."

Pea reached up and took Riley by the hand and drew her away from the edge. Then he invited her to sit. He pushed back the hood on his cloak.

"Riley, the Forbidden Zone is called that for a very good reason. It is forbidden to us because it is so dangerous. I don't doubt that you heard something, but there are creatures there that are beyond imagination. Some that may even sound like people."

"I didn't hear people, Pea, I heard my aunt."

Pea sighed. "Riley, you and Alfie washed ashore on the other side of Atlantis. If you were all in the water together when your boat went down, how could your aunt have made it around Atlantis, which is a very large island, and to the Forbidden Zone? With the tides around here, that would be impossible. Not to mention the Leviathan. It hunts all these waters."

"But—but it sounded like her," Riley said.

"Perhaps it is your wounded heart wishing it were so. But only the most vicious creatures are in the Forbidden Zone. Anyone unfortunate enough to be there wouldn't last a day."

Riley looked over to the dangerous island. She was sure it wasn't an animal she'd heard—it sounded like Mary. The Forbidden Zone was a distance away across the water, but she was a strong swimmer. She could make it there if she tried. There was only one problem. . . .

She looked back at the koala. "Pea, is it true the Leviathan pulled the *Queen of Bermuda* onto the island?"

Pea chuckled lightly. "What an odd question. Obviously Beresford has been telling his stories again. But in this case, it's true. It happened a very, very long time ago."

"So you could say the Leviathan helped the people."

"Yes, I believe he did, as many, including you, call the *Queen* your home."

"Then, if the Leviathan could go on land long enough to pull a big ship up there, couldn't he come back on land to hunt people if he really wanted to?"

Pea opened his mouth to speak, but then closed it again. "You know what? You're right. I wonder why I never thought of that."

Riley sniffed. "My mother says sometimes you can't see the forest for the trees."

Pea considered for a moment and then nodded. "Perhaps. Your mother sounds like a wise woman."

"She is," Riley agreed. She felt her throat constrict. "Pea, I want to go home. I want to tell my mom what happened to us and I want to see my brother, but I can't. Everyone in Atlantis doesn't understand. I didn't just lose my dad; I've lost my whole family."

"I wish I could send you home," Pea said. "I truly do. But I can't. I can't do much of anything anymore." The small animal sighed. "Did I tell you I used to be a carpenter?"

Riley shook her head.

"I was," Pea said. "Before the change and my hands became too small to work my tools. I helped build a lot of the boat homes back there. But that was a lifetime ago. You might say I lost my old life, too, and understand how you feel."

Riley frowned. "What do you mean before the change? What change?"

Pea brought his paw to his mouth. "Oh my, I've said too much. I am always saying too much. I'm sorry, child." He rose. "I must go."

Before Riley could stop him, Pea darted off into the jungle. She tried to follow him, to ask him what he meant about changing, but Pea vanished. She could find no trace of him in the trees.

By the time Riley reached the Community, people were up and walking around. They all smiled and greeted her as she walked past.

Back on the *Queen*, Riley climbed the stairs and made it back to her cabin. Alfie was still asleep.

"Alfie, wake up, I need to talk to you."

"No, leave me alone. . . ." He pulled the pillow over his head.

"Please," Riley said. "I have to speak to you. I don't think Aunt Mary is dead. . . ."

"What?" Alfie cried as he turned over. "What are you talking about?"

Riley told her cousin how she couldn't sleep and went for a predawn walk that led to the slope across from the Forbidden Zone. She told him about the shouting. "I couldn't hear everything clearly, but I did hear her shout no. I'm sure it was Mary. Pea tried to say it was an animal, but that was no animal."

"They said she was dead. Why would they lie to us?"

"I don't know. But think about it. We arrived on one side of Atlantis; how is it possible that Dad and Mary arrived on the other side, just across from the Forbidden Zone when we were together?"

Alfie sat up. "Atlantis is so big, it's not possible! Plus, why were they buried so quickly? We never saw them. It's like the people here didn't want us to look for them."

"Exactly," Riley said. "What if those creatures in the water brought us here, but took Dad and Mary to the Forbidden Zone?"

"Why would they?"

"I don't know. But there aren't many kids here. Maybe they wanted us but not Dad and Mary. Whatever it is, something strange is happening."

"No kidding!" Alfie said. "We have to check."

"What do you mean, 'check'?"

"Tonight," Alfie said. "We're going to dig up those mounds to see if they're really there."

15

BY THE TIME THE BREAKFAST GONG sounded, Riley and Alfie were ready. When Bastian knocked on their door, they opened it immediately.

Bastian's face was a puzzle when he entered and saw Alfie's bedroll on the sofa.

"You have your own cabin."

"So? Riley was upset. She wanted me to stay with her."

Riley looked at Alfie and raised her eyebrows. "Um, yeah, sure, I was really upset."

"I hope you are feeling better," Bastian said. "Today after breakfast, Lisette is going to assign you tasks."

Riley had completely forgotten about that. "Of course."

"Wonderful," Bastian said. "Let's get some break-fast and I can take you to Lisette."

They followed Bastian back through the ship and to the dining area outside. When they approached the children's table, everyone greeted them warmly. Everyone except Kerry, who scowled at Riley when she saw Bastian walking with her. "Bastian, I'm sure the newcomers have learned how to get here on their own. You don't have to stay with them all the time."

"It's only been a day," Bastian defended. "They have a lot to learn."

"Let someone else teach them. Why does it have to be you?"

Riley had known girls like Kerry at school. They were jealous troublemakers, always needing to be the center of attention. Even in the middle of nowhere, girls like that still existed. "Maybe he's just being nice," Riley said. "You should try it sometime."

Kerry gasped. "What did you say to me?"

"You heard me," Riley said.

"Shorty," Alfie warned, "let's just eat and not cause trouble. We have work to do."

Riley looked at Alfie and realized it was usually her stopping him. She nodded. "You're right, I'm sorry."

"You should be!" Kerry spat. She stood up and stormed off.

Riley watched her go, wondering if she had just made a mistake in angering her.

After a meal of fresh fruit and a kind of oatmeal, Lisette walked over to the table. "Are you two ready to receive your assignments for the day?"

Riley looked at her cousin before nodding.

"Very good." She looked at Riley. "Do you know how to sew?"

"Not really," Riley answered.

"Then it is time you learned. I'll take you to the sewing hut and you can get started." She turned to Alfie. "For today, you will stay with Bastian and do as he does. Tomorrow we will chat about other jobs for you."

"Do I have a choice?" Alfie said.

Lisette smiled. "Not really. We all work here."

"Fine," Alfie said, "I'll work with Bastian."

Riley followed Lisette away from the dining area.

"As you can imagine, with all these people, and limited supplies, we must make the clothing last. So we repair them just as soon as they show signs of wear."

"Where does everyone get their clothes? Is there a store here or something?" Riley had noticed the strange assortment of clothing on the people of Atlantis. Most of it was older styles. Nothing like she saw in the shopping malls with her friends.

"Stores?" Lisette said with a confused look. "There are no stores here."

"So where do you get your clothing and stuff?"

"It is washed ashore," Lisette said. "I am sure before long we will see some of the clothing that you had on your boat arriving here. That and other supplies."

"So you just scavenge?"

This Lisette did understand. "Yes, we have learned to accept what the ocean grants us. And if there isn't anything new washed ashore, we can weave some of our own fabrics from what grows in Atlantis. Do not fear: there will always be plenty for everyone."

Lisette took Riley back to one of the old, colorful stone buildings she had walked past yesterday. Inside were several women sitting in a circle. The doors and windows were open, and they seemed to be the only sources of light.

"Everyone, Riley will be joining you today. We want her to learn to sew."

The women in the room were of different races, and all smiled at her. Off to one side working alone was someone wearing a yellow cloak with the hood drawn up. Her hands were covered with gloves, but despite them she was sewing quickly with neat stitches. When she looked up, Riley nearly gasped. Her eyes were like cat's eyes, with slits for pupils, and her nose was almost flat on her face and jet-black. Her lips were shaped like a cat's as well.

The cat-woman smiled, and it showed long, canine-like teeth. "Welcome, Riley," she said softly.

"Um, thank you . . . ," Riley responded, unable to take her eyes off the strange woman.

"Don't stare, dear, you'll make Maggie uncomfortable." Lisette drew Riley away. She looked at the ladies. "So who would like to be Riley's teacher today?"

"I would."

Riley turned and her heart sank when Kerry entered the sewing hut.

"That's very kind of you, Kerry," Lisette said. "Thank you."

Kerry smiled sweetly at Lisette. "It will be my pleasure."

Lisette patted Riley's shoulder. "I will leave you in the care of Kerry and see you again at lunch."

When she was gone, Kerry caught Riley by the arm in a grip that was almost painful. "Come on, Riley, let's get started."

Kerry led Riley to a large basket filled with clothing. "This is where the clothes needing repair are kept. You come in the morning and take something. Then you repair it." Going through the basket, she pulled out some heavy-duty pants. "These are for you." Then she pulled out a lightweight plaid shirt for herself. "Take a seat and get to work."

Kerry showed Riley where to get the needles and thread.

"I—I really don't know how to sew."

"I know that," Kerry spat. "Watch me."

Riley sat down beside Kerry and watched her draw a line of thread through the needle hole and then tie a knot at one end. Then she started to repair the shirt with tiny, even stitches.

When Riley did the same, she realized why Kerry had given her the pants. The fabric was so thick and hard, she was constantly stabbing herself with the back end of the needle, trying to push it through the layers.

"You can work faster than that," Kerry said. "If we all took that long with a project, we'd never get anything done. Look at me, I've done two tops already, and you're still on that."

Riley said nothing but looked around the room. All the other women were working quietly with skills they'd had for years.

"I'm sorry. I've never sewn before and don't know what to do."

"Probably because you're too stupid," Kerry muttered softly so no one else would hear her.

Riley tried her best, but Kerry wasn't teaching her. All she was doing was criticizing her mistakes.

Finally, Maggie in the yellow cloak stood up. "Riley, why don't you bring your chair here? I'm sure I can help."

Kerry looked at Maggie and then whispered to Riley. "I hope she tears you to pieces."

Riley dragged her chair across the hut and settled down beside Maggie.

Maggie smiled at her, showing all her sharp feline teeth. "Don't let my cloak alarm you. I know it's yellow, but I am perfectly safe."

"I—I'm sorry if I stared. I didn't mean to offend you. It's just that . . ."

"It's perfectly natural for you to be curious." Maggie reached up and pushed back her hood.

The other women in the hut gasped and turned away quickly.

Riley was stunned to see that Maggie didn't have hair on her head. Instead she had short fur. And instead of normal ears, hers were on the top of her head, just like a cat.

"You may touch them if you like."

Riley couldn't help herself. She reached up and petted Maggie's head.

"See?" Maggie finally said. "I may look a little different, but I'm still a person inside."

Riley grinned at her. "I think you're beautiful."

Across the hut, Kerry smacked her lips against her teeth in disgust.

"Thank you, child," Maggie said. She looked at Kerry. "I haven't been called that in a very, very long time."

"But you are," Riley said sincerely.

Maggie chuckled softly. "So now let's teach you to sew."

Maggie patiently showed Riley how to match up the torn edges and make small, even stitches to bind them together and then tie it all off securely.

Within a very short time, Riley had forgotten about the cat-woman's appearance and realized that she really liked her. By the time the lunch gong sounded, Riley had several painful holes in her thumb from the needle, but she had managed to complete her first repair. When she placed the pants in the repaired basket, she was quite proud of what she'd achieved.

"You did well this morning," Maggie said as she and Riley walked outside the sewing hut. "You have a deft hand with a needle. In a little while, I am sure you will be able to make your own clothes from the scraps."

Riley was strangely happy with the comment. She knew she wouldn't be in Atlantis long enough to need new clothes, but Maggie's kindness meant a lot to her. While they chatted, Kerry stormed ahead and shot a mean look back at Riley.

"Ignore her," Maggie said. "Our dear Kerry has always been the oldest girl in her group and has her heart set on Bastian. Now that Bastian is paying more attention to you, she is jealous."

"I don't want to cause trouble," Riley said.

"I know," Maggie said. "The problem is Kerry's,

not yours. Just give her time and I'm sure you two will be the best of friends."

Riley doubted it, but she kept silent. Halfway to the dining area, Maggie stopped. "This is where I leave you."

"Aren't you coming to eat?"

Maggie shook her head. "I'm a Yellow Cloak, I'm not allowed."

"But that's not fair; you're working like everyone else."

"True, but this is the way it is in Atlantis. Don't worry, I have my own place. I will see you after the meal."

Riley reached the dining area and took her seat at the children's table. She wanted to speak with Alfie, but he was talking to Ellis and John. Kerry was speaking with Bastian, but every so often she would look over to her and glare.

When the meal ended, Riley only had a couple of minutes with Alfie to learn that he and Bastian had refilled all the water buckets in the cabins on the *Queen*, and in the afternoon, he was going to learn how to do some light repairs.

"I'm learning all I can," Alfie said quietly. "We may need it for when we . . . you know."

Riley nodded. She'd been thinking the same thing. If she knew how to sew, she could learn how to make sails for their big escape.

The afternoon passed much like the morning with Maggie teaching her how to do other types of repairs. When they put down their sewing for the day, Riley's fingers were sore from stabbing herself, but she was determined to learn.

She met up with her cousin after work. Alfie had a cloth bandage tied around his arm. "What happened to you?"

"When we get out of here, if I start to complain about school, remind me about this," Alfie said. "I was working with Shane, cutting some wood, and a branch we were working on snapped and caught me in the arm."

"Alfie, you could have been really hurt!" Riley said.

"I know, but it was worth it. Shane showed me where they store all the tools. The shed isn't locked. We can get in there anytime to borrow what we need."

"That's great news." Riley held up her fingers, which were covered in tiny pinprick scabs. "Actually, I didn't do much better. Sewing is harder than it looks. But I'm learning, so maybe I can make us some sails."

"Perfect," Alfie said.

Riley then told Alfie about Maggie and her yellow cloak. "You wouldn't believe her eyes and ears. She's like a big cat, but she's so sweet."

"I saw two Yellow Cloaks too," Alfie said. "One was walking stooped over. I couldn't see his face, but his hands looked like gorilla hands. He spoke to me in this really deep voice. The other, well, Riley, they put a cloak on a rhinoceros! His name is Kevin and he's really tame. He was helping us move heavy logs. Who are these Cloaks? Are they people or animals?"

"It's like they're both," Riley said. "Look at Pea."

"I know. I asked Shane about all the Cloaks and he said I could work with the Blues or Yellows but never the Reds. And that I'm not supposed to talk to or get involved with them." He stopped. "This place is so weird."

"It sure is," Riley mused.

Their conversation ended abruptly when Bastian came up. He was smiling brightly at Riley. "How was your first day?"

Riley held up her hand again. "Not brilliant, but

Maggie is teaching me. She's so much nicer than Kerry."

Bastian frowned. "What's wrong with Kerry?"

Riley laughed. "You're kidding, right? Bastian, she is mega jealous because you're spending time with me."

"Really?" Bastian said.

Riley saw the sincerity in his face. He really didn't have a clue. "Yes, really. And because she's jealous, she's been really mean."

"I can't believe that she would be mean on purpose."

"I know you're isolated on this island, but seriously? She's ready to kill me."

Bastian gasped. "She would never kill you!"

Riley sighed. "I didn't mean actually kill. But she's really mad."

"I should talk to her," Bastian said. "Perhaps explain."

"Yeah, and that won't make things worse," Alfie said. "Look, Bastian, just let it go. But maybe you should spend more time with her, so she doesn't get even more jealous."

"Do you really think I should?"

"Sure," Alfie said. "You should go right now. Let her know you still care."

Bastian hesitated, and then nodded. "All right, if you really think I should. But I was going to show you both around some more."

"Later. For now you should go talk to Kerry," Alfie said.

Bastian had a look of hurt and confusion on his face as he walked away.

"That wasn't nice," Riley said. "You hurt his feelings."

"So?" Alfie said. "Look, Shorty, we want to find out the truth about Mom and Uncle Andrew, right? How are we supposed to do it with him hanging around? I don't trust him. I don't trust anyone here."

Riley didn't quite feel the same. She liked Bastian. But Alfie was right. If they hoped to get off Atlantis, they needed to do it alone. "So now what?"

Alfie nodded toward the trees. "Let me show you the toolshed. We can grab some shovels and hide them near the graveyard. Then I'll get the lantern from my cabin and hide that, too, so we can use them tonight to dig up the graves."

At dinner, Bastian took a seat beside Kerry and not Riley. When he did, Kerry looked at Riley with an expression of triumph.

Riley shook her head. If she and Alfie didn't have bigger plans, it would have really annoyed her.

When they finished, there was another bonfire. New stories were told and there was more singing. Riley realized this was what they did because there was no television or internet. She also realized this was the longest she'd ever gone without her phone and was surprised that she really didn't miss it. The stories were interesting, and the singing was almost fun.

When it broke up, everyone returned to their homes or the ship. Riley and Alfie hung back and headed to where they had hidden the two shovels and lantern.

"We have to do this fast and get back to the ship before they close the doors for the night," Riley said as she carried a shovel. "I sure don't want to get stuck out here with those Red Cloaks running around, whether they're allowed around here or not."

Walking through the jungle at night was very different from the day. The lantern light flashed off large leaves, making them terrifying and monstrous-looking. There were strange sounds and the rustling of unseen animals.

Back home, Riley hated going across the backyard

in the dark and always forced her brother to go with her if she needed to. This was unbelievable—they were treading through a mysterious jungle in the middle of the night and going to a cemetery to dig up a grave.

Suddenly it didn't seem like such a great idea. "Are we sure we want to do this?" Riley whispered.

"Well, duh," Alfie snapped. "How else will we know the truth? Unless you're lying about hearing my mom's voice."

"I'm not lying," Riley snapped. "I'm sure it was her shouting."

"Then we gotta do this," Alfie said. "Come on."

When they made it to the clearing where the graves were, Alfie walked up to the mound that was supposed to be his mother's and pushed the shovel into the loose dirt.

Riley joined him and, working side by side, they started to move the dirt away. Each shovelful brought dread, but they forced themselves to keep going.

"I wonder how deep we have to go." Riley was covered in sweat from the heavy work. Even though Atlantis was cooler in the evenings, it was still very warm.

"I don't know. But shouldn't we have found something by now?"

They kept digging until they hit a hard area. "That's deep enough," Alfie said. "The ground is solid and hasn't been disturbed. She's not in here."

"Then it must have been her that I heard. Alfie, your mom is alive!"

Alfie couldn't speak for a moment as relief washed over him. "She's alive," he repeated. He looked like he might cry again.

"Yeah, but she's in the Forbidden Zone," Riley said. "That's why Shane didn't want to look for her. He must have known she was there and was too scared to go. Instead they made up the story of them drowning and being buried." She looked over to the other mound. "Do you think they lied about Dad too?"

Alfie nodded. "But there's only one way to be sure: we dig."

Once again they started to dig, and once again the grave was empty. Riley wanted to scream with joy. Her father wasn't dead! She just hoped he was with her aunt and that they were safe.

"We have to find them," Alfie said. "Which means we have to go to the Forbidden Zone."

"You haven't seen it over there," Riley said. "It's really wild."

"If you're scared, I'll go alone," Alfie snapped. "But I'm going."

"Would you drop the attitude, Creep?" Riley said. "I didn't say I wouldn't go. I'm just saying it's dangerous. I heard some pretty scary sounds coming from over there. We'll have to plan carefully and find weapons to take with us."

Alfie's anger softened. "You're right. Come on, let's clear this up and get back before they close the ship."

Once the graves were reset and looking undisturbed, they picked up their shovels and lantern and started back toward the cruise ship. They had only gone a short distance when they started to hear a slow, deep growl coming from the trees behind them.

They stopped.

"Uh-oh," Riley said as she held up the lantern. "Shane did say there were other predators on this side of the boundary fence, right?"

"What boundary fence?" Alfie whispered.

"The one separating the Community from the Red Cloak territory." Riley turned slowly as the growling increased. When they started walking again, the sound followed them. A flash of movement to her right caught Riley's eye. It was a filthy Red Cloak. "Alfie, it's Mada—"

Suddenly Riley was knocked to the ground by something very large and painfully heavy. Acting on instinct alone, she held up the shovel for protection just as a tooth-filled mouth came toward her. Snarling and hissing, it bit down on the shovel handle instead of her throat.

"Mada, stop!" Riley howled.

"Get off her!" Alfie brought his shovel down on Mada's head. There was the sickening sound of the metal meeting bone, but it didn't stop the attack.

Mada roared as his hood fell back, revealing a grotesque face that was a cross between a man and a tiger.

"You shouldn't have been on the beach, child!" Mada spat. "You shouldn't have seen my sorrow." He released the shovel handle and tried for Riley's throat again.

"We didn't know," Riley cried. "I'm sorry you lost Susan. . . ."

"Don't you dare say her name," Mada hissed. "You have no right."

As he moved, his rear claws raked down Riley's legs and she cried in pain.

"Yes, scream," Mada snarled. "It makes the kill more exciting."

Alfie brought the shovel down again on Mada's back. When he did, Mada swiped at Alfie and knocked him into the trees.

"You're next!" he roared at Alfie. Then he turned his golden eyes back on Riley.

"Stop!" Riley was still holding Mada back with the shovel handle, but her arms were growing weaker. "Please," she begged. "You don't have to do this! Yes, we saw you cry, but tears make you human; they show you still care!"

Mada threw back his head and roared. "I am not human anymore! I am a Red Cloak and I don't care about anything but hunting!"

His voice was distorted by the shape of his tiger mouth, but Riley could still understand him and hear the joyful menace in every word.

"I'm sorry we were there. We didn't know," Riley said.

"Save your apologies. You broke the rules and came into our territory. Killing you is my right." Mada threw back his head again and roared.

Riley shut her eyes just as Mada opened his mouth wider and his deadly teeth descended toward her throat.

16

"MADA, STOP!"

The new voice was just above Riley as the deadly mouth moved for her throat. Because of Mada's position, she couldn't see who or what it was that spoke. But it worked. Mada stopped his attack and turned to look up. "This is my kill!"

"No! You have trespassed into Community territory. It is forbidden!"

Mada roared in rage and then focused on Riley again. But before he could strike, Riley felt his weight lift off her as Mada rose in the air.

It all happened too fast for her to follow. But one moment Mada was about to kill her, and the next he appeared to be carried away into the night sky.

Riley sat up and saw Alfie several feet away. He wasn't looking at her, he was staring up with his mouth hanging open and his eyes wide.

"W-what was that?"

"It was a monster," Alfie said, pointing up to the sky. "It swooped down and caught Mada in these big claws on its feet and pulled him away from you. It was huge and had bat wings and big ears. Its legs were like tree trunks. . . ."

Riley was too frightened to stand or even follow Alfie's pointing finger. Her legs were on fire. Reaching for her lantern, she saw deep, bleeding gashes on her shins.

"Riley, you're bleeding," Alfie cried.

Riley winced as she looked at the damage. "It was Mada's claws."

Alfie pulled off his T-shirt and tore it into strips to wrap around Riley's wounds to stop the bleeding.

Every few seconds he would check the sky. "You should have seen that thing's face. It was terrifying."

"I was too busy trying not to be killed," Riley said.

When Alfie finished, he reached for Riley's hands.

"I hope you can walk, because we've got to get out of here before something else decides to eat us."

Riley was still shaking as Alfie helped her to her feet. Her legs were wobbly and throbbed with pain. But she didn't want to stay outside a moment longer. Leaning on her cousin, they returned the shovels to the toolshed and made their way back to the *Queen of Bermuda*.

Luckily, the doors on the cruise ship were still open and no one was inside. They climbed the gangplank and up the stairs to Riley's cabin. Alfie went into the bathroom and collected the bucket of clean water and carried it to the sofa where Riley waited. "We'll need more water. I'll go get some from my room."

While he was gone, Riley started to untie the T-shirt rags. Her legs were stinging from the deep scratches, but at least the bleeding had stopped. She dipped one of the rags in the water and rinsed it off. Then she gently dabbed the cuts.

Riley couldn't stop shaking as she tried to clean her wounds. The attack was on repeat in her mind, and she could still feel Mada's weight pressing down on her. If she hadn't had the shovel in her hand, he would have killed her.

Alfie returned with his bucket. He was also carrying a new shirt. Biting the bottom of it, he tore it into strips. "They gave me this to sleep in, but it would be a better bandage."

"Just don't expect me to sew it back together again." Riley tried to sound calmer than she felt.

"I won't. I don't know how I'm going to explain it missing. But I'll figure something out."

When her legs were cleaned and the last of the bandages were tied, Riley sat back on the sofa. She was in too much shock to think clearly. "Why do they let Mada stay here if he's so dangerous? Pea said they send the deadly creatures to the Forbidden Zone, but Mada is left here to do as he pleases. We're not allowed in their territory, but he came here to get us just because we saw him cry or because he's angry with the unicorn." She looked intently at Alfie. "What is Mada? What are all the creatures in cloaks? Where do they come from?"

"I don't know," her cousin said. "And what was the monster that took him?"

Riley shrugged. "I couldn't see. All I saw was Mada's teeth."

"This place is a nightmare," Alfie said. "I just wish

I could wake up on the *Event Horizon* with everything back to normal." He settled at the desk and pulled out a faded piece of paper. Reaching for a pencil, in the faint lantern light, he started to draw.

"The monster that took Mada was big," he said as he sketched. "With large bat wings. Its face was almost like a pig with pointy ears, but not quite. It was hard to be sure in the light, but I think it was gray, like an elephant or something."

"A flying elephant saved me?"

"Did I say it was an elephant? No, stupid, I said it was gray *like* an elephant."

"Cut it out, Creep," Riley said. "I can't deal with your attitude right now. Just leave me alone and go back to your cabin."

"Fine," Alfie said as he got up and left.

Riley felt bad for snapping at Alfie, but she was scared and feeling terrible. She'd nearly been killed by Mada, and her legs were on fire. Trying to distract herself, she reached for Alfie's drawing and looked at the strange creature. How could anything like that exist? But it did, and it had saved her life. Nothing in Atlantis made any sense. Pea, Maggie, the Red Cloaks—it was all so unbelievable.

Sitting alone in the silence, she started to think about all the strange things that everyone just accepted. Then something Pea said struck her and she had a random thought.

Before the idea fully formed, there was soft knocking on her door. Alfie popped his head in. "I'm sorry. Can I come back in?"

Riley nodded.

Alfie entered her cabin and sat back down at the desk. "I didn't mean to call you stupid. But this place and all the monsters are getting to me."

"Me too," Riley said. Alfie had never apologized to her before. But he looked genuinely sorry. "Alfie, I think I might know what's going on with the Cloaks."

"What?"

"Please don't laugh or call me stupid again. . . ."

"I won't—I promise."

"Okay, so like, I was talking with Pea and he said that he used to be a ship's carpenter and even helped build some of the houses here. But he can't now because he's changed too much and can't hold the tools."

"Pea was a carpenter?"

Riley nodded. "Alfie, I think he used to be a man

and somehow turned into an animal. I wanted to ask him more, but then he said he talked too much and ran away. Think about it. Pea, Maggie, Mada, and you saw a talking gorilla—"

"And Kevin the tame rhino," Alfie added. He looked at her and his frown deepened. "Didn't Bastian say that Miss Pigglesworth was his governess? Who ever heard of a dog as a governess?"

"I have, in *Peter Pan*," Riley said. "But that's just a story, and their dog was a nursemaid, not a governess. I know it sounds insane, but nothing else makes any sense. I mean, there are no elderly people here. . . . Maybe when people grow old, they change. When I was speaking with Maggie, she sounded a lot like Grandma. She definitely wasn't young."

"Pea sounds old too," Alfie agreed.

Riley shook her head. "But how is it possible? People don't turn into animals. . . ."

Alfie laughed. "Yeah, like ferocious animals don't wear red cloaks and talk. And big gray monsters don't fly in to save people. It's all bonkers."

"We have to find out what's going on and how it's happening," Riley said.

"Why?" Alfie said. "It's not like we're planning

to stay. We're just going to find Mom and Uncle Andrew and go."

"Yeah," Riley agreed. "But what if people *are* turning into animals? What if it happens to Dad or Mary?"

Alfie's face went even paler in the lantern light. "We have to find them, right away."

17

ALFIE SLEPT ON THE SOFA AGAIN WITH-
out asking permission, but Riley was grateful for the
company. Even with his cruel remarks, he was the
only other normal person in Atlantis.

Riley's legs were hurting, and sleep wouldn't come
as her mind kept replaying the attack. Mada wanted
to kill her, but why? Just because she and Alfie wit-
nessed him crying over losing Susan? Bastian was
there—was Mada going to try to kill him too? Or
was it something else completely? Maybe because
they were new here? And what kind of monster was
big enough to carry him away?

Turning over, Riley hoped that whatever the monster was, it had killed Mada or maybe dropped him in the ocean for the Leviathan to eat. Just so long as the tiger-man was gone.

Morning brought the usual knocking on her door, and Riley climbed painfully to her feet. She looked down at her clothes and saw that she was filthy. After she'd spent half the night digging in the dirt, and then been attacked by Mada, the lantern light hadn't shown what a mess she was. But the bright sunlight shining in the window did.

"Who is it?" she called.

"It's me, Bastian."

"Hi, Bastian. I—I'm not ready yet. I'll meet you at breakfast; is that okay?"

"Sure," Bastian replied. "But are you all right? Have you been hurt?"

"Um, why do you ask?"

By now Alfie was awake and standing beside her, looking just as filthy as she did.

"Because there is dirt and blood outside your door."

"Let him in," Alfie said quickly. He reached for the remaining water and what was left of his shirt. "Talk to him. I'll clean up outside."

"What should I say?" Riley whispered.

"Tell him the truth. Then ask him what he knows."

Riley opened the door. When Bastian saw her, his eyes went wide.

"What happened to you?"

Riley invited him and Miss Pigglesworth in. "We were attacked by Mada."

Miss Pigglesworth woofed as Bastian cried, "Mada? How? He's not allowed on the *Queen*!"

"Sit down," Alfie said. "It's time we had this out."

Bastian's face was a picture of confusion. "Have what out?"

Alfie stood before Bastian and poked him in the chest. "I don't trust you, Bastian. I don't trust anyone here. But we need answers and you're gonna tell us." He carried the bucket of water to the door and looked back at Riley. "I'll be outside cleaning. Try to get him to tell you the truth."

Riley sat down painfully on the sofa and patted the seat beside her. "Bastian, please sit. Alfie and I really need to know what's happening here."

"I—I don't know what you mean," Bastian said.

"Last night we dug up the graves of my father and aunt. . . ."

Bastian gasped. "What?"

Riley nodded. "Yesterday I heard shouting coming from the Forbidden Zone that sounded just like my aunt, so we had to be sure. Bastian, the graves were empty."

"That—that's impossible. Beresford said they died and were buried. He wouldn't lie."

"He did. They just piled up dirt to make it look like graves."

"Why would they?"

"Don't ask me," Riley said. "I need to ask you something and I want an honest answer."

"Of course," Bastian said sincerely.

"You said Miss Pigglesworth was your governess. But she's a dog—she can't be."

"She is," Bastian said. "She's always been."

"Yeah, but has she always been a dog?"

Bastian laughed. "What do you mean?"

"Was Miss Pigglesworth always a dog, or was she once a person?"

"Of course, she—" Bastian paused and frowned. "I mean, she—she's a dog. Yes, I can talk to her, but I don't think—Riley, this is crazy. Why would you ask such a thing?"

Riley looked at the dog. "Miss Pigglesworth, were you ever a person?"

When the dog wouldn't look at her, Riley continued, "Please tell us the truth. I know you can understand me, and Bastian and Pea can understand you. That's not normal."

The dog was still facing away from her.

"Miss Pigglesworth?" Bastian asked. "Look at me, please."

Miss Pigglesworth turned to Bastian and started whining as she lay her head on his leg.

Bastian gasped. "But I don't understand. We've always been together. How could I forget you wearing a blue cloak?"

After more soft barking and whining, Bastian stood up and started to pace the room. "Why can't I remember?"

"What is it?" Riley asked.

Bastian had the frightened expression of someone just awakened from a confused dream. "I—I don't understand. All this time together, I just accepted Miss Pigglesworth as she was. But she just said she used to walk upright like us. She was a person—a real person. She doesn't remember what happened to her. I don't remember anything at all. How could I forget something like that?"

The fear in Bastian's eyes told Riley he was telling the truth. But that, like everything else about Atlantis, didn't make sense.

"What do you remember?" Riley asked. "Do you remember your life before Atlantis? What about your parents? Were you born here or shipwrecked like us?"

Bastian sat and put his hands on his head. "I don't know. I was told my parents died and were buried, but I don't remember them. Or even what Miss Pigglesworth looked like before." His pleading eyes turned to her. "What happened to us?"

Alfie opened the door and entered. "Hopefully that should do it." He put down the bucket and walked over to the sofa. "So?"

Riley nodded. "Miss Pigglesworth used to be a person, and Bastian can't remember anything about his past."

Bastian looked up. "I don't even know my full name or where I come from. Atlantis is all I know."

"How can you not know your name?"

"I don't know!" Bastian cried. He stood up and started to pace like a caged animal. "Why haven't

I thought of this before? How could I just accept everything without question? Where do I come from? Who am I?"

Miss Pigglesworth was pacing beside him, whining.

Bastian stopped. "All Miss Pigglesworth can remember is having to take care of me. She doesn't remember her first name or where she comes from either." He started toward the door. "I have to ask Beresford. He should know."

"No!" Alfie rushed over to him and pulled Bastian by the arm. "You can't let Beresford, or anyone, know what you're thinking. They may be part of it."

"Part of what?"

"The big lie," Riley said. "Think about it. It was Beresford who said our parents were buried, but they weren't. We can't trust him or anyone. We have to figure this out on our own."

Bastian shook his head. "Beresford wouldn't do that to me. There has to be another explanation."

"Oh yeah?" Alfie said. "Like what?"

"I—I don't know," Bastian said.

Miss Pigglesworth whined, and Bastian became more irritated. "No, they wouldn't."

"Wouldn't what?" Riley asked.

"Miss Pigglesworth thinks they might have used Memory Berries on us. But—but that would be too terrible."

"What are Memory Berries?" Riley asked.

Bastian returned to his seat. "There are berries here that, when you eat them, you forget everything. We are a small community and we have to get along. If there is trouble, berries are used, and the trouble stops."

"What?" Riley cried.

"They drug people?" Alfie gasped.

"Not a drug, just berries. But—but why would they use them on me and Miss Pigglesworth?"

"I don't know," Riley said. "Nothing here makes sense."

"I must find out," Bastian insisted.

"No way," Alfie said. "Until we figure out what's happening here, you're not gonna say a word to anyone about anything. If they lied to you all this time, and to us about our parents, they could lie about anything."

"Or worse, they'll use the Memory Berries on all of us," Riley added.

Bastian knelt beside the dog and hugged her

tightly. "We're just as lost here as they are, Miss Pigglesworth." He looked up at Riley and Alfie. "We'll help you all we can to figure out what happened to your parents. Maybe we can find out what happened to Miss Pigglesworth and the others too."

Riley nodded. "Good. So it all starts now."

18

THEY AGREED NOT TO DISCUSS ANYTHING outside of their cabins. Going down to breakfast, they behaved as though nothing was wrong. Bastian came up with the idea of telling people that Riley fell down the metal crew stairs to explain the bandages on her legs. That excuse seemed to work, and although Riley received a lot of sympathy and well wishing, there were no uncomfortable questions.

After breakfast, Riley was once again assigned to the sewing hut to work with Maggie while Alfie was told to spend the morning with Bastian and afternoon with Shane.

They met up at lunch, and again nothing was

discussed. When the workday ended, Riley looked for Alfie and Bastian. She found Alfie returning tools to the shed.

"Where's Bastian?"

Alfie shrugged. "He's been acting weird all day. Quiet and moping around. I just hope he doesn't say anything."

"Me too," Riley agreed. "Alfie, I was wondering if you'd like to come with me to that slope across from the Forbidden Zone. It's in Community territory, so hopefully there won't be any Red Cloaks. Maybe we can hear your mom again. Or even swim over there to look."

"I'm in," Alfie said quickly. He reached back into the toolshed and pulled out a machete. "I asked Shane about the territories, and he told me the Red Cloaks aren't allowed over the fence. But that didn't stop Mada last night."

Riley reached past Alfie and pulled down a second machete. "Yeah, just in case."

They looked around to see if anyone was watching. When they were sure they were alone, they made their way through the trees to the slope where Riley heard her aunt.

They stood, overlooking the water. "That's the Forbidden Zone?" Alfie asked.

"That's it," Riley said.

The water below was calm and clear, and they watched the shoals of fish swimming. Across from them the Forbidden Zone rose much taller than Atlantis and was filled with the sounds of wild animals and loud, screeching birds soaring high overhead.

Riley nodded. "There are all kinds of wild animals there. I hope Dad and Aunt Mary are all right."

"So do I," Alfie said. He followed the path of the birds. "Are those condors?"

Riley looked at the big birds and shrugged. "I don't know. But they're so big. I wonder why the animals don't come here."

"They do," Bastian called. "During the Red Moon."

Riley and Alfie jumped as Bastian and Miss Pigglesworth trotted up behind them.

Alfie turned sharply and raised his machete. "Bastian! Don't you ever do that again; I might have killed you!"

"I'm sorry," Bastian said.

"Where've you been?" Riley asked. "I looked for

you after I finished in the sewing hut, but I couldn't find you."

"Miss Pigglesworth and I wanted to be alone to think and try to remember. But we still don't know how we arrived here."

"I don't care about how any of us got here," Alfie said. "I just wanna find my mom and go home."

He looked up at the Forbidden Zone again. "Mom!" he shouted.

Riley cupped her hands over her mouth and shouted, "Dad! Can you hear us?"

After each call, they stopped and listened, but heard only birdcalls and wild roars coming from the Forbidden Zone.

Alfie took off his shirt and started to climb down the slope to the water. "I'm going over."

Riley was about to follow, but Alfie stopped her. "No, Shorty, stay here. Your legs are still bleeding. You might attract sharks or something."

Riley looked down at her painful legs and saw trails of blood seeping from beneath the bandages.

Alfie handed her his machete. "You stay here; I'll go look for Mom and Uncle Andrew."

"Alfie, be careful."

"I will."

Riley stood with Bastian, watching Alfie climb down into the water. Her cousin seemed to be swimming hard, but not making much progress.

"Is everything all right?" Riley called.

"Yeah," Alfie answered. "But there's a heavy current just beneath the surface. It's hard to swim."

Moments later, Alfie turned quickly in the water, looking down. "Something just touched me!" he cried. "Something's here!"

Suddenly Alfie appeared to be pushed as he moved quickly back toward Atlantis.

"Stop!" Alfie cried. "Lemme go!" Alfie was thrashing in the water and trying to punch whatever was moving him. But no matter what he did, he was still being pushed back to shore.

Moments later, Riley caught sight of movement in the water farther down the channel. It was heading straight for Alfie. When it was several yards away, a massive head shot out of the water. Riley shrieked when she realized it was the same sea monster that had attacked their boat.

"The Leviathan!" Bastian cried. "Alfie, swim faster, it's coming for you!"

Alfie screamed as he fought to make it to shore. Moments later, he touched the ground and was climbing back up the slope. Just as he reached the top, the Leviathan's head reared out of the water and snapped at him.

They all jumped back as the Leviathan roared once and then dipped back down into the water. Looking down on the departing sea serpent, Riley thought she caught the glimpse of a long green tail and flash of blonde hair swimming beside it. But then it was gone.

"It—it was going to eat me!" Alfie cried.

"But—" Riley gulped. "Pea said it could come on shore anytime and didn't hurt anyone."

"He was wrong," Alfie cried.

"I told you the Leviathan hunted these waters," Bastian said. "There is no leaving Atlantis."

Alfie sat down and wrapped his arms around his knees. "I—I don't care what it takes. I'll get over there and find my mom. Then we're getting out of this wacky place and going home."

"How?" Riley said as she took several deep breaths to calm down. "How do we get out of here with the Leviathan out there?"

"I don't know." Alfie finally rose and looked back

over the water. "The Leviathan wasn't the only thing out there. I—I felt something before it came—like hands on my back. They were pushing me back to shore."

"Maybe it was one of those mermaid monsters I told you about," Riley suggested.

"Maybe," Alfie agreed.

"Whatever it is, we need to find another way over there."

"The only way is the causeway that appears during a Red Moon, but it's too dangerous then," Bastian said.

Riley looked at him and frowned. "That's the second time you've mentioned the Red Moon. What is it?"

Bastian became uncomfortable as he started to speak. "During the Red Moon the tide goes out so far that there is a land bridge between the two islands. That's why it's so dangerous. When the bridge appears, the wild animals from over there come here, and we're all in danger. When it starts, everyone boards the *Queen* and it is locked up tight until it's over."

Riley looked back over at the Forbidden Zone. "That's the only time they come over?"

Bastian nodded. "Birds can fly back and forth, but none of them seem dangerous. If predators try to swim, the Leviathan gets them like it almost got Alfie."

Alfie shivered at the mention, then shook his head. "If those wild creatures come here, how do you get rid of them?"

"We don't," Bastian said. "The unicorns do. They stop the creatures from breaking into the *Queen* and then drive them back to their island."

Riley frowned. "So why don't the unicorns stop them from using the bridge?"

Bastian shrugged. "I don't know. I don't even know why they help us. They're wild and can be vicious to us too. But they come, and they do help. I've always thought there was more to it, but no one here seems to know anything."

"Where do the unicorns live? Maybe they could help us find my dad and Mary," Riley said.

"Trust me, they won't. They live on the North Side, but it's on the other side of the Red Cloaks' territory. We are forbidden from going there. I once heard there were even stranger, more magical creatures there. But I don't know."

"So when's the next Red Moon?" Alfie asked. "Maybe we can sneak over to the Forbidden Zone."

"No!" Bastian cried. "Don't even think about it. Red Moons are the worst. We haven't had one in so long, there must be one coming any day now. Get through the first one and you'll understand why no one goes out during it."

Riley was still shaken from seeing the Leviathan again. Atlantis was filled with more terrors than she imagined possible. "We'd better get back. I need to change my bandages before dinner. Then we need to figure out how we're going to get over to the Forbidden Zone."

19

AFTER DINNER, THEY MADE THEIR WAY to the bonfire. Keeping their voices low, Riley and Alfie were still trying to figure out a way over to the Forbidden Zone.

"We could try building a raft," Alfie suggested. "But there are a lot of currents under the water, so it would have to be strong."

"How long will that take?" Riley asked.

Alfie shrugged. "How should I know? I'm not a carpenter and it's not like I could ask Shane!"

"Well, you suggested it," Riley shot back at him. "And I wouldn't ask Shane. I'd ask Pea—so there!"

"Will you two please stop arguing?" Bastian said.

"Honestly, how can you be from the same family? All you ever do is fight."

"We don't fight, we debate," Alfie said.

"Whatever you call it, it's really annoying," Bastian said. He turned to Alfie. "It will take too long to build a raft, not to mention the Leviathan. There is also something you both must consider, and it's not pleasant. If your parents have been in the Forbidden Zone since you got here, the chances of them still being alive are very slim. It is filled with predators and killers. It's not a place for people."

"You're wrong!" Alfie shot. "My mom is strong and she's smart. She'll fight and she'll survive. You'll see." He stormed off and ran toward the *Queen*.

"I'm sorry if I upset him," Bastian said. "But you both must know the truth. It is impossible to imagine anyone surviving long in the Forbidden Zone. When Red Cloaks become too dangerous, they are driven there."

"But I heard . . ."

"Yes, you heard shouting," Bastian said. "Doesn't that tell you how dangerous it must be over there? Have you heard anything since then?"

"Well, no," Riley admitted. "But you don't know

our family. If anyone could survive over there, it would be them."

For two days, Riley and Alfie tried to figure out a way across the channel. Each day after work, they met up at the slope and called over to the island, hoping to hear anything that sounded like their parents. But all they heard back were the calls of wild animals.

"We have to get over there," Alfie said as they walked together to breakfast.

"I know," Riley agreed. "I have an idea I want to try. Let's meet back there again after work."

"Tell me now," Alfie said.

"Later—I'm already late for work."

Alfie nodded. "Okay, Shorty, see ya later."

"Not if I see you first, Creep," Riley said as she smiled at her cousin and started to head toward the sewing hut.

With each new day, Riley felt more confident in her sewing and actually looked forward to spending time with Maggie. Besides, being friends with Maggie really irritated Kerry, so that was a bonus.

Just before lunch, as Maggie was teaching Riley how to do a French seam, a horn sounded. It was much like a cruise ship's horn that Riley had heard when they were in Miami at the port. Everyone in the sewing hut put down their work, and as fear rose in their eyes, they got up and left. Maggie stood up and reached for Riley with her gloved hand. "Come, child, we must move."

"What is it?"

"That is the call to the *Queen*," Maggie said. "It means the Red Moon is coming and everyone is being summoned aboard for protection. Her doors will shut and be secured against the invaders from the Forbidden Zone."

"I don't understand. It's not even lunchtime. Why do we have to go to the *Queen* now?"

"Because the fog comes long before the Red Moon rises. If you are not on board, you will not find the ship. Trust me, the fog is almost the worst part." Maggie smiled at Riley. "Though it pleases me that you will be safe."

Riley still didn't understand everything that was happening. She looked at the kind cat-woman. "All right, let's go."

Maggie shook her head. "No, child, not me. It is forbidden. All Cloaks are banned from boarding. We must take our chances with the Red Moon out in the open."

"What do you mean you can't board? That's not fair!"

Maggie took Riley's hand and it was quivering. "We—we are not welcome there because we are different. I must face this night alone as I have all the others since I—" Maggie stopped speaking.

Riley frowned. "Wait, just because you're turning into a cat, you can't go where it's safe?"

Maggie paused. "You—you understand what is happening to me?"

Riley nodded. "Of course. I've met Pea and seen him without his cloak. He's harmless. But they won't let him on board either?"

Maggie shook her head. "None of us can board."

"Why?"

"Those are the rules. I don't understand why they won't let Pea aboard, but for me it's because no one knows what kind of feline I will be when my change is complete. I may stop changing now and stay in this yellow cloak, or perhaps I might turn into a simple cat and be accepted as Miss Pigglesworth is accepted. But I may also turn into something more ferocious and not be able to control myself. Then I will be forced into a red cloak and eventually banished to the Forbidden Zone."

"But you're not dangerous now."

"No, I am not."

"Then you can't stay out," Riley said desperately. "Look, I have a cabin all to myself. There's plenty of room for you. And Pea, too, if I can find him. If this Red Moon is as bad as everyone says . . ."

"It is," Maggie said. "I was nearly killed during the last one."

"Then you must come with me."

"I can't. It is forbidden."

"I hate that word!" Riley stormed. "So many things here are *forbidden*. Those rules are wrong." She walked over to the basket of clothes that had been repaired. "Maybe there is something in here we can use to hide you, so you look like a person."

"But if I am caught breaking the rules . . ."

"You won't be." Riley pulled out several pieces of larger clothes. Then she found a straw hat that was set to be repaired. She also found a work scarf that came from those working in the vegetable fields.

"Please, let's just try."

Maggie allowed Riley to take her out of her yellow cloak. When she stood before her, Riley she saw that her entire body was covered in fur, much like a tabby cat, but Maggie could also look like a leopard. She had a long tail that twitched with nerves.

Riley tried not to stare, but when Maggie caught her, the cat-woman lowered her head. "I have not been seen by anyone for so long."

"You're just so beautiful," Riley said.

Tears rose in Maggie's eyes. "No, I'm not."

"Yes, you are—really, I mean it!" Riley insisted. She grinned and put the straw hat on Maggie's head playfully. It pushed her feline ears down and they poked out the side. "Now, how about we get you dressed?"

It took some time to find clothes that fit Maggie's feline form. But soon, with the scarf wrapped around her head and straw hat on top, she looked like she would pass.

"Oh, here." Riley bent down and took off her shoes. "I'll go barefoot. You wear these."

"I haven't worn shoes in ages," Maggie said.

Riley looked down at the woman's feline feet. "I can see why. But today, you're forcing your feet into these."

After a bit of struggling, Maggie was fully dressed and wearing Riley's running shoes.

"Perfect!" Riley stood back and admired her work. "Now, if you stay here for a few minutes, I'm going to get Alfie and Bastian. If we walk on either side of you, no one will ever know."

Maggie was wringing her hands. "If you are sure this will work. I do dread the thought of staying out tonight."

"We'll make it work!" Riley said, grinning. "I'll be right back."

Riley left the sewing hut to look for Alfie and Bastian. She ran past crowds all heading toward the *Queen* and found them waiting to board.

The ramp that was normally empty was filled with a long line of people slowly making their way aboard.

"Alfie, Bastian," Riley called, running up to them. "I need your help. Please come."

"Is anything wrong?" Alfie asked.

"You'll see. C'mon."

"No, Riley, we have to board," Bastian said.

"We will. Just come with me for a minute."

They made it back to the sewing hut. Inside they found Maggie standing there.

"Maggie, this is my cousin Alfie," Riley said.

"It's lovely to meet you, Alfie."

Alfie was staring at Maggie, unable to speak.

"Maggie?" Bastian cried. "Is it really you under all that?"

"Yes," Maggie said shyly. "Riley is trying to make me look like a person again."

"Where's your cloak?" Bastian asked.

"I took it off her," Riley said. "You keep saying how bad Red Moons are, but anyone wearing a cloak isn't allowed to board the *Queen*."

"I know," Bastian said. "But that's because they have their own place to shelter."

"No, child. That's what Beresford and the others tell you, but it's not true. We are left to fend for ourselves."

"Really?" Bastian cried.

Alfie finally snapped out of his shock. "Wait, that's not fair."

"That's what I said," Riley said. "So we're going to sneak her on board, and she can stay in my cabin with me. I just wish I knew where Pea was."

"I just saw him," Alfie said. "He was watching everyone going up the ramp. Are you saying Pea can't board the ship either?"

Maggie shook her head. "None of us in cloaks can."

"No way," Alfie cried. "Don't go anywhere without me; I'll be right back." He dashed out of the hut. He returned a few minutes later carrying a squirming Pea in his tiny blue cloak.

"Put me down," Pea protested. "Alfie, please."

Alfie lowered him to the floor. "I told you, you aren't spending the night outside."

"I must," Pea said. "Those are the rules."

"And I say it's a stupid rule," Riley said. She went over to the sewing basket. "We can't dress him as a child; there aren't enough children here. But . . ." She held up a large work shirt. "Alfie, if you wear this, we can hide Pea on your back. Especially if you're carrying something."

"Like a bag of fruit!" Bastian offered. "I'll go get one!"

"What?" Pea cried. "We can't do that. We will be caught and banished! I have survived many Red Moons before now; I will climb a tree and be safe."

Maggie sighed. "I remember, dear Pea, a few Red Moons ago when we found you half-dead at the base of a tree." She turned to Riley. "He was attacked. We all feared he would die."

"But that was a long time ago," Pea protested. "I must remain outside."

Alfie held up his hands. "Do you want to stay outside?"

"Of course not. No one does," Pea said. "But I have no choice."

"Now you do," Riley said. "Pea, we can do this. With a bit of work, we can hide you and Maggie and get you safely on board the *Queen*. Please let us try. I can't bear the thought of you outside if it's as bad as everyone says."

Maggie leaned down to him. "Look at me, Pea. I tried to tell Riley, but she won't listen. I think it is best to surrender to their will."

"Please, Pea, let us help you," Alfie said.

The ship's horn sounded again, reminding them of the urgency.

Bastian returned carrying a sack filled with fruit.

Pea pulled off his blue cloak, revealing his adorable furry body. "I surrender. But when this night is over, we are going to have some serious words."

Bastian smiled. "We shall look forward to it."

After a few minutes, Pea was strapped to Alfie's back and hidden under the large shirt. An extra-loose layer was added on top. Then Alfie lifted the bag of fruit and slung it over his shoulder to help hide the lump.

"Because we are young, we are never stopped," Bastian said as he finished with Alfie and Pea. He looked over at Maggie. "Your disguise is not perfect, but if you stay close to us and keep your head down, it should work."

"I haven't been this nervous in a very long time," Maggie said.

"Me neither," Pea's muffled voice called.

"It'll be fine," Riley said. "Just as long as you stay quiet."

They walked out of the sewing hut and toward the *Queen*. There were still a large number of people waiting to board the grounded cruise ship.

When they joined the lines at the rear, Riley looked up and saw Shane on one side of the ramp entrance and Beresford on the other. She leaned over to Alfie and Bastian. "I have an idea. When we go up, I'm going to distract Shane, so stay close to his side of the ramp and keep moving."

Bastian nodded. "Be careful."

"I will."

Maggie reached for Riley's hand and gave it a squeeze. "Whatever happens, I am grateful to you for seeing me as a person and not judging me by my appearance."

Riley squeezed her hand back. "You and Pea are the nicest ones here. Nothing is going to happen to you."

Further comment was cut off as they approached the ramp. Riley felt nerves bunching up in her stomach. Shane was just ahead. Moving a bit faster, she ran up to him.

"Shane, Shane, I'm so scared," she cried aloud. "No one will tell me what a Red Moon is. Are we in danger? Are we going to die? Why do we have to board the ship in the middle of the day?" She started to wail.

"Don't be scared, Riley," Shane said kindly. He dipped his head down to look into her eyes and lifted her chin gently. "We'll all be fine. The *Queen* has protected us for many Red Moons before now and will continue to do so for many more. Just go into your cabin and close your curtains. We will ring the bells when it's time to eat. I'm sure Bastian or one of the other children will show you the way to the dining hall."

"But I don't understand what a Red Moon is," Riley cried.

"You'll hear all about it at dinner," Shane said reassuringly. "Just stay off the decks and keep your curtains closed at all times."

Riley felt, more than saw, Alfie, Bastian, and Maggie making it past Shane and up into the *Queen*. She sniffed loudly and smiled up at him. "Thank you, Shane, you've made me feel a lot better."

Shane beamed at the compliment. "We are all in this together."

Riley finished walking up the ramp and into the *Queen*. She looked ahead and couldn't see any sign of the others. But there hadn't been a commotion or any kind of confrontation, so they must have made it.

When she entered her cabin, everyone was there. The curtains were drawn, and Maggie was taking off her hat and scarf. Bastian was helping to free Pea from Alfie's back.

"That was not entirely unpleasant," Pea said softly. "I rather liked the adventure of it."

Riley walked over to the window and pulled back the curtains slightly. Down on the ground were several Blue Cloaks and a couple of Yellow Cloaks standing back. Their hoods were facing the *Queen*. "Alfie, Bastian, come here."

They joined her at the window. Alfie looked down. "That's Jeff, the gorilla I told you about. He's in the yellow cloak. And farther back is Kevin the rhino, also in yellow. They should be on board with us, not down there."

"They all should," Riley said.

Bastian shook his head. "I never knew. They told us the Cloaks had a place to stay safe. Now I feel really bad for them."

Alfie looked back at him. "Can we go out there and get them?"

Bastian shook his head again. "We won't be allowed off. Once we're on board, we can't leave until after the Red Moon. That's why Shane and Beresford were on the ramp. To make sure we don't leave again."

"And to keep us off," Pea added.

"I hope they make it all right," Riley said.

"As do we all," Pea agreed. He walked up to one of the plush chairs and crawled into it. "I had forgotten just how comfortable the *Queen* is. I have not been aboard in a very long time."

"What about those serious words you wanted to have with us?" Alfie said.

"Hmm . . . yes," Pea said. "The words are—*thank you.*"

"You're very welcome," Riley said.

They heard a loud rumble and thump coming from the decks below them. It was close to what they heard each night, but there were more sounds. "What's happening?" Riley asked.

"They are bringing up the ramp as well as closing the doors," Pea said. "So many Red Moons have I watched with envy as those doors closed. Anyone who hasn't made it aboard must now find somewhere to shelter for this very long night."

Riley looked up at the sky. The sun was still shining, and it was only midday. "It's still so early."

Bastian opened the window and peered out. He craned his neck. "It's not coming from this direction."

"What isn't?" Alfie asked.

Riley said to her cousin, "Maggie says that a heavy fog comes before the Red Moon."

"Yes," Maggie agreed. "Soon it will be so thick you won't be able to see a thing."

"Fog?" Alfie said. "During a bright sunny day?"

Pea was still settled on the chair. "You have much to learn about Atlantis. Things change very quickly when it comes to the Red Moon."

"How many Red Moons do you get a year?" Riley asked.

Pea, Maggie, and Bastian all exchanged curious glances. Finally Bastian said, "We don't measure time. I don't know how long a year is."

"It is three hundred and sixty-five days," Riley answered.

"What an odd number," Pea said.

"Yes," Bastian agreed. "Why so many days?"

Riley shrugged. "I don't know. Maybe it has to do with seasons and stuff."

"Ah," Pea said. "As we only have one season here, perhaps that explains it. I do not know how many we have, but Red Moons stubbornly refuse to follow a schedule."

They all settled down and talked softly about the life Riley and Alfie used to have. They discussed their childhoods, school, and their families. Riley went into detail about her mother being a doctor and her father being a marine biologist trying to save whales.

"It all sounds wonderful, but very busy," Pea said. "I think I prefer the pace here."

"Until the Red Moons," Riley said.

"Indeed," Pea agreed. "Then everything changes."

A horn blared. It was different from the horn that called everyone to the *Queen*.

"Now what?" Alfie asked.

"That is the foghorn," Maggie explained. "It is coming." She looked at the window. "It is time you closed the window and curtains. The Red Moon is starting."

Tension in the cabin rose as the horn continued to sound. Every time it blared, there was a return call from the ground, a deep, mournful bellow that was filled with loss and suffering.

"What is that?" Riley asked.

"That will be Kevin," Maggie said. "I worry about him the most out there. I also believe it is unfair that he is forced into a yellow cloak when he is the gentlest of us all."

"It is his size and that sharp horn that betray him," Pea said.

"Yes," Maggie agreed. "I just hope he is not judged harshly because of it."

"What do you mean, 'judged'?" Riley asked.

Maggie nodded. "When those of us that are

transforming finally complete our change, we are judged by the community and then our fate is decided. If we are gentle and pose no threat, we are allowed to stay. If we are deemed too dangerous, we are banished to the Forbidden Zone or the ocean."

"Mada's really dangerous, so why is he still here?" Riley asked.

"Ah, Mada," Maggie said. "He is very dangerous, but since he has not completed his transformation, he can't be judged yet."

"But Susan was judged," Bastian said. He looked at Maggie. "We saw the other Red Cloaks carry her to the ocean to release her."

An expression of sadness shadowed Maggie's eyes. "Susan was a dear friend. I shall miss her greatly."

"What was she?" Alfie asked. "I mean, what did she become? We couldn't see."

"I believe she became a crocodile," Maggie said. Then she looked at Pea. "Or was it an alligator? I can't remember the difference."

"Me neither," Pea said. "But she became a danger to everyone. She surrendered to the change."

"I don't understand," Riley said.

Maggie inhaled deeply. "We don't know why the transformation happens or how. But we all change eventually. When it starts, we retain our humanity. But some embrace their change and give up what it means to be human. It is then they become a danger to all. Whereas Jeff, who has completed his transformation, chose to hold on to his humanity and can actually speak. He was judged safe and allowed to remain."

"Just like me," Pea said proudly.

"And Miss Pigglesworth," Bastian added.

"So does the change start when you get older?" Riley asked. "Is that why there are no old people here?"

Pea nodded. "Yes. And it is also why we are especially grateful when children come to Atlantis. Their innocence reminds us of what we used to be. But there are so few arriving these days, I fear what will happen to us in the future."

The mournful bellowing from outside the ship trailed off. "There he goes," Pea said. "Kevin will have to find cover before the moon rises fully and the wildlings arrive."

"Wildlings?" Alfie asked.

Pea nodded. "There are normal predators that come from the Forbidden Zone, but then there are the wildlings, which are much worse. They are those of us who transformed and surrendered completely to their change. But they retain their intelligence, which makes them more dangerous. It's almost as though they remember who they were and where they came from—but instead of wanting to return to visit old friends, they seek to destroy us."

"That doesn't make sense," Riley said.

"You are right, it doesn't," Maggie said. She smiled at her and reached for her hand. "I, for one, will never surrender to my change, whatever I turn into."

Riley smiled back.

Bastian stood up. "If you will excuse me, I'm going back to my cabin to try to get some rest."

"Now?" Riley said. "It's still the middle of the day."

"Yes, it is. But trust me, when the sun sets and the Red Moon rises, you won't be doing a lot of sleeping." He looked at Pea and Maggie. "Are you comfortable here? Or do you want to split up into other rooms? You are welcome to join Miss Pigglesworth and me."

"Thank you, Bastian," Pea said. "But if you don't

mind, I will stay here. We made it safely to this cabin. I don't wish to risk being seen and removed from the *Queen*."

"I feel much the same," Maggie said. "That is, if Riley doesn't mind sharing with us."

"Of course not," Riley said. "Everyone is welcome in here."

Alfie also stood. "I'm going to try to sleep a bit too. I'll come back later."

When they left, Maggie settled down on the sofa. She curled in a tight ball and placed her head on her hands. With her long tail wrapped around her tightly, she looked more like a large cat than a woman.

Riley smiled at her and Pea as she climbed onto the bed. She wasn't tired, but with the long night ahead, she thought she might try taking a nap.

20

THE SOUND OF A BELL ROUSED RILEY from her sleep. A few minutes later, there was a knock on her door.

Riley rose from her bed and opened the door a few inches. Bastian and Alfie were there. They slipped into the room.

"You should see it outside," Alfie said. "It's awesome."

Riley went to the window, and when she pulled back the curtains, she was faced with a wall of white. The fog was so thick she couldn't see anything. "Wow, you guys weren't kidding. That is solid out there."

The bell rang again. "That's dinner," Bastian said.

"I'm not hungry," Riley said. "I'm a little freaked about tonight. I think I'll stay here."

"Me too," Alfie agreed.

"You children should eat," Pea said as he yawned and stretched in the chair. "Do not stop because of us. Maggie and I are fine up here."

"Maybe later . . . ," Riley said.

"I have an idea," Bastian said. "What if Alfie and I go down and get some trays of food. Then we can bring it back and we can all eat together."

Riley nodded. "Perfect."

When they left, Maggie and Riley pulled the desk into the center of the room to make a table. Then the chairs were pulled closer.

"This will be lovely," Pea said, rubbing his hands together. "I am going to enjoy myself."

After several minutes, Alfie and Bastian returned. Riley stepped back to let them in and saw that Soraya was with them. She ran into the room and straight over to Pea. She gave him a big hug and petted his ears.

"Sorry," Bastian said. "Normally I sit with the others during the Red Moon. Kerry is with them now, but Soraya wanted to stay with me."

"I won't tell anyone about you," Soraya said to Pea and Maggie.

Riley closed the door and sighed. "Well, that's another thing for Kerry to hate me for."

Bastian and Alfie went back to their cabins to collect more chairs. They were set up around the desk, and the food was shared among everyone.

As they ate, Pea told stories of fun and adventure. There was something so sweet about the koala gesturing and performing the dramatic scenes. Riley realized Pea had missed his calling. He was a natural actor.

As the day faded into night and the fog outside turned dark, strange snarling and growling noises sounded from outside the *Queen*.

Soraya's eyes became large and filled with fear. "I hate this. I hope they don't get in."

"They won't," Maggie said. She held up her hands and pulled off her gloves, revealing long, sharp claws at the end of her fur-covered fingers. "Do you see these? I promise that I will use them and everything I have to protect you. Nothing will happen—you are safe with us."

Soraya smiled at Maggie, but the fear never left her face.

As the moments passed, the sounds from the ground increased. Another bell on the ship sounded. "Has everyone eaten enough?" Bastian asked.

When they nodded, he looked at Riley. "That bell means lights out. We must extinguish our lanterns so we don't attract predators."

Bastian rose and went to the three lanterns. One was from Riley's room, and the other two were from his and Alfie's. When they were extinguished, the room was cast into darkness.

An especially loud and threatening roar came from outside and seemed to be getting closer.

"And so it begins," Pea whispered.

Being in total darkness seemed to amplify Riley's fear. The roaring sounded like it was coming from just outside her window. She climbed to her feet and made her way carefully over to the window. She peered behind the curtain but could only see a wall of black fog.

"Close them," Pea warned quietly. "We can't see in that fog, but whatever is out there most likely can."

The sounds were even closer. But mixed in with the roaring, growling, snarling, and screaming were the sounds of horses' whinnies.

"And here they come," Maggie whispered.

"Who?" Alfie asked softly.

"The unicorns," Maggie answered. "They'll spend the rest of the night driving the others away from the *Queen* to keep us safe."

Riley was confused. Everyone said the unicorns were wild and dangerous, and yet they came here specifically to protect the *Queen*. Why?

Time seemed to stop as the sounds grew angrier and more intense. Riley wanted to ask what they were, but she was too frightened in case whatever was outside heard her voice. She fumbled her way to the bottom of the bed and sat down on the floor.

A while later there was pounding and scratching against the side of the ship. Riley found herself holding her breath, hoping and praying whatever it was out there stayed out there.

"Can the ship tip over?" Alfie whispered.

"No," Pea whispered. "It is seated too deep in the ground. We are safe as long as we stay quiet."

The long night moved at a snail's pace as their ears were assaulted by more noise. Wild, angry roars and howling.

Mixed in with the violent sounds was an almost-human voice snarling, "Let us in!"

Riley gasped. "There's someone outside."

"Hush," Pea called. "That is a wildling. Your voice will encourage him."

More angry whinnies rose from the ground. It sounded like the unicorns were all around the *Queen*.

Riley felt Alfie settle on the floor beside her, and he slipped his arm around her. He was trembling as much as she was.

Sitting in total darkness, Riley realized the Red Moon was more terrifying than she'd imagined. Her heart went out to all the Blue and Yellow Cloaks who were locked outside the ship and left to the mercy of whatever was out there.

If there were electricity and the lights came on, Riley was sure she would look like a frightened child. Because that was exactly what she was. She was frozen with fear unlike anything she'd ever experienced before. It was even worse than when she was in the water after being washed overboard.

Every glass-rattling roar from outside the window reduced her to a quivering mess.

Suddenly blood-chilling howls started. This was followed by loud thumps from above. The ship itself seemed to rock with each thud.

Riley shut her eyes and held her breath, waiting for the moment the big something broke through the ceiling and devoured them all.

Pea sighed. "We are safe now; the gargoyles are here."

21

RILEY'S LEGS WERE JELLY AND SHE FELT sick as she and Alfie sat together on the floor in complete darkness and total silence. She wasn't sure for how long. But after a while, she realized all the wild sounds were fading and replaced by the sounds of heavy rain hitting the window.

Then she heard movement and a soft tread on the floor. Soon weak morning light leaked in the window as Pea threw back the curtains.

He rubbed his hands. "Well, that's another Red Moon done. I'm starving. Is anyone else hungry?"

"I could eat," Maggie said.

"Me too," Bastian agreed.

"I would like a papaya," Soraya said. She was sitting beside Maggie, still holding her clawed hand.

Riley looked at them in disbelief. They had just gone through the most terrifying night of her life and now they were talking about food?

"Riley, are you all right?" Bastian asked.

"You—you're hungry? Really?"

Bastian nodded. So did Miss Pigglesworth.

"After—after everything we heard, you're actually hungry?" Alfie cried.

Pea chuckled and walked up to them. He placed his furry hand on Riley's arm. "That is the Red Moon, child. We are used to it. After the rain stops, workers will go out to look for damage to the *Queen* and the other buildings."

"Then we find out who we lost to the Red Moon," Maggie added.

"Indeed," Pea agreed sadly.

Maggie yawned and stretched. "Actually, I could also use a nice nap."

"Me too," Pea agreed. He walked back to the plush chair and settled down. Then he reached for a piece of leftover fruit and started to eat. "We still have some time before they open the outer doors. May I suggest we all get some rest? It was a long night."

Bastian rose and yawned. "Good idea. I'm going back to my cabin." He smiled at Riley. "Thank you for letting us share the Red Moon with you in here. It was one of the better ones, I think."

"Better?" Alfie barked, breaking his silence. "If that was a better one, I'd hate to see a worse one."

"Don't worry, you will," Bastian said. He looked at Maggie and Pea. "I'll be back later, and we can get you both off the *Queen*."

Alfie rose and said nothing as he followed Bastian to the door. "See ya later, Shorty."

"Yeah, see ya, Creep," Riley responded.

Soraya stayed in the room and settled down on the bed beside Riley, while Maggie returned to the sofa.

Curled up with Soraya, Riley realized just how exhausted she was after the night of terror. It was no wonder Bastian said they couldn't use the land bridge to go to the Forbidden Zone during the Red Moon. There was no way she would ever choose to leave the *Queen* during it.

They managed to get Maggie and Pea off the ship the same way they got them on. Though it was a lot easier as there was no one watching the ramp because of the heavy rain. On the ground, they made it back to the sewing hut so Pea and Maggie could collect their cloaks.

"Thank you again," Pea said. "I can't remember the last time I felt safe during a Red Moon."

"Me either," Maggie said. She looked at Riley. "May we try that again during the next one?"

"Sure," Riley agreed. "Maybe we can get more Blue and Yellow Cloaks on board. It's too cruel to leave them out here with all the monsters." She shivered again as she recalled the sounds of the night.

"That is very kind of you," Pea said. "Now, I am going to check if my home is still intact. I will see you later."

On the way back to the *Queen* they noticed all the damage done to the homes. There were claw marks on the stone walls, and doors had been torn off. One of the boat buildings was actually knocked over and torn open. If there had been anyone inside, they would have been killed.

Approaching the *Queen* again, Riley looked up at the ship and saw fresh gouges cut into the side. The outer skin of the ship held, but the paint had taken a beating.

Because of the heavy rain, everyone stayed on the ship. As Riley and Alfie entered the ship's dining hall, Kerry approached her. "You think you're so special keeping Bastian and Soraya in your cabin during the Red Moon. But you're not. Life was perfect until you got here. Now you've ruined everything."

Riley had reached her limit with the bully—especially after the terror of the previous night. She leaned forward and poked her finger in Kerry's chest. "Look, Kerry, just leave me alone. You got it? Leave me alone before I really lose my temper!"

Kerry opened her mouth to speak but shut it again. She stormed off and left the dining hall without eating.

The children's table was set up beside a large window. As the others settled around her, Riley looked outside. "It's coming down harder."

"It always rains for a few days after a Red Moon," Bastian said. "It means we don't have a lot of work to do. We can play or do whatever we want."

Riley looked at her cousin and then said, "Are we ordered to stay on board, or can we go out?"

"Why would you want to go out?" Ellis asked.

"I'd like to see the damage," Riley said. "What do you think, Alfie, you want to go check it out?"

Alfie looked out the window. "But it's raining."

"Yes, but Alfie, we don't have to work," Riley said, hoping to get him to agree. "We can *look around* more."

"Oh yeah, look around," Alfie said, finally understanding. "Sure, I want to go out."

"You two are crazy," Ellis said. He nudged John. "Maybe Kerry was right."

"I guess I am too," Bastian said. "I've never seen it out there right after the Red Moon. Let's eat and then we can go."

They ate quickly and then made their way off the ship. The rain was coming down in sheets and making it difficult to see.

"Tell me again why you wanted to go out," Alfie said.

"I want to go to the beach across from the Forbidden Zone and see if the land bridge is still there so we can cross."

"Good idea," Alfie said. "Let's go."

"But that beach is in Red Cloak territory," Bastian cried. "It's too dangerous, especially after a Red Moon."

Alfie said, "If you don't want to come, that's cool. But we're going."

"I do want to come," Bastian said. "But you should know, we will be risking our lives. Mada is in that territory."

"This whole place is dangerous!" Alfie cried. "What's the difference?"

Their first stop was to the toolshed to pick up machetes. Then they started through the jungle until they reached the split rail fence that marked the boundary between the Community and Red Cloak territory. Bastian paused and said, "Are you sure you want to do this?"

"Do what?" Alfie asked.

"This," Bastian said. "Cross over into the Red Cloak territory."

"Wait . . . ," Alfie cried. "Are you saying this puny little fence is all that separates us from the Red Cloaks? No wonder Mada came over to get us. There's nothing to stop him."

"This is an honorary boundary line. We all respect it."

"Um—Bastian, not all," Alfie said. "In case you forgot, Mada attacked us at the graveyard."

"He's not supposed to."

"Yeah, right," Alfie said.

"Let's just go," Riley said.

They climbed over the fence and crossed into the Red Cloak territory.

Riley's senses were on high alert as they made their way to the beach she'd visited on the first day. As they neared it, Riley thought she heard crying over the sounds of the rain. She stopped. "Do you hear that?"

"Hear what?" Alfie said. "All I hear is rain hitting my head."

It was soft, but it was there. "Someone's crying," Riley said. "It's coming from the beach. C'mon!"

They all started to run. When they burst through the jungle and onto the sand, they all heard the voice.

"Over there," Bastian called. "In the water, it's a girl!"

Just offshore a girl of about Riley's age was struggling and crying. Her arms were beneath the surface as she tried to keep her head above the water.

"She's drowning!" Alfie ran down the beach and straight into the water.

The girl saw him coming and there was terror on her face, but she still didn't move.

"Don't panic, I'm coming," Alfie called.

Despite the wounds on her legs, Riley entered the water right behind him. They swam over to the girl.

"Are you all right?" Riley called. Rain was making her hair run down into her eyes. Wiping it away furiously, she saw that the girl's eyes were filled with terror. The girl shook her head, and when she opened her mouth to speak, the only sounds she made were a series of soft singing notes.

"Can you speak?" Riley asked.

Again the girl shook her head and the soft singing emerged.

"She must be caught on something," Alfie said. "I'll go down and check." He looked around in the water and squinted. "Keep an eye out for the Leviathan."

"Be careful," Riley warned. She treaded water closer to the girl. "Don't be afraid; Alfie will get you free."

Moments later Alfie reappeared, and his face was ashen. "You are not going to believe this—" Before he could say another word, the girl cried out and her head dipped below the surface.

"She's gonna drown!" Riley warned.

"No, she's not!" Alfie said. "She can't. Riley, she's a mermaid!"

"What?"

"A real live mermaid!" Alfie repeated. "I swear, she's got a long tail that's swimming really fast. I think she's holding on to a statue. She'd be okay if she let it go."

The girl reached the surface again and her eyes pleaded with Riley. She looked down into the water and then back to Riley and made the soft singing sound again.

"Can you understand me?" Riley asked.

The mermaid nodded.

"The statue you're holding, let it go."

The mermaid's eyes went large and fearful again as she shook her head.

"Do you need us to help you with it?" Alfie asked.

The mermaid nodded urgently and sang a response.

"Shorty, we have to help her," Alfie said.

Riley and Alfie dove down into the water and caught hold of the statue's arms and helped raise it up. When its head broke the surface, Alfie gasped. "Riley, it's him, it's him! This is the monster that saved you from Mada!"

"It can't be," Riley grunted as she struggled to tread water and hold the statue.

"It is," Alfie said. "Let's get it to shore and I can show you."

Riley, Alfie, and the mermaid struggled to move the statue, but it was too heavy to carry, even in water. They could barely stay at the surface.

"Bastian," Riley shouted. "Help us—we need a rope or something."

"What is it?" Bastian called.

"A really heavy statue of the monster that saved Riley from Mada," Alfie responded.

The expression on Bastian's face changed. "Just hold on; don't let him go! We'll be right back!" He and Miss Pigglesworth vanished into the trees.

"I hope he hurries," Riley said as her head dipped beneath the surface and she took in a mouthful of salty water. "I can't hold it much longer."

A short while later Bastian returned carrying a long rope. He ran to the water's edge and paused. "I—I can't swim."

"Please, Bastian, try," Riley cried. "I can't hold it much longer."

Miss Pigglesworth took one end of the rope in her

mouth and charged into the water. When she was close enough, Alfie reached for the end and tied it around the statue's large head. "Bastian, pull!"

They worked together to get the large stone statue to shore. When Riley could feel the sand beneath her feet, it was easier to hold on to. But as more of it came out of the water, the heavier it became.

Alfie and Riley left the water and joined Bastian on the shore, towing the large statue as far as they could. But when it reached the shallows, its weight dug it deep into the sand until they couldn't move it farther.

"It's a gargoyle," Bastian said.

"That's a gargoyle?" Alfie said.

"It is, but I've never seen one during the day," Bastian said. "How did he get here?"

The mermaid swam closer but didn't come to shore. She sang out in a soft voice and then dove beneath the surface with a flash of her green tail.

"You're welcome!" Alfie called sarcastically. "Don't worry about us. We were happy to help!" He looked at Riley. "Nice, we save the statue and she vanishes."

Riley wiped the hair out of her eyes. "She didn't look anything like the others. She didn't have long teeth."

"You know about the mermaids?" Bastian asked. "I've never seen one myself, but I'm told they are scary-looking."

"They are," Riley said. She told Bastian about her encounter with the mermaid when she was on the *Event Horizon*. "I saw her again right before I passed out."

The mermaid reappeared at the surface and called out in her singsong voice. She raised her hand out of the water and pointed down.

Alfie frowned and looked out over the rain-swept water. "Don't tell me there's another one out there."

The mermaid shook her head and then flapped both arms in the air.

"Is she trying to fly?" Riley asked.

Miss Pigglesworth started to bark. Bastian looked at the dog and then to the stone statue they dragged from the water. "No, look. This gargoyle is missing a wing."

Riley called to the mermaid. "Is that it? Do you see the missing wing?"

The mermaid nodded and pointed down again.

Alfie untied the rope around the statue's neck and threw the end to the mermaid. "Tie this around it and we'll pull it ashore."

The mermaid caught hold of the rope and dipped down into the water.

While they waited, Riley wiped her hair from her eyes furiously. "This rain is really getting on my nerves."

"We shouldn't be out here," Bastian said. He looked around anxiously. "This was a mistake."

"It's too late now, we're here," Alfie said. "The question is, can we get over to the Forbidden Zone once we get that wing to shore?"

Further discussion was cut off when the mermaid reappeared. Riley and Alfie entered the water again and swam up to her. When they were close, fear flashed across the mermaid's face.

"Why are you afraid of us?" Alfie asked.

"We're just trying to help," Riley added.

After a brief hesitation, the mermaid nodded and offered part of the rope. Riley and Alfie took it as the three swam closely together while they hauled the heavy wing to shore.

When it was in the shallows, they saw the break.

"Now what?" Alfie said.

"Children, what in the heavens are you doing here? This is Red Cloak territory! And get out of the water—the Leviathan—" Pea ran onto the beach but struggled with his soaking-wet cloak. When he neared the shore, he noticed the statue and ran up to it. "Gideon! What happened to him?"

"We don't know," Riley called as she walked out of the water. "We were—um—exploring when we heard the mermaid crying. Then we helped her bring this to shore."

"Oh, Gideon," Pea said sadly as he patted the statue. "My old friend. This is just too sad for words." The small koala sat down in the sand and leaned against the statue as he started to weep.

"Don't cry, Pea," Riley said softly as she knelt beside him.

"You don't understand," Pea said miserably. "Gideon was my only friend before you came here. And now he will die."

The mermaid cried in the water.

Pea looked at the water. "Oh my, look at you . . . Was he your friend too?"

The mermaid nodded and lowered her head in sadness.

"I still don't understand," Alfie said.

Pea sniffed and looked up at them. "Gideon is a

gargoyle. The most wonderful and kind of creature. But they live only by night. When the sun rises, they turn to stone. He saved my life a very long time ago during a Red Moon." Pea looked at the damaged statue and drew his paw across a deep gouge in the gargoyle's side.

"He must have been fighting during the Red Moon, and the sun rose before he could get to safety. Now Gideon's wing is broken, and he will die." His words failed as he started to weep again.

"He's not dead now?" Alfie asked.

Pea shook his head. "Not yet. But if that wing isn't back in place perfectly when the moon rises, he will never awaken again. Gargoyles must be intact at moonrise or they are doomed."

"What if we hold his wing in place when the moon rises?" Bastian asked. "Will he come back to life?"

"Possibly," Pea said. "But if there is one piece missing, one little break we can't fix, Gideon will be lost."

"Then we'd better check him over carefully," Riley said. "He saved me from Mada. This is the least I can do for him."

"You would do that?" Pea said.

"Well, duh," Alfie said. He looked at Bastian. "Help me get his wing to shore."

Everything took longer in the heavy rain. Eventually they hauled Gideon's wing out of the water. But with the gargoyle dug so deeply in the sand, they couldn't check him fully for breaks. They tried to turn him over, but after a lot of straining, they couldn't move him.

"He's too heavy," Alfie panted.

"We can't leave him here," Riley said. "Maybe we should ask the others to help."

Pea shook his head. "They won't enter this area, especially right after a Red Moon. It must be—"

A shrill whinny sounded in the jungle beside them. Riley looked over and watched as a unicorn emerged from the trees. His ears were back, and his horn was blazing brightly in the gray light of day. He snorted angrily as he got closer.

Pea held up his hands to the unicorn. "Please forgive us. I know we have crossed the boundary, but it was only to help Gideon!"

The unicorn took a step closer and lowered his horn threateningly.

In the water, the mermaid started to sing as she

swam closer to the shore. She dragged herself up onto the sand and reached out to the unicorn.

The unicorn looked at the mermaid, and his golden horn stopped glowing. He took several steps closer and lowered his head to her.

Riley could hardly believe what she was seeing and had to wipe water out of her eyes. The dangerous unicorn allowed the singing mermaid to stroke his dark muzzle. She so wanted to touch him as well. But when Riley started to move, Pea caught hold of her. "Don't move a muscle. Unicorns are deadly."

After a few minutes the mermaid stopped singing and slipped back into the water. The unicorn raised his head and approached Gideon. He whinnied sharply.

Riley looked back at the mermaid and she nodded. She lifted the end of the rope and called to the mermaid, "If we tie this around Gideon, will the unicorn help us get him farther onto the sand?"

The mermaid nodded.

"Come on, everyone," Riley said. "Before the unicorn changes his mind."

Bastian untied Gideon's wing and secured the rope around his torso. Riley held the end out to the unicorn. "Will you pull this for us, please?"

Her hand was trembling as the unicorn took a step closer and reached out to take the rope in his mouth.

Working together, they hauled Gideon out of the water and farther up the beach. His wing was carried up and placed beside it. With the unicorn there to help, they rolled Gideon over so they could check every part of him. The rest of the gargoyle was intact. It was just the wing that had broken.

"Now what?" Alfie said. "We can't wait here all day; we'll catch pneumonia in this rain."

"Not to mention lingering in Red Cloak territory," Bastian said nervously.

"But we need to protect Gideon," Riley said.

The unicorn whinnied loudly and took a step closer to Gideon. He stood stone-still over the gargoyle.

"I do not think that will be a problem," Pea said cautiously. "Gideon has the best protection there is on Atlantis." He settled down in the sand and leaned against the gargoyle, oblivious to the rain drenching his cloak. "Now, I suggest you all return to the *Queen* before you are missed. Tell no one what you've seen here and be back before dark so we can hold Gideon's wing in position before moonrise."

"Of course," Riley said. She turned and gazed over the water.

"What are you looking for?" Pea asked.

"The land bridge to the Forbidden Zone. I, uh, I was worried about animals coming over and hurting you."

"The bridge was covered by the returning tide early this morning; it is deep beneath the surface now," Pea said. "I am perfectly safe. Run along and be back before dark."

Riley looked longingly at the Forbidden Zone but knew this was a dead end. Then she saw the mermaid in the water watching Gideon with deep sadness in her eyes.

"Don't worry," Riley called to her. "We'll be back later, and we'll save him."

22

THEY HAD TO SNEAK ON BOARD THE *Queen* and get back to their cabins without being seen. Climbing up to their deck, they hid in the stairwell as several passengers came and went. As it was, they were leaving trails of water on the floor wherever they went. Once they changed clothes, they used a rag to mop them up.

Riley had no chores to do on the boat, so she helped Bastian and Alfie with theirs, refilling the water buckets. As they worked, Bastian gave Riley and Alfie a full tour of the *Queen*. There were loads of people in the various activity rooms playing games and singing songs. Peals of laughter filled the ship as everyone celebrated surviving another Red Moon.

Lunch was a noisy, joyous occasion as more singing broke out in the dining hall. Despite being anxious over the events of the morning, Riley joined in and found herself having fun.

Throughout the day, Kerry would see Riley and shoot angry looks at her. Riley knew she shouldn't respond, but she couldn't help herself. On more than one occasion she stuck out her tongue at the bully.

As the afternoon dragged on, Riley was becoming too distracted to join some of the games being played by the other children. She was invited into a Ping-Pong tournament but declined the offer. Her mind kept going back to the Forbidden Zone. With the bridge covered, how were they supposed to get over there? Each passing day brought more danger to Aunt Mary and her father—if he was with her.

Throughout the day the rain never slowed. It was impossible to tell the time without a sun to follow. Finally, when the waiting became too much, Riley, Alfie, and Bastian agreed it was time to go.

Before leaving the *Queen*, Riley found Beresford and told him that she was exhausted from the long night and was going to bed early. Alfie and Bastian also said the same so their presence in the dining hall wouldn't be missed.

They made their way to the exit and were grateful to see that no one was there. Creeping forward, they dashed out of the ship before anyone arrived.

"The rain is coming down even harder!" Alfie complained as they walked through the trees. "Is it ever going to stop?"

"In a few days," Bastian said. "But it always gets worse before it gets better."

"Oh, that's just great," Alfie said. "So now I'll really get pneumonia."

Riley wasn't happy about the rain, either, but Alfie's complaining was getting on her frayed nerves. "If you want to go back to the *Queen*, I'm sure Bastian and I can hold Gideon's wing."

"Don't tempt me," Alfie said.

"Then go," Riley said.

"Please stop," Bastian cried. "We have to help Gideon. You two can fight later."

Alfie glared at Riley. "She started it."

Miss Pigglesworth barked.

"Well, she did," Alfie said.

Riley opened her mouth to retort, but held it in.

Bastian was right: their fighting wasn't going to help Gideon.

Instead she focused on walking through the rainy jungle. When they made it to the boundary, Riley gasped. On the other side of the fence was a unicorn. When it saw them, it whinnied and nodded its head.

"Um, any idea how we're supposed to get past that?" Alfie asked.

The unicorn whinnied again and backed up. It bowed its head.

"Look, his horn isn't glowing. I think he's here to help us." Riley took a tentative step closer to the fence. "Is that it? Are you here to escort us safely to Gideon?"

"Don't be stupid. He can't understand you!" Alfie snapped.

The unicorn snorted and took another step back.

Miss Pigglesworth slipped through the fence and approached the unicorn. She barked a few times and then came back to Bastian.

"Miss Pigglesworth thinks you are right. She believes he is here to protect us from Red Cloaks. They know we want to help Gideon."

"I hope you're right," Alfie said. "That's one mean-looking horn!"

Riley moved first. She cautiously walked forward and slowly climbed over the fence. Touching down on the other side, she kept her eyes on the unicorn. He didn't move.

Bastian went next, and then Alfie. When they were all over, the unicorn turned and started to walk through the jungle.

"No one would ever believe this back home," Riley said as they followed the unicorn.

When they reached the beach, they received another surprise. Four more unicorns were standing around Gideon, protecting him on all sides.

"Wow," Riley said softly. "It's like they're working together or something."

"They are," Bastian said.

"How many unicorns are there?" Alfie asked.

"I don't know," Bastian said. "They live on the North Side, and we're not allowed to go there."

Up ahead, Pea was out of his cloak and holding it over his head for shelter as he sat beside Gideon. "You're back!" he cried excitedly.

The unicorns around Gideon looked at Riley and the others warily and their ears went back, but at least their horns didn't start to glow.

But when their escort unicorn whinnied loudly, they calmed, and their ears came forward.

Pea rose to his feet. "This day has been endless. But at least I've had some company." He trotted over to Riley and whispered behind his hand. "But I must say, they are not the best conversationalists." He led them back to Gideon.

"Bastian, Alfie, I need your help, please. I was looking at this earlier and fear we may not have all the pieces. But I can't be certain until we check."

Gideon was lying on his side, and it was difficult to maneuver the wing into place. When they finally did, Pea crawled beneath it and felt the break with his furry hand. He sat up. "It is as I feared. There is a shard missing. If we don't find it, Gideon will never wake again."

They searched the sand first, and when they didn't find it, Riley ran into the shallows. The mermaid was drifting in the current farther out. "Please," she called, "there is still a piece missing from Gideon. Would you go down and check all around the area? Without it, he won't awaken."

"Riley, get out of the water," Pea warned. "The Leviathan may come. . . ."

Riley checked the water, but the rain pounding the surface hid any movement of the Leviathan if it was in the area. She stepped back.

As the time ticked away, everyone watched the sky. The solid gray above them was darkening. But was it the sun going down, or just more storms moving in?

While they waited, they all strained to get Gideon turned onto his front so they would have easy access to the gargoyle's back and the wing break.

After a time, the mermaid surfaced again and sang out. She swam closer to shore but paused before reaching the shallows.

"I'll go," Riley said. She ran down to the edge and called to the mermaid, "Is the Leviathan around here?"

When the mermaid shook her head, Riley entered the water. But then the mermaid swam back into deeper water.

Her constant fear was almost as irritating as Alfie. "Why are you so scared of us after everything we've been through today? We want to help Gideon as much as you do."

The mermaid lowered her head and then looked up again. To Riley it was almost as though she was arguing with herself. Finally the mermaid swam closer and held out her webbed hands.

Riley saw several stones and sharp pieces of rock that were the same color as Gideon. "Thank you. Now, let's hope it's one of these." She carried the pieces back up the beach and handed them to Pea.

The small koala inspected each one carefully. "Here. This one!" He looked at Alfie and Bastian. "Boys, hold up the wing again and I'll check."

Alfie and Bastian strained to hold up the heavy wing. Riley joined them and caught hold of the tip. With a bit of maneuvering, they placed it against the break.

"And now this," Pea said as he slipped the shard into place. "Perfect!" He wrapped his small hands around the join to keep it secure. "Now we just have to hold it steady until the moon rises."

"How are we supposed to tell in all this?" Alfie complained.

"Alfie, please," Riley said.

Alfie shot her a look but then calmed. "I'm serious, how can we tell when the moon is rising?"

"You will know when you feel Gideon move," Pea said.

Riley's arms started to tremble with the strain as she, Alfie, and Bastian held the wing as still as possible.

While they waited, Miss Pigglesworth started to let out a soft growl.

"Uh-oh," Bastian said. "We may have a problem."

"What is it?" Riley asked.

Her question was answered by a loud roar sounding in the jungle just to their left.

"I thought Gideon got rid of Mada," Alfie said nervously.

"It may not be Mada," Pea offered. "There are several other Red Cloaks just like him."

"That's just perfect," Alfie said.

Miss Pigglesworth's growling intensified.

"Oh no," Bastian said. "Not again. Stay here, Miss Pigglesworth. Do you hear me?"

Before the dog could respond, a Red Cloak emerged from the jungle. Its cloak was filthy and soaked as it clung to a body that was much larger than Riley expected. She recognized him immediately. It was Mada. He started across the beach on all fours, but then rose onto his back legs as he neared.

The five unicorns gathered closer around them.

"Stay right where you are, Mada," Pea called. "You are not welcome here. Please go away."

Riley was stunned by Pea's bravery. He showed no fear of Mada as he faced him down.

"This is my territory, Pea," Mada hissed. "My hunting ground. It is *you* who are not welcome here."

Miss Pigglesworth started to bark.

"Control her, Bastian," Mada warned. "Or I will."

"Miss Pigglesworth, please," Bastian begged. "Don't do it."

Riley couldn't see under the cloak's hood and didn't want to. She'd seen him once; that was plenty. Just hearing his distorted voice was sending chills down her spine.

Mada took a step closer and hissed, "So Gideon is broken—"

"We're going to save him, and you can't stop us!" Riley heard herself speaking and was shocked. It was as though her mouth had a will of its own.

Mada snarled at her, "I am so going to enjoy killing you!"

"Please stop," Bastian said. "The unicorns want to help him too. They won't let you near him. Remember what happened to you on the beach—do you want to be touched again?"

Mada threw back his head and roared in rage. His wet hood fell off, revealing his half-man, half-tiger face. His mouth was distended and filled with pointed teeth, but his eyes still looked human, though they were golden yellow. Then he paused and looked back at the darkening sky. "I will forgive you that, just this once, Bastian," he hissed. "And I will make a deal with you all. Leave here now and you may live."

Bastian looked at Riley. "If we go, Gideon will die."

"Exactly," Mada hissed. "Now go before I change my mind."

"We're not leaving him," Riley said.

"Good," Mada said. "I had rather hoped you would want to fight. It makes the meat more tender."

As Mada started to charge, the horns on the five unicorns started to blaze brilliantly. They whinnied loudly, and the one that had escorted them reared and slammed down to the sand.

Mada stopped mid-charge and roared furiously. "No! They have broken the rules and are in Red Cloak territory. Leave me to my hunt!"

The lead unicorn snorted and lowered his horn threateningly. He took a step forward.

"You have no right to stop me!"

With one more whinny from the lead unicorn, Mada returned to all fours and started to trot away. "I will not forget this. . . ." With a final roar, he disappeared into the trees.

Riley couldn't imagine a more horrifying sight than Mada's grotesque face. It was a thing of nightmares that would haunt her forever.

"Everyone, please," Pea called. "We must set Gideon's wing again."

Riley looked at the join and realized they'd moved the pieces apart when Mada came.

As the stormy gray sky darkened, they settled Gideon's wing in position again. The stone was wet and slippery, and Riley's hands were trembling from the encounter with Mada.

"All of you, calm down," Pea said softly as he held the shard in place. "It is over. Mada will not trouble us again tonight."

"What about tomorrow?" Bastian said. "Or the next day?"

Pea nodded. "Mada will always be a danger until he is banished to the Forbidden Zone. Right now, Gideon is our only concern. Shaking hands will seal his fate and Mada will have won."

The sky darkened further, and a rough wind started to blow. The lead unicorn came forward and touched the lantern with his golden horn. Instantly, it burst to life with a brilliant flame that drove back the darkness.

"Wow, that's really bright," Riley said.

"It's unicorn magic," Bastian grunted. "Is it just me, or is this wing getting heavier?"

"Much heavier," Alfie complained.

"We're almost there," Pea said. "We may not see it, but the moon is rising. If Gideon is going to wake, it should be any moment now."

Riley didn't want to say anything, but she doubted she'd be able to hold the wing much longer. But dropping it would mean the death of the gargoyle. With her hands aching, she wasn't sure if she felt movement beneath her fingers, or whether it was a cramp.

"Wait," Bastian called. "I felt something. . . ."

"Me too," Alfie said.

A song, unearthly and sweet, rose from the water behind them and Riley knew it was the mermaid. The notes were so beautiful, tears rose in her eyes.

"She is calling to him," Pea said softly. "In all my life, I never imagined that I would hear the song of a siren. It is truly enchanting."

As the music carried them away, the statue started to grow warm. The gray stone wing turned leathery and batlike. There was a soft moan.

The unicorns nickered and Pea called, "You may release him now. Stand well back—we can't be sure how he will react when he wakes."

Riley was grateful to release the wing. Her hands were cramped, and she could barely move her fingers. As she stepped back, she watched in wonder as stone came to life.

Gideon's back rose and fell as he took deep breaths. The once-broken wing moved and folded neatly into place, nestled beside the other wing.

Gideon's hands flexed in the sand. "Wha— what . . . ?"

His head turned and he looked up at the unicorns surrounding him. He gasped.

When the lead unicorn whinnied, Gideon turned his massive head and looked at Pea. "Pea, what are you doing here?"

Pea stepped forward and put a small furry hand on Gideon's muscular arm. "Take it easy, my old friend. You have suffered a break."

"A break?" Gideon climbed slowly to his feet.

Riley wiped the rain from her eyes and had the feeling she was watching a mountain rise. The gargoyle had to be at least seven feet tall and was more muscular than the biggest wrestlers on television. His voice was deep like rolling thunder, and it sounded like it was coming from inside a bottomless well.

Gideon's eyes came to rest on Riley, Alfie, and Bastian. Then he looked over at the unicorns and back to them again. "Pea, I do not understand. What is happening here?"

Riley was struck silent by the sight of the immense gargoyle. As a statue, its face had been horrifying with big eyes and an even bigger nose. It had sharp fangs in a mouth that was drawn back in a vicious snarl.

Now that Gideon was awake, he was still a sight to see, but he wasn't horrifying at all. The look of confusion on his face made him almost endearing.

Gideon turned back to the water. "Galina? Galina, are you all right?" He jogged a few paces to the water's edge, and Riley was sure she felt the earth shake.

The song stopped as the mermaid called to him in her singsong voice.

"I am fine, child," Gideon said. "Though I don't understand what has happened."

The mermaid kept speaking. After a time, Gideon turned and walked back up the beach. "I owe you all my life," he said somberly. "How can I thank you?"

"You did the same for us," Riley said. "When you stopped Mada from killing Alfie and me."

"That was nothing," Gideon said. "But this . . . you risked your lives coming her for me."

"Not really," Alfie said. "We just went in the water and—"

"Where the Leviathan waits," Gideon said.

"I guess," Alfie said. "But the mermaid was crying; we had to help. What happened to you?"

"It was the end of the Red Moon, but one of the wildlings from the Forbidden Zone refused to return. I drove him to the land bridge, but then as the dawn arrived, he attacked me and broke my wing. Had you not helped me, I would now be dead."

"It was the mermaid, Galina," Riley said. "She held you up until we came."

"I am grateful to all of you," Gideon said.

Riley stepped closer. "I'm Riley, and this is my

cousin Alfie." She looked at Bastian. "And this is Bastian. He's from Atlantis."

"I know of Bastian," Gideon said. "And I know that you two are the newcomers."

The unicorns whinnied and started to walk away. Before they did, Riley ran up to them. "Thank you for helping us. If you hadn't been here, Mada would have killed us."

The lead unicorn paused and looked at Riley. He took a step closer and then bobbed his head. A moment later he turned and trotted off into the jungle with the others.

Riley came back to the group. "He's so beautiful. I wonder, if I reached out my hand, would he let me stroke him like Galina did?"

Gideon looked back to the water and then said to Riley, "Galina is a siren: She can charm anyone or anything, including the unicorns. You must never try to touch them. They are dangerous and unpredictable. As guardians of Atlantis, they take their responsibilities seriously. They keep the peace between the territories. They also enforce banishment when necessary. Believe me, child, they are not to be taken lightly, and they do not tolerate distractions or friendships."

"But where do they come from? How did they get here? Where do they live?" Riley asked. "Unicorns are from fairy tales, but here they are real."

Gideon shook his head. "I see that look in your eyes. You are hoping to know them. But they will not welcome your attention. The unicorns were here long before we gargoyles came and much longer than the people. They live on the North Side with the other magicals. That is a dangerous territory you must never enter. Trust what I say. Stay away from the unicorns."

Riley nodded, but she couldn't help how she felt. She was drawn to the unicorns in a way even she couldn't understand.

"Can you understand the mermaid? I mean, Galina?" Bastian asked.

Gideon nodded. "Much like you and Miss Pigglesworth. I have known her from the day she washed ashore on Atlantis. The others in the ocean rejected her because she is not from here."

"Really?" Riley said. "Where's she from? I've seen one of the ocean creatures that I thought was a mermaid, but they looked completely different and a lot scarier."

"They are different," Gideon said. "I do not know where Galina comes from. She was but a young child when I found her. I have done my best to protect her and make a home for her here. She's become a daughter to me, and I love her dearly." Gideon paused and stared into the lantern light. "Though it seems that she is the one who has protected me."

Riley was getting used to the large gargoyle. His face was no longer shocking to her, any more than Pea's or Maggie's were. "Can Galina speak, you know, like us?"

"No," Gideon said. "I have tried to teach her, and she does understand us, but she is unable to speak. If you got to know her, after a time, I am sure you might learn her language."

"Would she let us?" Alfie said. "I mean, she seems really scared all the time."

Gideon sighed and it sounded like a wind through a deep cavern. "That is my fault. I told her she must keep hidden from the people of Atlantis. I feared what they might do if they found her." His eyes landed on Pea. "You have seen how they treat those of us who are different."

"Indeed," Pea said. "You were wise to teach her

to fear. But please tell her that we are safe."

"I will," Gideon said. "It worries me that she spends so much time alone. I think it would be lovely for her to have you as friends."

"I'd like that," Riley said.

Bastian and Alfie nodded. Finally Bastian said, "It's getting late. I'm soaked and starting to get cold. We had better get back to the *Queen* before they shut the doors."

Gideon nodded. "And I had best get back to the Crucible. The others will be wondering what happened to me."

"What is the Crucible?" Riley asked. "I've seen the top of it from the *Queen*. It sparkles like diamonds in the sunlight. I'd love to see more of it."

Gideon smiled, and it showed his long fangs. "The Crucible is ours. We keep books and instruments of knowledge there that have been recovered from the wrecks. It is in our territory."

"How many territories are there?" Alfie asked.

"A few," Gideon said. "There is the North Side, the gargoyle territory, the Red Cloak territory, and then the Community. We tend to stick to our boundaries and keep away from each other except during the

Red Moon. Then we merge to protect Atlantis from the Forbidden Zone. That is a danger to all of us."

"I didn't realize Atlantis was so big," Alfie said.

"Oh, it is," Pea said. "Very big."

Gideon nodded. "And we all keep to our own areas—most of the time."

"Except when you're out saving us," Riley said.

"That was just good fortune," Gideon said. "I was out for a flight to stretch my wings and saw what Mada was doing. He is becoming a problem."

"No kidding," Alfie said.

"So you've got books in your Crucible, like a library?" Riley asked.

Gideon nodded. "Yes, you might consider the Crucible a library. But one that only gargoyles use."

"Why? Books should be for everyone. I love reading. May I see it one day?" Riley said.

"Perhaps," Gideon said. "But I would need to seek the permission of the others before you enter our territory."

Alfie frowned. "Why are all the territories kept apart? I mean, okay, I understand about the Red Cloak territory. But why do you stay away? And the North Side?"

Gideon looked at Pea.

"Go ahead and tell them," Pea said.

Gideon shrugged. "It is safer this way. We gargoyles were persecuted by humanity for so long."

Pea nodded. "People knew their weakness of turning to stone during the day and used it against them. They attacked and broke them."

Riley gasped. "No . . ."

"Yes," Gideon said. "We were facing extinction until we found sanctuary here. But even in Atlantis, the people are uncomfortable around us. It is safer if we keep apart."

"That is so sad," Riley said.

"Indeed," Gideon agreed.

Miss Pigglesworth started to bark impatiently.

"Yes, we're coming," Bastian said. "We really must get back to the *Queen*."

Gideon nodded. "I shall escort you back to the Community."

They hadn't told Gideon about Mada's threat, but Galina might have. As they carried the torch into the trees, they were grateful for the gargoyle's presence. Gideon stayed with them over the boundary fence right up to the edge of the Community.

"I will wait here while you go ahead." He reached out to Riley. "Give me the lantern. It contains unicorn light and cannot be extinguished. If the others see it, they will know you have been with them and there will be questions."

Riley handed over the lantern, marveling at just how much bigger Gideon's hands were than hers.

"Thank you again for saving my life," Gideon said. "I will never forget your kindness."

They waved at Gideon and ran toward the ship. Before they got there, Pea excused himself and vanished in the trees.

Alfie was shivering as he said, "This has been the weirdest day!"

"It sure has," Riley agreed.

They walked up the ramp and entered the *Queen* just as the guards arrived to close the doors. Across from the doors, Lisette was seated with her arms crossed over her chest. She rose and charged forward. "Where have you been? We've been worried sick. When Kerry told me that she'd seen you leave the *Queen*, we feared the worst. There are dangers outside this ship right after a Red Moon. What would inspire you to go out in this terrible weather?

Look at you all: you're soaked to the skin!"

"I—I'm sorry," Riley said. "But we were curious to see what happened and then we got lost."

"Your curiosity could have gotten you all killed! As it is, Beresford is arranging a search party." Her eyes landed on Bastian. "You know better than to leave after a Red Moon. Why did you let them talk you into this?"

"I am sorry, Lisette," Bastian said. "But I've always been curious too."

"But you know how dangerous it is. The Red Cloaks . . ."

"It was my fault," Riley cut in. "I talked Bastian into coming with us. We just wanted to see all the damage done by the monsters."

Lisette inhaled deeply. "You will all return to your cabins immediately. There will be no more adventures. Do you hear me?"

"Yes, Lisette," Riley said softly.

Reaching her cabin, Riley went inside, changed out of her wet clothes, and sat down on the side of her bed. She was starting to shiver from the cold and pulled the bedcovers around herself. She was aching all over from the muscle strain of holding on to

Gideon's wing. But it had been worth it. Meeting the gargoyle and Galina had been beyond amazing. If they could get the siren to trust them, then maybe, just maybe, she could help them get over to the Forbidden Zone and they could finally search for Riley's father and aunt.

23

THE NEXT MORNING, RILEY WOKE AND peered out the window. It was still raining. A few minutes later there was a soft knock on her door. When she opened it, Alfie pushed past her. "We have to talk."

"Good morning to you too. Come in," Riley said.

"Yeah, whatever," Alfie said. He sat down on one of the chairs.

Her cousin had dark circles under his eyes and looked like he hadn't slept. "What's wrong?"

"Everything," Alfie said. "How are we supposed to get to the Forbidden Zone now? The land bridge is gone, the Leviathan is in the water, and after so many days of going to the slope and hearing nothing—"

"Don't say it!" Riley snapped. "They're there and they're alive! Don't you go losing hope. Yes, this place is really dangerous, but they're smart. They'll find somewhere safe to hide."

"But what if they didn't?"

Alfie looked on the verge of tears.

"Look, Creep," Riley said sharply, "if you wanna give up and believe Mary is dead, fine. But I don't. They're there and I'm going to find them."

"How?"

Suddenly Alfie, the big toughie, looked young and vulnerable. "We can do it, Alfie," Riley said. "I'm going to ask Galina to take us there. She's a siren. Gideon said she could charm anything. Maybe if the Leviathan comes, she can charm it."

"How can you be sure she can charm it?"

"I can't, but we have to try. After breakfast, I'm going to the slope to call her. If she comes, I'll ask."

"I'm coming with you," Alfie said.

Riley nodded. "Good. Now we just have to watch out for that little sneak Kerry and we'll be fine."

Seated at the breakfast table, Kerry sneered at Riley triumphantly. "Trouble last night, Riley?"

"No one likes a snitch, Kerry," Riley responded.

"Yeah, running to Lisette wasn't cool," Alfie put in. "If you have a problem with us, you talk to us. But if you try that again, you're gonna regret it."

Kerry gasped and turned to Bastian. "Are you going to let them talk to me like that?"

Bastian looked at her. "Why did you tell Lisette?"

Kerry's lower lip trembled. "Well, because . . . because you're not allowed to leave the ship when it rains."

"Says who?" Alfie said.

"Those are the rules," Kerry said.

"No, they're not," Bastian said. "You're just saying that because you don't like Riley or Alfie. But they're here with us now. There is nothing you can do about it."

"Not if the Red Cloaks eat them!" Kerry said. She stood and leaned closer to Riley. "I hope Mada gobbles you up!"

"Kerry!" Bastian cried.

Tears filled Kerry's eyes as she turned and ran away.

"What is her problem?" Alfie said.

"She's jealous," Vadin said as he ate his porridge. "Just ignore her. We do."

Riley looked at the others at the table and they all nodded. But Kerry was more than just jealous. She was a troublemaker who could really cause some problems for them if they weren't careful.

After breakfast, Riley and Alfie told Bastian their plan.

"So are you in?" Alfie asked.

"In what?" Bastian asked.

"No, I mean, do you wanna come with us?"

Bastian nodded. "Yes, I am in."

24

TO AVOID BEING FOLLOWED AND SPIED ON by Kerry, they snuck off the *Queen* separately and met up just inside the jungle.

The rain stayed heavy all the way to the slope where Riley heard the voice. The beach would have been better, but it was deep in Red Cloak territory and they couldn't risk an encounter with Mada. They just hoped Galina would hear them.

They reached the slope and listened to the strange hushing sound as raindrops struck the water.

"Galina," Riley called. "Can you hear me?"

"Galina?" Alfie repeated.

After a few minutes, the mermaid surfaced, showing none of the fear from their first encounter.

They started down the slope, but the rain made the trail slippery and Alfie slid down and crashed noisily into the water.

Galina swam closer and her laughter came out as beautiful singing.

Riley couldn't keep her laughter in, either, as she, Bastian, and Miss Pigglesworth made it down to the water.

Alfie stood up, covered in mud. But he was laughing too. He looked at the mermaid. "We can't understand you, but you sure have a pretty voice. Gideon says in time we can learn your language."

Miss Pigglesworth treaded into the water and swam up to the mermaid. Fear returned to Galina's face.

"It's all right," Bastian said. "Miss Pigglesworth just wants to say hello."

Galina hesitated, but then she reached out her hand and stroked the dog. But then when Miss Pigglesworth licked her hand, the mermaid giggled.

"See?" Riley said as she swam out into deeper water. "We're all friends here." She approached the mermaid. "Galina, I know we're only just getting to know each other, but we really need your help. Would you be able to take us over to the Forbidden Zone? Or at least stop the Leviathan if it came after us?"

The mermaid's eyes went large and she shook her head furiously.

"Please," Alfie said. "We think our family is there. Riley heard a woman shouting over there a while ago."

"Did you hear it?" Riley asked.

The mermaid nodded.

"That could be my mother," Alfie said. "We were all together on our boat when the Leviathan sank us. Riley and I washed ashore here, and the people here said they were dead. But then Riley heard the voice."

"We don't believe they're dead," Riley added. "We think they're over there. But we can't get there without your help."

Galina started to speak in a quick singing voice that they couldn't understand. She pointed to the Forbidden Zone and then made a circular gesture.

"We don't understand," Riley said. "Please, Galina, will you help us get there?"

The mermaid hesitated and shook her head.

"We helped you with Gideon," Alfie said. "It's only fair that you help us find our family."

Galina dropped her head and slipped beneath the water.

"That's just great, Alfie," Riley said. "Well done. You drove her away."

"What?" Alfie cried. "We *did* help her with Gideon. . . ."

A series of roars sounded in the jungle behind them. Everyone looked back. Three Red Cloaks stood at the top of the slope. Mada was in front. They all pulled off their cloaks and cast them aside.

Riley gasped at the sight. Mada's body was all tiger, with a long striped tail. It was only his head and hands that showed remnants of the man he used to be. One of the others was a black panther in transition, and the last was a leopard or perhaps jaguar. The creatures' eyes were focused intently on them.

"There are no unicorns to help you now," Mada hissed through his distorted mouth.

"You can't be here," Bastian cried. "This is Community territory. It is forbidden."

"But you had no problem coming to our territory yesterday," Mada growled.

"That was to help Gideon," Riley said.

"I don't care," Mada said. "We will have our hunt,

and everyone will believe the Leviathan got you. It is perfect."

"Please," Riley begged. "We just want to go home. Our parents are in the Forbidden Zone. We'll get them and then leave. You won't have to deal with us again."

Mada growled, "You aren't going anywhere." He roared and climbed down the slope, followed by the other two. They entered the water and started to swim.

Riley and Alfie moved, but when Bastian hesitated, Riley called, "Bastian, c'mon!"

"I can't swim!" Bastian cried. He turned back. Mada and the others were right behind him, and he screamed.

"I'll help you, Bastian," Mada teased.

Miss Pigglesworth started to bark furiously. She swam up to Bastian and caught him by the arm and pulled him into deeper water.

Alfie looked back. "They're cats—why are they in the water?"

"Foolish boy," Mada teased. "Don't you know? Tigers and leopards like water!"

Riley looked back and saw how Mada and the others were using their tails to direct their paths in the water. The thrill of the hunt was on their terrible faces as they moved. "No!" Riley cried. "Leave us alone!"

No matter how fast they swam, the Red Cloaks were faster. When they made it halfway to the Forbidden Zone, Galina resurfaced.

"Galina, get down!" Alfie warned. "They're coming!"

The mermaid ducked back down into the water. Moments later, the water around them seemed to move and swell.

Riley felt a strange pressure around her. She stopped and looked around.

"Riley, keep going!" Bastian cried.

She turned to the right and saw movement in the water. Moments later, the Leviathan's head rose above the surface. Its eyes blazed and its serpent's body cut through the water like a snake as it moved toward them.

Mada stopped swimming and turned quickly. "Go back," he roared.

The three hunters turned back toward the shore. As they swam, Galina surfaced beside Riley and started to sing.

The Leviathan looked back at the siren, and when Galina pointed at the Red Cloaks, it focused on Mada and the two other hunters. It glided past Riley,

Alfie, and Bastian without pausing, and gained on the Red Cloaks.

Mada was by far the fastest swimmer and reached the shore first, making it up the slope in a single leap. He was followed closely by the black panther. But the leopard lagged behind. Before it reached the safety of shore, the Leviathan picked up the Red Cloak in its fearsome mouth.

The leopard roared and howled as the Leviathan changed direction and dove down into the depths, taking the leopard with it.

Riley was too stunned to speak. She had hoped that Galina might be able to charm the Leviathan with her song, but she never imagined she'd be able to command it.

On the shore, Mada roared in rage. "You will have to come out of the water eventually. I will be waiting!"

Galina caught Riley by the arm and started to draw her forward. "I—I think she's going to help us."

Galina turned back and nodded.

"I'm too scared to swim," Alfie said.

"You're gonna have to, because we can't go back there yet," Riley said. She looked back at Mada and the black panther. "I bet they do wait for us."

"We'll have to go to shore in a different place," Bastian said. "Take us back, Miss Pigglesworth."

"No!" Riley said. "We've come this far; let's get to the Forbidden Zone and look for our family!"

Alfie turned to Bastian. "Riley's right. We have to check."

"You two are too stubborn for your own good," Bastian complained.

"No one's forcing you to come," Alfie said. "You can go back if you want. I mean, I'm sure Mada would love to see you again."

Bastian hesitated and glanced back to shore, and then toward the Forbidden Zone. "All right. Miss Pigglesworth, will you help me?"

Miss Pigglesworth drew Bastian along with her as they moved into deeper water. They stayed close together as they slowly made their way across the channel toward the Forbidden Zone.

Even though the rain was coming down in heavy sheets, the wild sounds from the ferocious neighboring island could still be heard. Just before they reached the opposite shore, Galina changed direction and started to swim along the edge of the Forbidden Zone.

"I thought we were going to the Forbidden Zone," Alfie said.

Galina paused and nodded. Then she raised her hand out of the water and made the same circling motion she did before.

"Do you want to take us around the Forbidden Zone?" Riley asked.

Galina nodded again and made a soft singing sound.

"How far?" Bastian asked. "It's not fair to make Miss Pigglesworth carry me."

"We'll help you when she gets tired," Alfie said.

The journey took much longer than Riley expected. With the dull gray sky above them, they couldn't tell how long they were out. But it felt like an age. Finally they reached the end of the Forbidden Zone and started around the opposite side.

Riley looked back and dreaded the return journey. Her arms felt like jelly from the long swim, and they were facing the same trip back.

After a time, they all stopped when they were faced with a surprise.

"What is that?" Bastian asked.

"It's a ship's graveyard!" Alfie said. "I've seen a

show about them on TV, but I never thought I'd ever see one in person."

"What is it?" Bastian repeated.

"Sometimes currents take wrecks to the same area, and they call it a ship's graveyard."

Ahead, at a circular cove, they saw a large collection of ships and boats. Some small, some very large. Some looked in good condition while others were rotted wrecks with only their skeletons showing above the surface. Most were on their side, floating or sunk in the shallows.

"Look how many there are!" Alfie cried. "How long have these islands been eating boats?"

"Not the island," Riley said. "The Leviathan. Remember what it did to our . . ." Riley paused as her eyes landed on a sight. "Alfie, look, do you see it? There, beside that big brown sailboat. It's the *Event Horizon*!"

Though she was exhausted from the journey, seeing their sailboat gave Riley renewed strength to swim closer.

"Wow, it's been totaled," Alfie cried as they moved around their sunken sailboat.

The water around them was filled with debris

from the *Event Horizon* and the other ships that had washed to shore. They swam past the tall mast of a sailboat that was fully submerged beneath them.

"There have to be at least fifty boats here," Alfie said.

While Riley and Alfie looked at the *Event Horizon*, Bastian's eyes were locked on the large brown boat lying at an angle beside it. He was frowning.

"You okay, Bastian?" Riley called.

"I—I . . ." He looked at the dog treading water beside him. "Does that brown one look familiar to you?"

Miss Pigglesworth barked loudly and paddled toward the wreck. As they got closer, Alfie whistled. "That's a seriously large boat!"

Riley read the name on the back. "*Moon Dancer*. That's a pretty name."

Bastian gasped. "*Moon Dancer*—I know that name!" He looked at Miss Pigglesworth. "Do you recognize it?"

The dog barked excitedly.

"Wow," Alfie said. "Look at the size of it. It makes our boat look puny."

They approached the *Moon Dancer* and Riley realized it wasn't just a sailboat, it was a yacht. Sleek, beautiful, and elegant. It was an antique made of polished wooden planks. The yacht had three tall, undamaged masts, though the fabric sails were shredded and hanging off in pieces. But apart from that, it looked to be in perfect condition. It was leaning over on one side, but that could have been the tide or unseen damage.

They moved around the yacht until they were on the side lying lower in the water. The ornate brass railing was green with age and covered in algae, but still intact.

Miss Pigglesworth and Bastian reached the boat first and struggled to crawl up onto the tilted deck.

"It still looks new," Alfie said when he crawled aboard.

Before Riley climbed up, she said to Galina, "We'll be right back. Will you wait here?"

The mermaid nodded and helped push Riley onto the sloped deck.

Bastian was frowning deeply. "I'm sure I know this boat." He stood up carefully on the tilted deck. "I have been here before, but I don't remember when."

He walked as if in a dream along the oak deck.

There were luxury cabins running most of the length, and when Riley peered in a porthole, she could see antique furniture and lovely curtains and furnishing.

"How can you remember it? It's really old," Alfie asked.

"I don't know . . . ," Bastian mused.

Reaching the stern, they found a solid carved-oak door leading to the inside. It was nothing like the *Event Horizon*, with its sliding hatch going down to below deck. This was a real, large door with brass handle. They pushed it open, revealing a wide, wood-paneled passage.

"It's like we've traveled back in time," Riley said. "Everything is so elegant and fancy."

Bastian pushed past her and walked confidently down the corridor. At the end, it opened into an ornate lounge. A solid-oak bar stood on one side. All the liquor bottles and glasses had fallen off the shelves and broken on the floor. But there were still photos mounted to the wall.

Bastian walked right up to one and pointed. "I knew I remembered this boat. Look, that's me!"

Riley stood beside him and gazed at the photo. It was black and white and showed a happy family.

The father was dressed in a dark jacket over white pants and was wearing a dark sea captain's hat. There was a pipe in his mouth. The mother was standing right beside him, wearing an old-fashioned dress and hat with feathers and flowers. Beside her was another woman who looked to be in her fifties. She was holding the hand of a little boy who couldn't have been more than five or six. They were all grinning and enjoying life.

"That can't be you," Alfie said. "This was taken long ago."

Bastian looked at them. "It is! And right there, holding my hand, is—is . . ." He gasped. "Miss Pigglesworth, that's you!"

The dog started barking again.

Bastian looked at Riley and Alfie. "The *Moon Dancer* belonged to my family."

25

"BASTIAN, THAT'S IMPOSSIBLE," RILEY said. She leaned closer to the picture. The young boy did look a bit like Bastian. But when she read the writing on the bottom of the photograph, she shook her head. "This says *Moon Dancer, Bahamas, February 15, 1929.*"

Bastian looked at her, not understanding.

"Bastian, that photo is . . ." Alfie started to count on his fingers. "It's over ninety years old. That would make you an old man."

"And it would mean that Miss Pigglesworth is like a hundred and forty years old," Riley added. "No one lives that long."

Bastian shook his head. "That is me and Miss Pigglesworth and my parents. I can prove it."

"How?" Alfie asked.

Bastian started to walk away. "I remember my cabin was first on the left." He walked back to the corridor. "Inside I carved my name on the back of the door. My father was furious when I did it. There's also a miniature model of the *Moon Dancer*. My parents gave it to me on my birthday."

He reached the door and pushed it open. Everything in the room was on its side. Bastian peered behind the door and pointed. "See? There it is." Faded in the wood was the name *Sebastian*.

"And there!" Bastian climbed over spilled tables and against the slant of the yacht to reach a smaller version of the sailboat. Every detail was as he'd said, including the name at the back, done in the same writing style as the large yacht: *Moon Dancer*. Then Bastian went to the bunk. "I remember this too!"

It was another wood model, this time of a double-winger airplane. "My father built this for me. He said one day we would have our own and go flying around the world together."

Bastian's eyes were wide as he went through the

cabin. There were loads of toys and clothing that would fit a child. He looked back at Riley. "How could I have forgotten this? The carving on the door means that I knew how to read and write. But I can't now."

"You can't read?" Alfie said.

Bastian shook his head. "None of us here can. There are no books."

"How is that possible?" Riley said. "Everyone reads."

"We don't," Bastian said.

Miss Pigglesworth started to bark.

"I don't remember," Bastian said. He looked at the others. "Miss Pigglesworth says that a long time ago people in the Community gave up their books and burned them. Before they were all gone, the gargoyles came and took the rest."

"They took them to the Crucible," Riley mused.

Bastian frowned. "How could I forget all of this?"

"If the dates are right, it has been a long time," Riley said.

"But I've forgotten everything. My parents . . ." He looked at the dog. "I didn't remember that you used to be a person. How is that possible? Do you remember what happened to my parents?"

The dog whined and went back into the corridor and to the door opposite. She scratched at it.

Alfie went out and opened the door for the dog and followed her in. "Riley, Bastian, come here."

When Riley entered the room, she saw more antiques. A lot of pictures in ornate silver frames were scattered on the floor. Most showed a very young Bastian. Always with Miss Pigglesworth and always laughing. There were photos of him sitting on her lap and reaching up to her face. Another showed a three-year-old Bastian held in Miss Pigglesworth's arms, kissing the older woman on the cheek.

"You two were always together," Alfie said. "No wonder it's still the same."

Bastian picked up the pictures one by one, holding them up for the dog to see. "That was you, Miss Pigglesworth. You and me . . ." Tears trickled down his face. "I don't remember details, only that I was happy."

The dog whined and licked his face and tears.

Leaving the room, they walked down the corridor to the cabin beside Bastian's. He paused. "I remember this too. It was my parents' cabin!"

They pushed open the door. Clothes were scattered

on the floor, and a desk was tipped over. Riley walked over and reached for some of the papers. They were all dated from the 1920s. Among them was a small passport-like booklet. When she opened it, Riley discovered that it was a passport, issued in 1928. But it wasn't anything like the one she had. This one had a black-and-white photograph of three people. The same man and woman from the photo by the bar and Bastian standing with them. The names written in the passport were *Mr. and Mrs. Adrian Wolfe Fleetwood and child.*

Bastian gasped. "I remember my full name! I'm Sebastian Shelley Fleetwood, and I'm from 1129 Acorn Street, Boston." He looked excitedly to Riley. "My mother made me memorize my full address in case I was ever lost."

"So you're from Boston," Riley said. She looked at the document again. "Only one passport for three people? It doesn't say your mother's name here. Just your father's."

Bastian received the passport and studied it. "I—I don't remember my mother's name."

"I'm sure if we look around here, we might find it," Riley offered.

"But not today," Alfie warned. "I want to look around the Forbidden Zone for my mom."

"Me too," Riley agreed.

They made their way out of the yacht and crawled over the side into the water. Galina was there waiting for them.

"We're going to shore to look for our family," Riley called to the mermaid over the noisy rain pounding the surface.

Galina shook her head wildly and then raised her hands out of the water and made claws with her fingers.

"I know it's dangerous," Riley said. "But we have to check."

When they made it to shore, the sounds of wildlife were much louder than in Atlantis. Even with the rain, there was more roaring and what sounded like monkey calls. Climbing up onto land, Riley looked into the dense jungle. She couldn't see more than few feet in front of her. Cupping her hand over her mouth, she shouted, "Dad, can you hear me?"

"Mom!" Alfie cried. "We're here. Can you hear us?"

Each time they called, the jungle grew silent for a moment, then the sounds returned.

"They could be anywhere!" Alfie complained. "How do we find them in this?"

"I don't know," Riley said. "I really don't want to go walking around in there. It sounds worse than the Red Cloak territory."

"That's because it is," Bastian said nervously. "Remember, those judged too dangerous to stay in Atlantis are sent here."

"Dad!" Riley shouted.

"Daaaaadddd . . . ," a strange voice mimicked back. *"Daaaad . . ."*

The sound was heavily distorted and immediately put Riley on full alert.

Miss Pigglesworth lowered her head and started to growl.

"What was that?" Alfie said.

"I don't know, and I don't think I want to know," Riley said.

"Mom, where are you . . . ," the voice teased. *"Come here, children. . . . I am waiting."*

Bastian took a step back into the water.

Behind them, Galina sang out. When Riley turned to look at her, the mermaid was pointing farther down the shore. A massive alligator was entering the water and heading right for them. But the voice was from straight ahead. There were at least two creatures after them.

"Swim!" Riley shouted.

The three ran into the water and started to swim. Galina caught hold of Riley's and Alfie's arms while Miss Pigglesworth helped Bastian. As they moved into deeper water, Alfie was suddenly yanked beneath the surface.

"Alfie!" Riley cried.

Galina stopped. She pointed to the open water and screamed at Riley. Then she dove down beneath the surface.

Riley kept swimming but was looking back. "Alfie, Alfie!"

Suddenly the water behind her erupted in struggle as Galina was wrapped around the alligator that was holding on to Alfie's leg and spinning.

"Alfie!" Riley cried as the struggle moved deeper beneath the surface. Moments later, Galina lifted Alfie to the surface. He was unconscious.

"Alfie!"

"Alfie . . . ," the voice teased from the shore. Riley looked back and saw what might have been a bear standing upright where they had just been. *"Come back . . . ,"* the bear called, waving its arms. *"Come back and play with me. . . ."*

Ignoring it, Riley focused on Alfie. While Galina held him at the surface, Riley checked him over. He was alive and breathing. But he was pale. Behind him the water was turning red.

"He's bleeding!"

When Bastian swam closer, Riley said, "Watch his head. I'm going to see what happened." She dove beneath the surface, but the water before her was too red to see anything. Riley felt down her cousin's body. When she reached his left leg, she felt deep cuts.

She lifted it to the surface and gasped. Alfie's leg had been badly injured by the alligator.

Bastian tore off his shirt. "I don't know if this will stop the bleeding, but it might help." He tied it around Alfie's leg. "This is bad. We have to get him back to Atlantis."

Galina was still holding Alfie at the surface. She looked back to the open water and started to sing. A few minutes later, several dolphins arrived.

Riley was too frightened for Alfie to realize just how magical the moment was. Instead, she did as Galina directed and held on to the dolphin's dorsal fin while Bastian held on to another. Then a third dolphin caught hold of Miss Pigglesworth's front paws.

With Galina holding on to Alfie, moments later they were tearing through the water much faster than if they'd tried to swim.

When they reached the slope, Riley looked up and remembered that Mada said he'd be waiting for them. But this was the closest place to the Community— they had to try.

"Stay here," Bastian said. "I have to go to the *Queen* to get help; we can't get Alfie up that slope alone."

"But Mada," Riley warned.

Bastian nodded. "Mada's known me for a long time. If he's still around, I hope he won't attack me and Miss Pigglesworth."

Riley nodded. "Be careful!"

"I will."

With the rain pelting down, Bastian and Miss Pigglesworth struggled up the slippery slope. When they reached the top, Bastian nodded back to Riley and then disappeared.

While they waited, Riley reached for Alfie's leg and said to the mermaid, "My mom is a doctor. She says when someone is bleeding, you hold that part above the heart if you can. Will you keep his head above water?"

Galina nodded and cradled Alfie's head in her arms while Riley lifted his injured leg above the surface. Bastian's shirt was red with blood. "Hold on, Creep," Riley said. "Just hold on."

After what seemed like hours, they heard voices. Fear rose in Galina's eyes. Riley lowered Alfie's leg and reached for his head to keep it above the surface. "I understand. You have to go before they see you. Thank you, Galina, thank you for fighting the alligator for us. You saved Alfie's life and I'll never forget it."

Galina smiled gently and slipped beneath the surface just as Bastian, Shane, and three others arrived. Shane was holding a rope and slid down the muddy slope into the water. His wary eyes looked all around.

"The Leviathan isn't here," Riley said.

Shane gave her an expression that was chilling. "We will talk about this later."

26

BY THE TIME RILEY CLIMBED OUT OF THE water, Shane and the others had carried Alfie away. Bastian stayed behind to help her up the slope.

"What did you tell them?" Riley asked as they hurried back to the *Queen*.

"That we tried to swim over to the Forbidden Zone and Alfie was bitten by something in the water."

"Bastian, no!" Riley cried. "Why did you tell them that?"

"What else was I supposed to say? We were in the water. I didn't mention Galina or going over to see the *Moon Dancer*. Just that you'd heard what you thought was a woman crying and we tried to help her."

"Do you think they believed you?"

"They know I've never lied before. I think so."

Running through the sodden jungle, Riley called, "Where will they take Alfie?"

"The *Queen*; it's too wet and dark to use the medical hut."

"Let's go!"

It was only now that Alfie's life was in danger that Riley realized how much he meant to her. After years of fighting, their relationship had now changed completely. She relied on him for so much, and even though they still argued, even that had changed into more of a banter than actual fighting. The thought of losing him tightened her chest like a vise.

"He looked really bad," Riley said as they cleared the jungle and trotted toward the *Queen*.

"He's young and strong. I'm sure he'll be all right," Bastian said.

When they arrived at the *Queen* and walked up the ramp, Lisette and Beresford were waiting with expressions that were a mix of fear and rage.

"What—have—you—been—doing?" Lisette harshly demanded.

"You've been in the water?" Beresford cried. "Are you mad?"

"Please, not now. I need to see Alfie," Riley cried.

"Alfie is with the doctor. From what I have seen, his leg is a mess and he may lose it," Lisette said.

Beresford took a step closer and looked from Bastian to Riley and back to Bastian again. "Riley is a bad influence on you, Bastian. I am ashamed of you. Go to your cabin and get out of those wet clothes. We will talk later."

As Bastian walked away, Riley tried to follow, but Lisette caught her arm. "Not you . . ."

"Please, I have to see Alfie."

"Later. Right now, I must tell you how disappointed we are. We had hoped you would settle in, but you haven't. You and Alfie are a disruption here and you are leading Bastian astray. He no longer spends time with his friends. . . ."

"You mean Kerry," Riley said defensively. "She's the one who's been causing trouble for us and the reason we keep trying to leave the Community. She's jealous over Bastian and is making my life here impossible."

"I have never seen this," Lisette said.

"Because she doesn't do it when you're around. Ask Maggie, she'll tell you. She had to take over teaching me to sew because Kerry was so cruel. She's always saying that she wishes I would be eaten by the Red Cloaks."

Lisette frowned. "I had not heard this. I will of course be speaking with Maggie to confirm your words."

Beresford added, "But Kerry's behavior does not excuse what you've done today. You all could have been killed."

"You still don't get it, do you?" Riley cried. "Alfie and I lost our family and our homes. We don't belong here. When I heard a woman crying from the Forbidden Zone . . ."

"You thought it was your aunt," Beresford finished. "But Riley, your aunt is dead. You must accept it."

Riley looked from Lisette to Beresford and had to bite her tongue to keep from saying she'd seen the empty graves. "I just want to go home."

Lisette inhaled deeply and let it out again slowly. "This is your home now. Like it or not, there is nowhere else for you to go. Until you start to accept it, things are going to change. I am adjusting your work schedule. Obviously, you have too much spare time, which is leading you to wander into dangerous situations. When the rain stops, we are going to increase your workload until things settle down and you become part of this Community."

"That's not fair!" Riley cried.

"We must not have disruption," Beresford said.

Lisette nodded. "So when you finish your work in the sewing hut, you will work with me."

"But . . . ," Riley started.

"No buts," Beresford said. "You will do as Lisette says or there will be greater punishments."

"Indeed," Lisette agreed. "As well as working more hours, we are going to separate you from Bastian and Alfie. Your things are being taken to a cabin on the top deck, and Alfie is being relocated elsewhere. If you aren't together, you won't get into trouble. Finally you will no longer be seated with the other children. You will take your meals at my table."

Riley realized there was no point in arguing with them. It wouldn't change the outcome. Instead all she could do was agree, knowing that soon, somehow, they would be leaving Atlantis. "May I see Alfie now?"

"You will see him when he recovers—if he recovers," Beresford said.

"But I need to see him now! He's my family."

"You have brought this upon yourself, Riley," Lisette said. "There is no one to blame but you. You will take your punishment and then we will move forward."

"This just isn't fair. I heard someone crying out in the Forbidden Zone, and because we wanted to help them, we are being punished. What this says to me is that in the future, if I hear you or anyone else crying in the jungle, or if I see you hurt or wounded, I should just walk away and leave you there to die and rot or I'll be punished for helping."

"That is not the same thing at all," Beresford said.

"Yes, it is."

Shane appeared from the stairs. "The doctor thinks Alfie will live, but it was close."

"Oh, thank heavens," Lisette said. Then she said to Shane, "Would you please escort Riley to her new quarters?"

"Of course," Shane said.

Lisette focused on Riley. "We will continue this conversation later."

Riley walked toward the stairs. "There's no point. I understand how it works here now, and it is ugly." She didn't wait for Shane as she started up the stairs.

27

SHANE SAID NOTHING AS HE LED RILEY to her new cabin. They kept climbing the stairs past her normal deck and up two more flights. When they entered a narrow corridor, Riley saw how few doors there were. Shane stopped before one with an ornate sign on it.

"King's Suite?" Riley read aloud.

"What?" Shane said.

She pointed to the sign on the door. "It says this is the King's Suite?"

"Does it?"

"Can't you read either?"

"I don't need to read," Shane said coldly. "Now,

you will remain in here until the lunch bell sounds and then you will come down to the dining deck. It that clear?"

Riley nodded.

"Oh, and in case you have any plans for sneaking out again, we have closed the outer doors to the ship." Saying nothing more, he turned and left.

Riley entered her new cabin and was stunned. This wasn't a cabin; it was like an apartment. There was a lounge with a hall that led to two bedrooms with a separate dressing room and a spacious toilet. Like everything else on the *Queen*, it all looked opulent and expensive.

There was also an outer door that opened onto a private promenade that led to the public deck. Had this been an active cruise ship, this move would have been considered a mega upgrade, as this was a luxury suite. Instead, it felt even more like a prison. She was the only occupant on the entire deck, adding to her complete isolation.

Riley stood at the window and peered out but couldn't see much of anything because of the heavy rain. Her mind kept replaying the alligator attack. If Galina hadn't been there, Alfie would have been killed.

Tears trailed down her cheeks as fear for her cousin rose. Suddenly the years of fighting, of him tormenting her and breaking her toys, didn't matter. She loved him and was frightened about what would happen to him. Yes, the doctor had helped Miss Pigglesworth, but Alfie's wounds were much worse. Without a hospital, how could he help him? Alfie needed surgery in a sterile operating room to close his wounds. He needed antibiotics to fight the infection. Instead she feared the doctor would use more leaves and tie dirty rags around his wounded leg.

Riley took a seat in one of the cushioned chairs before the window. She left the outer door open because the sound of rain was better than the maddening silence of the suite.

Sometime later, the lunch bell sounded.

Part of Riley didn't want to go down to see anyone. But another part thought if she didn't, things could get even worse. To gain her freedom back, she was going to have to play their game. It would be difficult, but it would be the only way.

She left her suite and followed the same route back down the stairs to the dining hall. Lisette was standing at a table and nodded to Riley the moment she arrived.

Riley nodded back and walked past the children's table and over to Lisette's.

"Are you all settled in your new cabin?" Lisette asked lightly as though the conversation of earlier had never happened.

"Yes, thank you," Riley said.

"Good. Now, please, take a seat beside me."

Riley sat beside Lisette and peered over to the children's table. Kerry was looking at her smugly as she sat beside Bastian, speaking to him animatedly. It was obvious Bastian wasn't listening, and it seemed as though a dark cloud was hanging over his head. Because of the alligator attack, they hadn't had a chance to talk about how he felt learning about his family and seeing the *Moon Dancer*. Though his expression said more than words.

At the end of the meal, everyone got up and drifted away. Lisette had other jobs to attend to and told Riley she could join the children heading to the game room. There was also an undercurrent of a threat when she finished by saying, "I believe Shane told you the outer doors have been sealed?"

When Riley nodded, Lisette said, "Run along now and have fun."

Riley nodded again but couldn't force a smile. Everything was falling apart. They had made it to the Forbidden Zone, but it had nearly killed Alfie. Her father and aunt were there. Were they still alive? Or was it a desperate dream she was holding on to?

When Riley entered the game room, some of the children were playing Ping-Pong while the twins were playing checkers. Riley hadn't played games like this since she was a child. Bastian was taking on Kerry but didn't have any enthusiasm in his game. Kerry quickly beat him. When she asked to play again, he shook his head and sat down.

Riley wanted to speak with him, but it felt like everyone was watching her. Instead she took a seat by one of the ship's windows and stared out at the rain. Occasionally she would look back at the others playing as though they didn't have a care in the world. Part of her wished she could feel that way. But she couldn't. She and Alfie didn't belong in Atlantis.

The evening meal came, and once again Riley sat beside Lisette.

"How was your afternoon?" Lisette asked.

"Fine," Riley said. The last thing she wanted was

to speak with Lisette. But she did need to know about Alfie.

"May I see Alfie this evening?"

"No, dear, he is sleeping and needs his rest. We don't want to disturb him."

"I won't disturb him; I just want to see that he's all right."

"I have seen him, and he is recovering. Now, eat your meal. You must stay strong."

Lisette cut off any further conversation about her cousin. Riley started to fear that maybe Alfie wasn't so well. Would they tell her if he'd died?

Across the room at the children's table, once again Kerry was talking a mile a minute to Bastian, who couldn't have been more disinterested. He focused on preparing a plate of food for Miss Pigglesworth as she sat beside him at the table.

Watching the dog eat, Riley wondered what it was like for Miss Pigglesworth to live as a dog while still having the intellect of a person. She had paws instead of hands and relied on Bastian to prepare her plate. Did it frustrate her, or was she used to it?

After the meal, Riley excused herself from the games, saying she was too worried about Alfie to join the nightly singing. She returned to her new cabin and paced the floor like a caged animal.

This was the worst possible thing to happen. What about finding their parents? How could she get back to the *Moon Dancer* with the Forbidden Zone being so dangerous?

After a while there was a knock on the outer door. Riley ran to it and found Bastian and Miss Pigglesworth standing in the pouring rain.

"Come in!" Riley said, standing back.

Bastian was holding a cover over his head. "I snuck up the back way. I don't think anyone saw me."

Riley threw her arms around him and hugged him tightly. "I'm so glad you're here. Everything has gone wrong. They won't let me see Alfie."

He returned the hug, and his arms around her felt strong and sure. "They won't let me see him, either, but Shane says he's doing much better."

Riley sat down again. "What are we going to do?"

"I don't know, but we'll figure something out." Bastian looked down. "Riley, when you leave, Miss Pigglesworth and I want to go with you."

Riley gasped. "You want to leave Atlantis?"

Bastian nodded. "We've talked a lot about it. I don't

remember what happened to us, but Miss Pigglesworth and I had a family. Somehow we lost them like you did, or they were taken from us. I just can't stay now that I've seen the *Moon Dancer* and know who I am."

Riley looked at the window. "When we first got here, you and, well, everyone said how dangerous the Forbidden Zone was. I didn't really believe you. But I do now. You saw that bear. It talked like a person, but I know it wanted to kill us. That alligator nearly killed Alfie. Was that Susan? Has she become that deadly? It seems the wildlings are worse than the deadliest predators."

"I don't know if it was Susan," Bastian said. "It might have been her."

Riley sighed and started to pace. "How do we get back there and stay safe while we look for my dad and aunt? And how do we even try? I have a feeling we're being watched all the time now."

"It won't be easy, but we'll do it," Bastian said. "Besides, we've got Miss Pigglesworth. She can tell when people are around before we can. She's going to help us."

Riley reached over and stroked the dog. "Thank you, Miss Pigglesworth."

"But we have to be extra careful," Bastian said. "If Beresford and the others don't think we're cooperating or behaving ourselves, they might try something against us."

"Great, that gives me something else to worry about."

Bastian smiled. "We have to find a way to communicate so they don't see us together."

"I just wish you could read," Riley said. "Then we could pass each other notes."

"I wish I could too," Bastian agreed. "But we'll figure it out. Now, I'm going to ask you to do something, and you're not going to like it."

"Go on," Riley said cautiously.

"We know that Kerry is causing a lot of trouble for us. She's been running to Lisette and telling her everything. I need you to be extra nice to her. Try to be her friend. It might stop them from watching us so closely."

"You want me to be nice to Kerry?" Riley cried. This was a big ask, and Riley wasn't sure she could manage it. "You're right. I don't like it."

"It's the only way. Maybe if you can get her on your side, she might leave us alone."

"No, Bastian, the only way she'll leave us alone is if she thinks you like her and hate me—" The casual comment caused a storm of ideas. "That's it! Bastian, that's how we'll do it. Tell Kerry that you and I had a big fight and that you don't like me anymore. Ignore me and give her all your attention. Then we can meet up in secret."

Bastian nodded. "If it's the only way, I'll do it."

Riley spent the rest of the evening in her new cabin. She stood by the open door leading onto the deck and gazed out over Atlantis. Even in the rain, it was strangely beautiful. Yes, there were problems here, but if her whole family were here—her mother, father, and brother—would she be in such a hurry to leave? Atlantis gave them everything they needed. She realized she no longer cared about TV or her phone. Maggie and Pea were wonderful. So were Galina and Gideon. All that was calling her home was her family.

Riley thought of her mother and brother and wondered what was happening for them. Had they given up hope? Did they think everyone on the *Event Horizon* was dead? She ached to speak with them and tell them about Atlantis. She smiled, remembering how her mother always talked about hygiene and hand-washing. What would she say if she saw the doctor's hut and how he treated Miss Pigglesworth after a man and didn't seem to wash his hands? Had he cleaned himself before working on Alfie?

By the time Riley went to bed, she had resolved to try to blend in and appear to have accepted her fate. To get more involved, even. It would be difficult, but if she hoped to get back home, this would be the only way.

Riley awoke early and walked out onto the promenade. The rain had finally stopped, and the sky was the predawn gray. Birdsong was starting from the trees as the jungle slowly awoke.

This was the first time she was able to walk around the open deck. The air was salt-washed and clear. Making her way to the bow of the ship, she looked out over the trees to the ocean rising in the distance.

The sun was on the horizon, and as she stood there, leaning on the railing, she watched it rise. The ocean was calm and beautiful as the first rays of dawn sparkled on the surface.

If Lisette and Beresford thought this move to the top deck was a punishment, they were wrong. The beautiful view gave her a chance to get her thoughts in order and solidify the plan in her head.

When the breakfast bell chimed, Riley was ready. If this worked, it might make Lisette loosen the leash a bit. Going down to breakfast, she took her seat beside Lisette and asked her questions about her life and tried to get to know her better. Lisette responded with smiles and warm conversation. By the end of the meal, Riley realized that Lisette had no true memory of who she really was or how she came to be on Atlantis.

She wondered why Lisette, like Bastian, had lost her memory. Was it time that made them forget? Whatever the cause, Riley hoped to get away before it happened to her.

After breakfast, Lisette invited Riley to join her in visiting Alfie. Making their way to his new cabin, they knocked first and then entered.

Tears of relief filled Riley's eyes when she saw Alfie sitting up in bed. He was sipping a drink. He turned and looked at them and a strange smile crossed his face.

"Hi, Creep!" Riley said brightly. "How are you feeling?"

Alfie frowned. "Creep? I'm sorry, that's not very nice."

"W-what?" Riley said. There was a peculiar expression on Alfie's face that she'd never seen before.

"Alfie," Lisette said. "I am sure your cousin wasn't being cruel." She looked at Riley. "Were you, Riley?"

"No," Riley said quickly. "That's my pet name for him, and he calls me Shorty."

"But you're not short," Alfie said seriously. "You are average."

Each word out of Alfie's mouth terrified her. This was Alfie, but it wasn't Alfie. There was a blankness in his face. As though he knew her but somehow didn't. "So how are you feeling?"

"Much better," Alfie said. "Thank you for asking. The doctor said I will be up and back to work in no time."

With Lisette standing right beside her, Riley couldn't ask Alfie why he was speaking so weirdly. "Would you like me to come back later to see you?"

"Certainly," Alfie said. "If it would be all right with Lisette."

"Let's see how you're feeling before we decide," Lisette said. "Now, Alfie, say goodbye to Riley. It is time she got to work."

"Of course," Alfie said. "Goodbye, Riley. I hope to see you later."

"Yeah, bye, Alfie," Riley said as Lisette directed her to the door.

When they were back in the corridor, Riley asked, "Is he all right? He seems, well, kinda off."

"He is recovering well. Though he has been a very sick young man and lost a lot of blood in the accident."

"Accident?" Riley asked.

"Yes, well, we're telling him it was an accident. There is no point in upsetting him. Now, it's time for you to get to the sewing hut. After a Red Moon, there are always a lot more repairs to be done."

Riley moved as though she were in a dream. This was unbelievable. Alfie wasn't himself, and knowing him as she did, Riley knew that it wasn't an act. He was different. And with Lisette calling the alligator attack an accident, it really didn't help. They had done something to him. But what?

Riley made her way to the sewing hut and tried to focus on work instead of letting her fear for Alfie take over. But the moment she sat down with a shirt to repair, she looked up and saw Kerry seated on the opposite side of the room, glaring at her.

Maggie looked from Kerry and then back to Riley. "Do you want to tell me what's going on?"

"Kerry is making my life miserable because she's jealous of me and Bastian. She is constantly reporting me to Lisette and—"

"And . . . ?" Maggie asked.

Riley looked at Maggie but couldn't see her face because of the hood. She felt her eyes starting to well up. "I—I—" Unable to speak, Riley got up and ran out of the hut.

She had only gone a few yards when Maggie caught up with her. For being older, Maggie was remarkably fast. "Riley, please tell me what's wrong."

Riley turned to the cat-woman in the yellow cloak and threw her arms around her. "Everything," she wept.

Maggie embraced Riley and held her tight while her tears fell. Soon the hiccups started. "Oh, Maggie, what am I going to do . . . ?"

"You start by talking to me," Maggie said kindly. "Tell me, what's happened?"

Riley told Maggie everything—from opening the empty graves and hearing Mary shouting in the Forbidden Zone, to finding Gideon, meeting Galina, and right up to their trip over to the ship's graveyard. She spoke about Bastian and the *Moon Dancer* and finished by talking about Alfie being attacked by the alligator, and her morning visit.

"They've done something to him, Maggie." She sniffed. "I'm sure of it. He just wasn't the same and I know it wasn't pretend. But I don't know what. Now I can't even talk to Bastian about it. We have to pretend to not like each other."

Maggie continued to hold on to Riley. "You know you can always talk to me," she said softly. "Oh, child, I am so sorry. It grieves me to see you suffer so. But I fear I may know what has happened to Alfie."

"What?" Riley sniffed.

Maggie inhaled deeply. She hooked her arm in Riley's and said, "Walk with me for a while."

While they walked, Maggie asked, "Have you ever been told about Memory Berries?"

Riley nodded, then gasped. "You don't think they gave Alfie the berries?"

Maggie nodded. "It sounds like it. I knew a couple of people who were given them, and they changed completely. Lately, after speaking with you, I've started to suspect that I've been given them. Pea too. Neither of us can remember our lives before we were here in Atlantis."

It was terrifying, but it made sense. "I spoke with Lisette at breakfast and asked her a few questions—she couldn't remember her past life either. But she doesn't care." She paused and looked at Maggie. "Do you think they give them to everyone here to make them forget their past?"

"It wouldn't surprise me," Maggie said. "Child, listen to me. You be extra careful. If they've already given them to Alfie, they may be planning the same for you. Watch what you eat and don't eat anything that is brought to you especially. Just eat what everyone else is eating. I would be devastated if you changed."

"Is there an antidote? A way of reversing it?"

"I don't know."

"We can't leave Alfie like that. It's not him. He's like a zombie or something."

"I don't know if there is anything we can do. My memory has never returned. I just stopped asking myself the question of my past. It was only after talking to you on the *Queen* that I realized how much I've forgotten."

Maggie paused. "You must be especially careful around Kerry. She is not a friend. If there is more trouble, I fear Beresford may resort to using the berries."

"I'm going to try to blend in and see if that will help," Riley said softly.

"Very good," Maggie said. She paused and then said, "Do you really believe your father and aunt could still be alive in the Forbidden Zone?"

"I did," Riley said. "But now I'm not so sure. There are so many dangers over there, I don't know how they could survive. But I still need to try. I just don't know how with Kerry and the others watching all the time."

"It is difficult," Maggie agreed. "But I'm sure we'll figure something out."

"We?" Riley said.

Maggie patted her arm with her gloved hand. "Yes, my love, we. Now, dry your eyes. We don't want to give Kerry the satisfaction of seeing you upset. Hold you head high, Riley. You can do this."

Riley gave the cat-woman a tight hug. "Thank you, Maggie."

They walked back to the sewing hut and picked up the work they'd started. After a full day of repairing clothes, they finished, and Riley walked out with Maggie. Lisette was waiting for her.

"Are you ready to get to work?"

Riley looked at Maggie. "Thank you for teaching me today," she said softly.

Maggie nodded her hooded head and said to Lisette, "Riley is a good student. She has learned a lot."

"I am pleased to hear that," Lisette said. "Now we'll teach her to work in the orchards. We are gathering the fallen fruit. Nothing must ever be wasted."

"Indeed," Maggie agreed. "I will see you tomorrow, Riley."

Riley spent the balance of the day picking up mangos and papayas, as well as an unfamiliar bumpy fruit called jackfruit, and many other kinds of fruit that grew exclusively on Atlantis. The orchards had been attacked during the Red Moon, and as the bulk of the food that they ate came from them, everything that could be salvaged was gathered up and damaged trees were cared for.

It wasn't difficult work, but it was tiring as Riley filled basket upon basket of fruit. It was then loaded onto Kevin, the yellow-cloaked rhino, who carried the baskets back to the *Queen* and then returned for more.

The sight of an enormous rhinoceros with the yellow cloak draped over his back was both charming and frightening in equal measures. At first meeting, Riley was nervous to approach him, but she soon discovered that he was as gentle as Pea or Maggie. There was something especially charming because of his name. How could anyone fear a rhino called Kevin?

Unfortunately, he could no longer speak, but he could understand what was being said to him and he nodded or shook his head in answer to any questions. Riley thought if she wasn't planning to leave Atlantis, she might try teaching the others to read so that those who couldn't speak could still be understood by using some kind of alphabet tiles on the ground. It would be slow, but at least those like Kevin could do more than nod.

When the job was finished and the dinner gong sounded, Riley patted Kevin on the head and invited him to join her in the outdoor eating area. The rhino shook his head sadly and drifted away into the jungle.

Riley watched him go and felt bad at how the people of Atlantis treated those who were changing. They were happy to use their help when it was needed with jobs like picking fruit, lifting, or moving heavy items and carrying things. But when the work ended, they were expected to leave.

If it ever turned out they couldn't leave, Riley was going to do anything in her power to change things. This discrimination was wrong and cruel. As it was, all she could do was be friendly to the nonhuman people and treat them like normal.

After dinner, Riley joined the others at the big campfire. She was trying her best to take part and sang when needed and clapped during the stories. Several seats away, poor Bastian was trapped with Kerry. She was holding on to him like he was a chocolate candy that she was scared would be stolen.

Riley wished she could save him, but for the moment, they were pretending to not get along. It was hard on both of them, but if it kept Kerry from causing trouble, they would do it.

After the campfire, Riley walked back to the *Queen* beside Lisette.

"You worked hard today," Lisette said. "Thank you."

"You don't have to thank me," Riley said. "We're all in this together."

Lisette smiled at her and nodded. "Yes, we are."

Making her way back to her cabin on the uppermost deck, Riley was exhausted, and her arms and back were aching from lifting the heavy baskets. But Lisette seemed happier. If this kept up, Riley might have a bit more freedom.

Her cabin was dark and undisturbed. It seemed whoever lit the lanterns in the evening either didn't know she was up here, or they didn't care. But it was only the light from the bright moon overhead that lit her way.

Changing into her long nightshirt, Riley climbed into bed and drifted right off to sleep. She was unsure how long she'd been asleep when a soft knocking on the outer door woke her. Riley sprang from her bed, hoping it was Bastian and Miss Pigglesworth. But when she opened the door, she received the shock of her life.

"Gideon!"

"Good evening, Riley," Gideon said. He was standing outside her cabin and had to stoop over to talk to her through the doorframe.

Riley stepped outside. "How are you? Are you all healed?"

"I am well, thank you. And you?"

"Sore from working in the orchards, but I'll live."

Gideon grinned. "I'm sure you will. Please, come, walk with me for a bit."

Riley felt no fear in the presence of the massive gargoyle as she left her cabin and walked along the promenade with him. When they reached the bow of the ship, Gideon stopped. He rested his thick gray arms on the railing. "Maggie found me this evening and told me what happened to Alfie in the Forbidden Zone. She suspects he has been given Memory Berries."

Riley tensed and said nothing. She felt betrayed that Maggie had told him what they discussed.

As though reading her mind, Gideon said, "Don't be angry with Maggie for telling me. She cares deeply for you and is grateful for what you did for her and Pea during the Red Moon. She is concerned for you. So am I. The Forbidden Zone is incredibly dangerous."

"I know. We saw a talking bear; he was terrifying."

"Ah, that will be Austin. He is gentle in comparison to the others—he's more a mischief-maker than a killer—though I would never trust him. The greatest threat in the Forbidden Zone isn't from the creatures living there. It is the Forbidden Zone itself. We have been studying it for years and still can't figure out what is happening over there."

Fear rose in Riley. "What do you mean? Why is it dangerous? Are there, like, poisonous plants or something?"

"Not any more than here," Gideon answered. "I'm talking about what the Forbidden Zone does to people."

"I don't understand. What are you saying?"

"You are aware of how people here in Atlantis change when they grow older."

"You mean the Cloaks? Like Pea, Maggie, and Mada? They turn into animals."

"Exactly," Gideon said. "Over here, the change is gradual and takes many years. But in the Forbidden Zone it is greatly accelerated. We don't know why. What takes decades here takes only weeks there."

Riley looked down, trying to count how long she'd been in Atlantis, but she'd lost track of time. "So you're saying that if my dad and Mary are alive, they'll be changing?"

Gideon nodded. "For reasons we don't understand, Galina, the unicorns, those on the North Side, and us gargoyles appear unaffected by the Forbidden Zone. But for humans, the change is fast and drastic. Riley, you are not immune to the effects. If you spend time there, you too will change."

"But what if I'm only there a little while?"

Gideon shrugged. "I don't know how long it might take. We've never measured it in the young. Though you are as human as your parents, so I must assume the de-evolution will be just as swift."

"De-evolution?"

"That's what we call it," Gideon said. "This certainly isn't an evolution. People regress back into animal form."

Riley's heart was racing. Her father and aunt, if they were still alive, were over there. "I—I don't care," she said. "I'm still going over to find them."

"It is too dangerous for you."

"You don't understand," Riley insisted. "I have to go. It's my father. I need to find him and then we can finally go home."

"Maggie told me you wished to leave Atlantis."

Riley nodded. "It is beautiful here, but we don't belong. Especially if they've given Alfie Memory Berries just to make him cooperative. Maggie's scared they'll give them to me too. That's so barbaric. And look how they treat those who are changing. Today

I met a rhino called Kevin. He was so sweet, but he's not allowed to eat with us, and none of the Cloaks are allowed on the *Queen* during a Red Moon. That's not fair. They used to be members of the Community. How could the others treat them so badly? And you, all the gargoyles, should be welcome here too—I mean, this is just one island. But everyone lives apart."

"It is said that if something is wrong, you should change it," Gideon said. "I don't like how the Community treats the others as well. But I am a gargoyle; it is not my place to make the change. But you, Riley, you can."

"Me? How?" Riley said. "If I tried anything, I'm sure Beresford or Lisette would use the Memory Berries or something else to stop me."

Gideon inhaled deeply and once again it sounded like a bottomless cavern. "Perhaps you are right. No one should stay if they are unhappy."

"Bastian wants to leave too," Riley said. "We found the yacht he and his family arrived on. He's seen pictures of his mother and father and realized that he's lost family too. He feels like the Community has betrayed him."

"There is no evidence that the people of Atlantis

have done anything to Bastian or any of the new arrivals."

Riley raised her eyebrows. "What about Alfie?"

"Ah yes," Gideon said. "Are you sure he wasn't just confused from his wounds?"

"I'm pretty sure. He didn't sound like himself at all."

"You must be sure before you accuse Beresford of using the berries."

Riley considered and nodded. "You're right. I have to be sure. But one thing I am sure of is that we want to go home. Bastian's family's yacht, the *Moon Dancer*, looks intact. If we do find our family, we hope we can refloat her and might be able to leave."

"There are two problems with that plan," Gideon said. "First, the Forbidden Zone and what it will do to you. Then there's the Leviathan. It will never let you leave."

"I know," Riley said. "But I was hoping . . ." She paused, unsure what she should say.

The tall gargoyle grinned, and his black eyes sparkled in the moonlight. "Ah yes, Galina. You are going to ask her to sing to him."

Riley nodded. "I know it might be wrong to ask

her, but we have to try. We have family back home that we really miss. I have a mother and a brother. I just want to find Dad and go home."

"Well," Gideon said, "as it seems you are determined to go back to the Forbidden Zone to search, the only thing I can do is help you."

"Will you?"

Gideon smiled again. "I owe you my life. Of course I will help. This evening, I will fly over there and look for your father and aunt."

"Can I come with you?"

"I have told you of the dangers. Spending time there . . ."

"I know," Riley said. "But please, I have to come with you. I can call out to them. They'll know my voice."

Gideon sighed again. "There is no stopping you, is there?"

Riley grinned. "Not when it's this important."

"You must be a siren just like Galina, because I can't say no to you. Yes, you may come with me. Hearing your voice may help in the search."

"Thank you, Gideon!" Riley ran back to her cabin to change. Then at Gideon's suggestion, she climbed onto his back, piggyback style, settling between his large bat wings. She wrapped her arms around his thick neck and her legs around his waist.

Gideon reached up and grasped her arms. "All set?"

"You betcha!" Riley said.

"Hold on tight." Gideon carefully flapped his bat wings and took off.

Riley never imagined the thrill she could feel flying with the gargoyle. They climbed higher in the sky and flew over the jungle. The trees were moonlit, but the ground was too dark to see. She wondered where Maggie, Pea, and Kevin lived. Were they safe at night with Mada and the other Red Cloaks out hunting?

Moments later they were crossing over the dark channel, and Riley saw the moonlight glinting like diamonds across the water's surface. The Forbidden Zone lay dead ahead. The sounds from the trees were loud and terrifying, as animal calls mixed with deep roars and screeching. Dark flying figures darted across the sky, but Riley couldn't see what they were. The one good thing was that they parted quickly when Gideon flew toward them.

"Start calling out to your family," Gideon said.

Riley peered down into the dark jungle and shouted, "Dad? Aunt Mary? Can you hear me?"

Her calls were answered by even more roars. Despite the din from below, Riley kept shouting and then pausing to listen.

It seemed to take half the night as they flew the length of the Forbidden Zone. The island was much bigger than Riley imagined, and finding her family was like searching for a needle in the haystack.

Riley kept calling and then waiting for a response. She was just about to start again when Gideon held up his arm. His tall, pointed ears moved and then stopped. "Wait, I hear something."

He changed direction in the sky and tilted downward. "Call again."

"Dad! Aunt Mary! Can you hear me?"

"Riley? Riley is that you? Where are you?" The voice was faint, but it was there.

"That's my dad!" Riley cried. Tears rushed to her eyes, and her heart pounded fiercely in her chest. "He's alive, Gideon, he's alive!"

Gideon continued down. Then he stopped descending and flapped his wings and hovered above the trees.

"There, I see them!" Gideon called.

Riley strained her eyes but couldn't. "Where? I can't see them!"

"They are hiding in the top of that tree. I will go down to them. But Riley, do your aunt a favor. Say nothing about Alfie. Until we know for certain what has happened to him, telling her will only frighten her."

"I understand."

"Good, now hold on tight. I'm taking us in closer."

Riley tightened her arms and legs around Gideon and continued to peer down into the darkness. Despite the moonlight, she couldn't see any details.

"What is your father's name?" Gideon called.

"Andrew," Riley answered. "And my aunt is Mary."

"Andrew and Mary," Gideon called. "I have Riley with me. Please do not fear me. I am here to help!"

"Yeah, Dad, he is!" Riley added. "Can you hear us?"

"Yes!" Riley's father called. "Thank heavens you're alive!"

"Is Alfie with you?" Mary called.

"No, but he's safe."

"We'll explain everything shortly," Gideon called.

"For now, we need to get you out of there and somewhere safe!" He craned his neck to look back at Riley. "Hold on extra tight. This is going to be awkward, as I need to work my wings hard to hover over the trees."

"I'm okay, just be careful with my dad and Mary."

Riley felt the massive gargoyle's muscles tense and then his wings beat harder with short, fast wingbeats. She could feel the pressure pushing against her and had to tighten her grip to keep from being knocked off his back.

"Get ready," Gideon called. "I want you both to catch hold of my feet as tight as you can."

"We understand," Andrew called.

When Gideon lowered himself into the trees, Riley couldn't see anything. She was holding tight to the gargoyle's neck and tucked her head into his shoulders to keep from falling off.

"Andrew, look at him," Mary squealed fearfully. "I can't, I just can't!"

"Aunt Mary, it's all right," Riley called. "Gideon is kind. He's here to help you."

"Come on, Mary, just grab his foot!" Andrew called.

Riley heard a strange kind of whine coming from her aunt. Finally Gideon called, "My toes are going to grasp you; do not be alarmed."

More whining from Mary followed, but then Gideon started to climb higher in the trees. The pressure against Riley lessened and she was able to look down. It was too dark to make out the finer details, but she rejoiced seeing her father and aunt holding on to Gideon's feet.

"Just hold on, Dad, we'll get to Atlantis in a few minutes."

Once again, Gideon craned his neck to look back at her. "We cannot take them to Atlantis."

"Why not?" Riley cried.

"You will understand when you see them. For now, I have an idea. You said Bastian's boat is here?"

"Yes, the *Moon Dancer*. It's in the ship's graveyard along the coast."

"That is where we will land."

They reached the ship's graveyard in a few minutes. Riley peered down and saw moonlight glowing on the white wreck that was the *Event Horizon*. The *Moon Dancer* was much darker, but she could make out the shape of the large yacht.

"Down there." Riley pointed to the yacht. "It's leaning over, but you can still stand on the deck if you're careful."

She looked down to her family again. "Dad, Mary, we're going to a sailing yacht. It's mostly intact."

"Please hurry," Mary said fearfully.

Moments later they touched down on the deck of the *Moon Dancer*. Riley barely let go of Gideon before her father grabbed her and held her tightly. "We thought we'd lost you," he cried in her hair.

"Us too," Riley sobbed. "Alfie and I were so scared."

Mary threw her arms around her as well. "We're together now. That's all that matters." She was trembling, and somehow, in the dark of the night, she seemed much shorter than before.

When Mary released her, Riley turned and hugged Gideon tightly. "Thank you, Gideon. Thank you so much!"

"Yes, thank you, Gideon," Mary said.

"It was my pleasure," Gideon said. "I am so pleased to find you both alive."

"Yeah," Riley agreed. "How did you survive in the Forbidden Zone for so long?"

"Forbidden Zone?" her father repeated.

"That's what the people in Atlantis call it. They say it's wild and there are monsters here."

Her father said, "They're not kidding! There are creatures here we never imagined possible." He looked at Gideon. "Like you. You're a . . ."

"Gargoyle," Gideon said. "It is an honor to meet you."

"And you," Andrew agreed. "I am so grateful to you for saving me and my sister."

"It only seemed fair," Gideon said lightly. "Riley, Alfie, and their friend Bastian saved my life."

"Riley, where is Alfie?" Mary asked.

"He's still on Atlantis."

"Atlantis?" Andrew repeated. "What do you mean, 'Atlantis'?"

Riley told her father and aunt everything that had happened, from waking up on the beach in Atlantis, living on the *Queen of Bermuda*, meeting Gideon, the unicorns and the Red Moon, and hearing Mary's calls in the Forbidden Zone.

Mary turned to her brother. "That was probably when the lions were chasing us."

"Lions?" Riley said.

"Yes," her father said, nodding. "There are lions,

bears, crocodiles—you name it and they're here. I won't even mention the insects!"

Riley almost agreed about the dangers but stopped herself from speaking.

"Atlantis," Andrew repeated. "I've heard the myths about the lost city of Atlantis, but I can't believe it's real."

"It is," Riley said. "It's right behind this island."

"We haven't made it all the way to the edge of the island yet. We've been too busy trying to stay alive," Mary said. "I'm just so glad you heard me over all the other sounds."

Andrew nodded again. "We've seen such impossible things."

"Me too," Riley agreed.

Her father looked around the ship's graveyard. "We didn't even know this was here." He paused and then said, "There she is, the *Event Horizon*."

"You can see her?" Riley asked. "I can barely see you."

"Yes, she's right over there. Maybe we can salvage her somehow and get home."

Riley shook her head. "I've seen her in daylight. She's all but destroyed and filled with water. But there's this yacht. It looks intact. We haven't searched it all because we couldn't stay here long, but we haven't seen any real damage."

"We'll check it out," Andrew said.

"Dad," Riley asked, "have you seen any other people here? The *Moon Dancer* used to belong to my friend Bastian and his family. His parents and their crew are missing too. I'm hoping they might still be here."

"It is highly unlikely," Gideon said. "I told you what happens here and how the metamorphosis is infinitely quicker. Which is why I must now get you away from here."

"What metamorphosis?" Mary asked nervously.

"Well," Riley started, "the people in Atlantis live a *really* long time. But instead of growing old, they start to change. I know it sounds unbelievable, but they turn into animals. I've met a koala called Pea, who is really cute; then there's Maggie, who is wonderful and teaching me to sew, but she's a big cat. Today I met Kevin, who has turned into a rhino. Pea and Maggie can talk, but not Kevin. Then there's Miss Pigglesworth, who used to be Bastian's governess, but now she's a dog. And Mada, but he's really terrible and dangerous. He's turned into a tiger."

Riley paused, expecting her father to say she was making up stories or that it was impossible. Instead he nodded. "Now I understand. We've heard human-sounding voices here, but we never found the source and only encountered animals."

"Yeah, I saw a talking bear," Riley said.

"There is definitely something strange happening here. The sooner we leave, the better."

"Andrew, we have to leave now—we're already changing!" Mary's voice was high-pitched and almost squeaky.

Riley's heart skipped a beat. "What do you mean you're already changing?"

Gideon said, "In this darkness you can't see it, but your father and aunt have started to morph into animals. Looking at your father, I would say he is going aquatic."

"What?" Riley cried. "No! We have to get them over to Atlantis before it's too late."

"I am so sorry, Riley, but we can't," Gideon said. "The Atlanteans will not accept them. Especially if Beresford told everyone they were dead. Their arrival would prove the lie. There is no telling what Beresford and Shane would do. But I can assure you it will not be pleasant."

"I want to stay here," Riley's father said. "Mary and I need to work on this boat to make it seaworthy. Then we can all go."

"We'll help," Riley said.

"Oh no you will not!" her father insisted. "This change is happening quickly. I forbid you to come over here again until we're ready to leave."

"But, Dad . . ."

"Riley, no. This is deadly serious. You must stay away." He came forward and embraced her. "Go back with Gideon. Mary and I will be fine now that we have this yacht. We'll start to work on the *Moon Dancer* first thing tomorrow."

"But you'll need supplies, tools."

"I can bring them food and anything they need," Gideon said. "They will be safe."

"Go on now," Mary said. "Listen to your father and Gideon. We'll see you soon."

Riley embraced her father and then her aunt. "I love you."

"And we love you too," Mary said. "Please give Alfie a big kiss for me and tell him I love him."

Riley sniffed back tears at having to leave. "Can I just give him a punch in the arm instead?"

Mary laughed lightly. "Of course, just as long as it's not a hard punch."

"Okay." Riley turned to the gargoyle. "I'm ready."

It was still dark when Gideon dropped Riley off on the top deck of the *Queen*. She hugged him tightly. "Thank you so much for giving me back my family."

"It was my pleasure," Gideon said. "Now, tomorrow I need you to see Alfie—but make sure you're alone. If he behaves the same way, we will know they have given him the Memory Berries. But use caution. If it's true, he may become suspicious of your questions and tell the others, so keep your conversation simple and friendly. I will be back tomorrow evening and you can tell me what you've found."

"If it is true, is there anything we can do?"

"Perhaps," Gideon said. He walked up to the railing. "Until tomorrow evening."

The gargoyle leaped gracefully into the air and flew high into the sky. The moon glinted off his wings and it should have been a terrifying sight, but instead, to Riley, it was beautiful.

The excitement of seeing her family mixing with her anxiety over Alfie left Riley too restless to sleep. She needed to speak with Bastian to let him know what had happened, but she couldn't risk it. Instead she paced the length of the *Queen*'s deck until she was too tired to continue. She slipped back into her cabin and went to bed.

28

MORNING CAME, AND WITH IT, A RENEWED determination for Riley. She sprang from her bed and dressed quickly. She couldn't wait to see Alfie and find out the truth, but she had to control herself and take it slow. Breakfast and friendly conversation with Lisette first, and then, if she was lucky, she could slip in to see Alfie.

Going through the corridor to the passenger stairs, Riley made her way down the many decks to get to the exit. Along the way she saw Bastian and Miss Pigglesworth in the stairwell. This was the first time she'd seen him without Kerry clinging to his side.

"Bastian!" Riley whispered. She ran down the steps to catch up with him. "Where's Kerry?"

"She went back to her cabin to get something. We don't have long." He smiled at her. "I've missed talking to you."

"Me too." Riley bent down and stroked Miss Pigglesworth. "And I've missed you too. I have so much to tell you. . . ."

"I'm back!" Kerry called as she entered the stairwell. Her face dropped when she saw Riley. "What are you doing here?"

"You don't own the stairwell, Kerry," Riley shot.

"Riley, don't be so rude to Kerry," Bastian said sharply. "And I already told you to leave me alone!"

Riley caught on immediately to what Bastian was doing. "I didn't want to speak with you, Bastian, I wanted to say hello to Miss Pigglesworth, and you can't stop me!"

"Maybe not, but I don't have to listen to it." Bastian looked up at Kerry. "Come on, you and I can go to breakfast. Miss Pigglesworth can join us later."

Bastian and Kerry stormed off together. Before rounding the bend in the stairs, Kerry turned back and stuck her tongue out at Riley.

"She does that once more and I don't think I'll be able to control myself."

Miss Pigglesworth barked softly and then whined. Riley nodded. "I know. I won't hit her. But I want to." She looked down at the dog. "I really do need to speak with you. Would you come back up to my deck with me?"

Riley turned and ran back up the stairs, with Miss Pigglesworth moving easily beside her. When they reached the open deck, Riley knelt before the dog. "I need you to get a message to Bastian, please. . . ." She quickly told Miss Pigglesworth the events of the previous evening as well as her meeting with Alfie. "Maggie and Gideon think it might be Memory Berries, but I have to test Alfie today. Gideon is coming back here tonight. I thought you and Bastian would like to know."

Miss Pigglesworth barked softly and licked Riley's face. Riley couldn't help but smile at her. There was a person inside all that fur, but at times she was still an excited dog. Perhaps Miss Pigglesworth was the best of both. "We should go down to breakfast before Kerry makes up a lie about me."

By the time Riley and Miss Pigglesworth arrived

at the breakfast gathering, Kerry was sitting close to Bastian, and Lisette was standing and waiting for her.

"Are you all right?" Lisette asked.

"Yes, thank you," Riley said. "I'm sorry I'm late, but my muscles are really sore after working in the orchards yesterday. I couldn't move down the stairs very fast. I think I need to do more exercises."

"It was hard work," Lisette said. "Are you up to doing it again today?"

Riley nodded. "Sure, I'll be fine by this afternoon, even if I am slow now."

"Wonderful," Lisette said. "Have some breakfast and we can all get to work."

When she arrived at the sewing hut, Riley wanted to give Maggie the biggest hug in the world. Maggie had done more for her than Riley could've imagined, but because Kerry the Spy was there, all Riley could do was sit beside Maggie and say, "I don't know how to thank you."

"Did it help?" Maggie asked softly as she pretended to show Riley how to do a delicate stitch.

"Yes," Riley said. "He thinks it's Memory Berries too. But he wants me to carefully test Alfie today. I have even bigger news. . . ." Riley leaned closer to Maggie and showed her the work she was doing. "He carried me over to the Forbidden Zone last night. We found our family—they're safe."

"Thank heavens."

They settled in to work. Riley looked over at the repair basket and it was full again. Before long, some of the pieces wouldn't be able to be repaired anymore. It was frustrating, as there was a lot of clothing on the *Moon Dancer*, not to mention everything they had on the *Event Horizon*. She wondered if there was a way to bring some of it over without it leading to her.

The day dragged on. At lunch, Riley saw Bastian at the kids' table, but he was trapped with Kerry. Miss Pigglesworth trotted over to Riley as she arrived. She bent down to pet her. "Did you give Bastian the message?" Riley whispered.

Miss Pigglesworth barked softly, and her tail wagged.

Riley wanted to ask more, but Beresford came up to her. "I see you've made a friend."

"I love Miss Pigglesworth," Riley said as she stood up. "She's so friendly."

"Indeed, she is," Beresford said. "Lisette told me that you've been helping in the orchards."

Riley nodded, wondering where this was leading.

"That is good. Hard work makes for a settled mind."

"I guess," Riley said, now more perplexed. "I—I'd better get to the table before Lisette wonders what happened to me."

Beresford swept his arm open. "Please don't let me detain you."

Riley gave Miss Pigglesworth a final pat and then headed to lunch. She looked back and saw Beresford was still watching her. It gave her the shivers. Had she been seen last night with Gideon? How much did they know? Or were they planning to give her the berries and maybe changed their minds because she was working hard?

Gideon's words came back to her from last night: *If something is wrong, you should change it.*

Riley wished she could. But she wasn't going to be here long enough to get involved.

The rest of the day was a repeat of the previous day. And just like yesterday, Riley was exhausted by the time she finished. But she was determined to see Alfie. So right before the dinner bell sounded, she slipped onto the *Queen* and climbed up to the deck that had Alfie's new cabin.

When she arrived at his door, she knocked softly. "Alfie, it's me. May I come in?"

"Of course," Alfie called back.

Even before she opened the door, Riley knew it was bad. Just the tone of his voice said so. She entered the cabin and found Alfie was out of bed and sitting in one of the lounge chairs. There was a blanket on his lap. He was alone.

"Good afternoon, Riley," he said formally. "Please take a seat."

"Hi, Cre—I mean, Alfie. How are you feeling today?" Riley pulled another chair close and sat opposite him.

"Much better. The doctor says I can try walking tomorrow."

"So soon?"

Alfie nodded. "I am healing well. It hardly hurts anymore."

Riley recalled Gideon's warning not to say too much that could alarm him. Then she had a thought. "I'm sorry, I'm not really sure what happened to you."

"There is no need to apologize," Alfie said. "I was working with Shane and we were cutting down a dying tree. It twisted and the trunk cut into my leg."

"Oh, how awful," Riley said. She felt sick to her stomach. Alfie didn't even look like himself anymore. Yes, his face was the same, but it was the expression and blandness of his eyes. "It must have been terrifying. I bet your leg looked like it was bitten by an alligator."

"A what?" Alfie cried. "Heavens no, it was a tree trunk. But I am recovering."

"Heavens no?" Riley repeated quietly to herself. That was Beresford speaking, not her fiery cousin.

"Well, I'm so glad to hear it. It's almost dinner. Do you want me to bring you your meal like I did on the *Event Horizon?*"

Alfie grinned. "That is kind, but no, thank you, Riley. Vadin usually brings my meals to me."

As if on cue, the meal bell rang.

"There it is," Alfie said calmly. "You had better go. It would be rude to keep everyone waiting."

Riley rose up and walked toward the door. She peered into the bathroom and looked all around the room. Finally she came back and said to her cousin, "The moon is almost full. Maybe when you can walk again, you can become a *Moon Dancer* again, just like we used to." She had hoped saying the yacht's name might trigger a memory in him. But his face remained unchanged.

"Maybe," Alfie said.

Riley left the cabin and walked slowly down the corridor. There was a chunk of lead seated firmly in her stomach. They had given her cousin Memory Berries. The Alfie she knew, the troublemaker, the tormentor, the boy she used to hate but now cared deeply for, was gone.

As she entered the stairwell and descended, she prayed that Gideon might know a way to stop or reverse the effects of the terrible berries.

She took a seat beside Lisette and said all the right things as they ate. After dinner she applauded the stories and sang at the bonfire. All the while her rage at Beresford, Lisette, and Shane grew. How dare they poison someone just because they behaved differently than what they wanted? That wasn't freedom. It was brainwashing.

After Riley returned to her cabin on the top deck, she lit her lantern using the old-fashioned spark starter and started to pull together a package for Gideon to take to her father and aunt. At dinner she'd slipped a few extra rolls into her pocket. She'd also hidden a few pieces of fruit from the orchard. She put these into a pillowcase and added another lantern, a starter, and the machete they'd taken from the supply shed a few days ago.

When she finished, she took a seat in one of the chairs and waited. After what seemed an age, Bastian arrived at her cabin.

Once again he embraced her. "I'm so sorry for what I said in the stairwell."

Riley held him tightly. "You don't have to apologize. I know what you were doing. It's working, so please keep it up."

When they separated, Bastian said, "Miss Pigglesworth told me everything. Do you really think they gave Alfie Memory Berries?"

Riley nodded. "I'm certain. I saw him today. We were alone, but he still talked strangely. He sounded more like Beresford than himself. I even mentioned the *Event Horizon* and *Moon Dancer* just to test him, and he didn't react at all. Then I asked him how he had been hurt, and he said it was an accident with a tree."

Bastian started to pace. "This is terrible. I fear we may have lost Alfie. There is no way we can tell him about the Forbidden Zone and wanting to leave Atlantis. He might tell Beresford or the others.

"We can't leave him behind," Riley said.

"I know, we'll just have to figure something else out."

"I hope Gideon can help us. He said he'd come back tonight."

The wait for Gideon seemed to take ages. But it did give them time to add extra items into the pillowcase going to the *Moon Dancer*.

When Gideon arrived, he was surprised to see Bastian and Miss Pigglesworth with Riley.

"I understand you wish to leave too," said the large gargoyle.

Bastian nodded. "I just can't stay any longer. Especially now."

Gideon focused on Riley. "What has happened?"

Riley welled up when she started to tell Gideon about Alfie. "He knew me, but didn't know me," she explained. "Gideon, he talked like Beresford and had no memory of being bitten by the alligator. He believes he was hurt by a tree. Alfie is gone."

Gideon said gently, "Alfie is not gone, he's just

been hidden in his mind by the berries. I feared it was true when you told me last evening."

"Is there an antidote?" Riley asked.

Gideon nodded. "I believe so. When the people in Atlantis started using the Memory Berries to control the rowdier members of the Community, we gargoyles felt it prudent to ensure there was a cure in case they tried to use them on us. We believe we've found it. Nature is wonderful that way. For every poison it creates, it also creates an antidote."

"Why did they start using the berries?" Riley asked. "Was it Beresford?"

Gideon shook his head. "No, it was long before him. It started when a shipwreck arrived on the shores of Atlantis. Walston Greeves and his wife, Sophia, were passengers on that ship. He was a small-minded, unforgiving little man with a cruel nature. After being here for some time, he rose to power and became head of the Community. Soon after, he started to make changes. Walston was responsible for putting those who are transforming into the Cloaks—starting with his own wife—and shunning them. He made them feel ashamed for their 'weakness,' as he called it. He also destroyed the relationship between the Community and us, and the Community and those on the North Side. He put up the boundaries we have today. He was also responsible for the use of the berries to ensure he stayed in power."

"He used the berries to maintain power?" Bastian cried.

"Indeed," Gideon said. "There is very little that someone who craves absolute power wouldn't do to get it. He destroyed the harmony and peace in Atlantis. Now we are all separate." He turned to Riley. "It only takes one person to destroy something good. Just as it only takes one good person to heal something bad."

Riley understood the message. Gideon was still encouraging her to improve the Community. But she wasn't going to stay. She softly mused, "So they are still using the berries today to control people."

Gideon nodded. "Though I doubt Beresford or the others remember the true origin of their use. Now it's just to keep harmony in the Community."

"That doesn't excuse it," Bastian said.

"No, it doesn't," Gideon agreed.

"But you have the antidote?" Riley asked.

"I *hope* it is an antidote. We've never actually tried it on a human."

"So it could hurt Alfie?"

"No, there is nothing toxic in it. But we can't be one hundred percent sure it will reverse the effect of the berries. We also don't know the dosage."

"If it won't hurt Alfie, I want to try it," Riley said. "Alfie isn't Alfie anymore and he'd hate what he's become."

"Of course," Gideon said. "I will bring some tomorrow evening. Now, I am heading over to the *Moon Dancer*. Do you have anything for your family?"

Riley nodded and held up the pillowcase. "Can we come with you?"

Gideon shook his head. "I am sorry, but the less time you stay there, the better. Your father and aunt have only been there a day. I doubt there is much they have achieved apart from checking the boat for damage."

"But—"

Gideon smiled gently. "I understand you want to see them again. But it is too dangerous for you. Perhaps when Alfie is himself, you might go over to ease Mary's mind. But not tonight. Stay strong. I shall see you soon."

29

AFTER GIDEON LEFT, BASTIAN AND MISS Pigglesworth stayed a bit longer. They walked around the deck together and finally settled at the side.

"I know Gideon is only trying to protect us, but I need to see my dad again."

"How?" Bastian asked. "Swimming takes too long and is too dangerous for us."

"I know," Riley agreed. "But there has to be some way."

They fell into a comfortable silence, just standing and watching the moonlight glinting off the ocean in the distance.

"It's really pretty up here," Bastian said. "I wonder why I never came up here before."

"Maybe you didn't have a reason," Riley suggested. She turned to him. "Bastian, do you think they gave you Memory Berries when you first arrived here to make you forget your family?"

He didn't answer for a long time. Miss Pigglesworth was sitting beside him and started to whine.

"Could be," Bastian said to her. He looked at Riley. "Miss Pigglesworth thinks we were given the berries. How else could we both forget our lives before Atlantis?"

"Lisette can't remember her past either," Riley said. "I wonder if they gave them to all new arrivals in the past. I know they didn't give them to me or Alfie until—well—you know. But that guy Gideon was talking about, Walston Greeves, he sounded really bad. Maybe he was giving them to everyone."

"Could be," Bastian agreed.

Miss Pigglesworth started to whine again, and Bastian nodded. "We had better get back to our cabin. I have a lot of work to do in the morning. Without Alfie, I'm back to filling the buckets alone. I'll see you tomorrow, even if I can't talk to you."

Just as he walked away, Riley teased, "Say a big hello to Kerry for me."

Bastian turned sharply and only laughed when he saw Riley's smile. "I will, don't you worry about that."

Riley woke early as she always did, just before dawn. While getting dressed, she heard the clanging and thudding from below deck as the outer doors were opened for the new day.

It was still too early to head down to breakfast. Instead she wanted to take a walk on the deck and do some exercises. But when she opened the door to the promenade, she found a small wooden box sitting against her door.

The box was tied with a bow and had a lovely flower on top. Riley carried it inside and untied the box and opened the lid. There she found a cream-colored parchment, and beneath it, some wilted leaves.

The parchment was old and faded but had the most beautiful handwriting she'd ever seen in her life.

Riley,
I didn't want to wait until tomorrow night.
These leaves are what we hope will work against
the effects of the Memory Berries. If successful,
they should restore Alfie to his old self.

As I said, we don't know the dosage, so I would suggest you dry all these leaves, grind them up, and put them in his food.

The rest is up to Alfie.

Your father and aunt send all their love.

I will see you soon,

Gideon

Riley looked up and then closed her eyes. "Thank you, Gideon."

She laid the leaves out on the table beside the window and hoped the morning sun would dry them. She felt confident leaving them out, as so far it appeared that no one else visited her cabin, except perhaps Bastian to refill her water bucket.

The rest of the day followed the new normal. Working with Maggie in the sewing hut, then into the orchards and vegetable gardens with Lisette. During lunch she slipped back into her cabin to check on the leaves. They were drying, but not enough to be ground up. She hoped by evening they might be ready. Then there was the worry of how to get them into Alfie.

Despite her resentment for what had been done to Alfie, she realized that life in Atlantis wasn't completely terrible. A bit boring at times, but not bad. Everyone seemed to enjoy themselves. But then again, if anyone dared showing anything but joy, they risked being dosed with Memory Berries.

By the end of the evening when the last song had been sung around the campfire, Shane surprised everyone by pushing Alfie in a strange kind of rattan wheelchair. His damaged leg was still wrapped in bandages, but the color was back in his face and he looked healthy.

Everyone rose to their feet and clapped when they saw him.

Riley approached her cousin. "I'm so glad to see you, Alfie!"

Alfie's face was beaming under all the attention. "I am pleased to be here."

Beresford came forward and greeted Alfie. "You are looking wonderful, young man. Welcome back to the fold."

Again Alfie blossomed under the attention.

But the expression on his face was all wrong. Riley stepped back, looking at the stranger in Alfie's body. The Memory Berries had changed him completely. She tried to hide her reaction and smile and clap along with the others, but it was difficult, knowing what had happened to him.

Riley glanced over to Bastian. He was standing with Kerry and clapping, but Riley could see the sympathy in his eyes.

Then Kerry caught Riley looking at Bastian, and she put her arms possessively around him and stuck out her tongue.

With the way Riley was feeling, it was just too much. Then she saw Lisette standing only a few feet away from Kerry, and it gave her an idea. She walked up to Kerry.

"Good evening, Kerry," Riley said sweetly. "Isn't it wonderful to see Alfie again? We've all been so worried. To celebrate, maybe we could all play Ping-Pong together tonight."

Kerry snorted. "Why should we celebrate? I wish Alfie had died in that accident! And I would never play with you—*ever*! It's just me and Bastian. Now, go away before I tell Lisette you've been sneaking off the *Queen* and causing trouble again!" Without another word, Kerry pulled Bastian away.

Riley went into an act of looking hurt. Then she looked over at Lisette. "See what I mean? She hates me."

Lisette followed Kerry with her eyes and stepped over to Riley. "I might have been wrong about you and her. Perhaps you weren't the problem."

"I told you she wants to get me in trouble. All I want is to live peacefully. But she won't let me. She's even turned Bastian against me."

"We'll see about that. Just go back to the *Queen* and have fun."

Riley watched Lisette follow Kerry and Bastian. She hoped this might just get her some more freedom.

Pea approached her in his blue cloak. "That was well played, Riley. It's about time someone had a talk with Kerry."

Riley nodded. "I just wanted Lisette to see that she's not the little princess everyone thinks she is. I'm sure Kerry was hoping they'd give me the Memory Berries too."

"Indeed," Pea agreed. "And Maggie told me about Alfie. I am so sorry. He is quite changed now."

They both looked over to Alfie chatting with the other boys.

"Now," Pea continued, "I haven't seen you in ages and would love to hear all your news. Would you like to come to my house for some tea?"

Riley glanced at the others. Everyone walking past them smiled and didn't seem to mind her speaking with Pea. Riley leaned down. "If it won't get me in trouble, I'd love to."

"It won't. The others know I would never lead you astray."

Pea reached up and caught Riley by the hand. They walked away from the campfire and deeper into the trees. This was somewhere Riley hadn't been before. She looked nervously around. "What about Mada?"

"This is still on the Community side of the boundary. He can't come here."

"That hasn't stopped him before," Riley said.

"I am sure we are safe tonight; I believe he is hunting on the other side of the island."

After a few minutes, they entered a small clearing and Riley couldn't have been more surprised. Her mother used to collect small ceramic English cottages, and Pea's house was just like one. The light shining out of the small leaded windows offered a warm, welcoming glow.

A picket fence encircled the clearing, and neatly groomed flowerbeds led up to the door. There was something otherworldly and magical about it. If there had been snow, it would have looked like a scene from a Christmas card.

"Do you like it?" Pea asked.

"It's magnificent!" Riley cried. "Did you build it?"

"I did," Pea said proudly. "Remember, I used to be a carpenter. I started it just as the first changes appeared. I knew I wouldn't be allowed to live in the Community once I'd changed, so I made my own home. Do come in. It's a bit bigger than I need, but I made it so friends could still fit inside. Sadly, no one ever comes to visit."

"Why is that?"

They entered the cottage and it was as beautiful on the inside as outside. It was warm, but not too hot, and there was a fire burning brightly in the hearth with a cooking pot hanging on a hook over it. The furniture was just as pretty as the house. Pea had not only built everything for function, but it was also decorated in intricately carved designs. It was, in a word, perfect.

Pea pulled off his blue cloak and tossed it across a chair, and Riley still marveled at the talking koala.

"The others don't like those of us in cloaks. We remind them of what is coming. Even my old friends don't speak to me."

"That's so wrong. I think it's really dumb and unfair that you have to wear the cloaks," Riley said. "Gideon told me about Walston Greeves."

"Ah yes, that is a name I haven't heard in a very long time. It is true he was responsible for these cloaks. The only justice he received for his cruelty was that he became a Red Cloak and was eventually banished—by his own rules—to the Forbidden Zone. I imagine he is still there tormenting the others, even now."

Pea walked over to an ornately carved shelf and pulled down a book and handed it to Riley. "Things were so much nicer before him."

"I thought you couldn't read?"

"I can't. But I can look at the lovely pictures. This was made ages ago by a very dear friend of mine. His name was Adam. In his old life, he was a bookmaker. I used to laugh because I wasn't interested in reading, yet a bookmaker and I were the closest of friends. I did so admire his art. He made this in a time when some of those in Atlantis could still read. Adam showed us how to make paper and bind books. Then Walston arrived and things changed, and all the books were burned. The gargoyles gathered up what few they could find and took them to the Crucible. I managed to save this one for myself."

Riley opened the book and gasped. The date on the title page was from 1641. She looked at Pea. "You really knew him?"

"I did," Pea said.

"But—but this book is hundreds of years old!"

"We do live a long time in Atlantis. Though Adam arrived here long before I did. We used to have the most wonderful conversations. It was painful to watch him suffer the change—but then in time my own started, and we stopped talking completely."

Riley leafed carefully through the pages. Along with the text, there were watercolor paintings. "These are beautiful."

Pea nodded. "Adam did them. He was very talented."

Some of the paintings showed people looking much the same as they did today, and some showed others among them who were in the process of turning into animals. There was what looked like a half woman, half goat. A bear-headed man, and some creatures Riley couldn't identify. They were all walking and eating together.

"It looks better without the cloaks," Riley said.

"It was. We were all one community, one people, no matter what we were turning into."

Riley continued to turn the delicate pages. She stopped on a painting of a beautiful woman with long dark hair and green eyes. At the bottom of the painting was one word, written in an old style of English: *Beloved.*

"Beloved?" Riley said.

"That is Susan," Pea said. "I believe you saw her being taken to the ocean on the day you arrived."

"That is Mada's Susan!" Riley cried. "It says 'Beloved.' Did Adam love Susan too?"

"Very much," Pea said.

"What happened to him?"

"He's still here," Pea said. "Well, partially. And you know him. Or rather, you don't want to know him. When Adam started to change, he said if he was reversing into a wild animal, his name should reverse too."

Riley frowned and thought. He reversed his name. Then she gasped. "Mada? The bookmaker Adam is now Mada?"

"Indeed, he is," Pea said. "He leaves me alone

because of our old friendship, but he's becoming more animal than man now. I don't know how much longer I will be safe around him." He walked into the kitchen area. "I am forgetting my manners. I invited you here for tea."

Riley took a seat at the table and watched the koala fill a cast-iron pot with water and exchange it with the cooking pot over the fire.

"That won't take long at all." He carried over a dish of sweet rolls. "Please have one or two, if you like. It has been an age since I've entertained and I'm so happy you are here."

"So am I." Riley took a roll. She was still full from her large dinner, but Pea was so eager for her to enjoy herself that she couldn't say no.

When the tea was brewed, Pea took a seat opposite her. His furry fingers wrapped around a small porcelain cup, and he smiled as he sipped the tea.

"So, please, I haven't seen you in days. I know about Alfie and that is too tragic for words. How are you now?"

Riley looked into the warm eyes of the koala. Everything about Pea told her she could trust him. As she had done with Maggie, she told him everything, including finding her family in the Forbidden Zone and how they hoped to repair the *Moon Dancer* and go. She also mentioned the leaves Gideon brought to her.

"I just have to find a way to get them into Alfie and then hope they work."

"May I suggest my special vegetable soup?" Pea offered. "I just made some this morning; you could take a bowl with you. I always put in lots of things, so the leaves won't be noticed."

"Thank you, I will!"

"I just hope the leaves work," Pea said. "Memory Berries are dreadful things."

They both sipped their tea. After a time, Riley said, "When Alfie is normal again, we hope to get over to the Forbidden Zone and help repair the *Moon Dancer*. We need to take tools and supplies. But—" She paused. "Gideon doesn't want us going back because we'll change much quicker. So we have to find another way over."

"I don't blame him for being concerned."

"I know. My dad and aunt have already started to change. Actually, I am kinda scared about it too. But we have to try. Dad and Mary can't repair the boat on their own; they need help."

"I understand." Pea lowered his head and peered into his steaming tea. Finally he looked up at Riley. "When you go, I will be so sad and alone. It will be like it was before. I will be tolerated here, but not liked. I don't want that. I don't want to lose you."

"You have the other Blue and Yellow Cloaks," Riley said. "And Maggie."

"True, but I'm sure after a few more Red Moons, we'll all be gone." Pea hesitated and then said, "Please, Riley, will you take me with you?"

Riley could hardly believe what she was hearing. "You want to leave Atlantis?"

Pea nodded his furry head. "I once tried to leave. It was a long time ago. I even built a small boat for myself. But the Leviathan kept pushing me back. Now I'm too small to do anything."

"Pea, I would love to take you, but it will be very dangerous for you out there. Maybe even more dangerous than here. If they found you, they might lock you in a zoo or maybe even a laboratory. I couldn't stand that."

"But I could stay with you? You could hide me like you did on the *Queen*."

Riley saw the pain and begging in Pea's sweet face.

She so wanted to help him. But would it be fair? He would be risking so much to go into the modern world. "Could you be happy always hiding and living in fear of being caught?"

"You don't understand. I already live in fear," Pea said. "For one, I was nearly killed during a Red Moon. If you aren't here to bring me back on the *Queen*, it's only a matter of time before it happens. Or for two, I haven't finished changing yet. What if I lose myself and become just an animal—the thought is terrifying." He clambered down from his chair and padded over to her. "Haven't you ever wondered why there aren't more Blue or Yellow Cloaks here? After all this time, there are only a handful of us."

"I thought it was because the change is slow and not many have turned."

Pea shook his head. "No, child, that's not it. There were more of us. Many more. But because they won't let us on the *Queen* during the Red Moon, we are hunted and killed by the wildlings. It is their way of getting rid of us."

Riley's hands went up to her mouth. "They want you killed?"

Pea nodded. "Please take me with you when you go."

Riley could hardly believe what she was hearing. Pea was right: There weren't many Blue or Yellow Cloaks around. Or Red, for that matter. "Of—of course, if we can go, you can come with us. But Pea, I don't know how bad the *Moon Dancer* is. It might need a lot of repairs. If it does, we're in trouble because we don't know how to do it."

"It sounds to me like you need a carpenter. If only there was one around—oh, wait, I am a carpenter. Isn't that handy!"

"Could you do it?"

"Of course. I still have all my tools. My hands may not be good with them anymore. But my mind still works perfectly, and I can teach your father and aunt what to do. My only concern is the Leviathan. How do we get past him?"

"I am going to ask Galina for help. She can sing to him to stop him."

Pea grinned and it made him even more adorable. "If Galina will help us, we can take my little boat over to the Forbidden Zone, and I promise you I will make the *Moon Dancer* float again."

"That's a deal! Riley left her chair and went down

on her knees and hugged Pea tightly. "Thank you, Pea. Thank you for everything!"

Riley left Pea's cottage with a bowl of his fragrant vegetable soup. She made it back to the *Queen* and returned to her cabin to check on the leaves. After a full day of direct sun, they were dry.

Riley crunched them up and rubbed them in her hands the way her mother showed her how to rub oregano and basil to put in her special spaghetti sauce. In fact, the leaves smelled a lot like fresh basil.

When they were reduced to powder, she poured it into the soup and stirred it. It smelled delicious. "Please work," she said softly as she picked up the soup and left her cabin.

Riley's heart was pounding like a freight train when she reached Alfie's deck. She saw several people in the corridor and they all greeted her warmly.

"A late-night treat?" one of the women asked.

Riley nodded. "It's for Alfie."

"Tell him hello for me."

"I will," Riley said. She knocked on Alfie's door,

and without waiting to be invited in, she pushed it open.

"Riley?" Alfie said. "It's a little late for a visit, isn't it?"

"I know," Riley agreed, "and I am sorry to disturb you. . . ." She felt like she was talking to the principal of her school. It couldn't have been more formal. "But I saw the doctor this evening, and he suggested I bring you some of this special vegetable soup. He said it will help you get back on your feet much quicker."

"But I have already eaten."

"I know, but he said . . ."

"And I am not hungry."

Riley nodded and then had a thought. "Of course. I'll take this back and tell Beresford that you weren't hungry."

"He wants me to eat?"

"Yes, Alfie. We all want you back to normal as soon as possible."

"Oh, all right, if Beresford wants me to eat . . ." Alfie reached out for the bowl, and the moment Riley handed it to him, he started to eat. "It is cold, but it tastes good."

It didn't take long for Alfie to finish the entire

bowl of soup. He held up the empty dish for Riley to take, but before she reached it, his eyes closed, and he fell into unconsciousness.

"Alfie?" Riley said. She checked his breathing and it was steady, deep, and even. Alfie was asleep. She leaned forward and kissed her cousin on the forehead. "Come back to me, Creep, I need you."

30

INSTEAD OF RETURNING TO HER CABIN, Riley spent the night with Alfie, seated on the chair opposite his bed. She prayed Gideon's antidote worked. The one thing he didn't say, probably because he didn't know, was how long it would take if it did work.

As the long night dragged by, other anxieties rose to the surface. What if the change didn't happen right away—and what if he was with Beresford or Shane when his memory returned? Would they find out? Would they berry him again?

There was only one way to find out—to wait and see.

At some point during the endless night, Riley fell

asleep in the chair. She woke when she heard a soft moan. She stole a look to the window. The sky was gray as dawn arrived.

"Alfie?"

Alfie moaned again. "Ouch, my head."

Riley crossed over to the bed. "Are you unwell?" She tried to sound formal like he did.

"Riley?" Alfie turned to her and frowned. He rubbed his forehead. "W-what happened? My head is exploding."

Riley tried to be very careful with what she said. "What do you remember?"

"I remember . . . I mean . . ."

His brows knit together in a frown. "I'm not sure."

"What would you say if I called you 'Creep'?"

"You do call me 'Creep,'" Alfie said.

Riley gasped. "Alfie, is it you? Is it really you?"

"What are you talking about?" Alfie demanded.

Riley almost cried for joy. "It is you! What do you call me?"

He snorted and winced at his headache. "I call you stupid for waking me up. Why are you in my cabin?"

Riley couldn't let herself believe it. Not yet. "Alfie, tell me, what happened to your leg?"

"My leg?" Alfie moved his leg and then winced in pain. "I was attacked by a giant alligator!"

"You are back!" Riley threw herself down on the bed and hugged her cousin.

"Shorty, get off," Alfie snapped. "My leg is killing me!"

Tears filled her eyes at the name.

"What is wrong with you? Why are you crying now?"

Riley pulled her chair closer to the bed and wiped away her tears. "You gotta listen to me now, Creep, closer than you've ever listened before. Your life depends on it."

Alfie sat up in bed as Riley told him everything that happened to him.

When she finished, his eyes went over to the bowl. Then he looked at her. "Those monsters drugged me. . . ."

"Yes, and they've been doing it to people here for years." She told him about Walston Greeves and his arrival on Atlantis and the changes he started. "Alfie, I'm serious, you must behave the same as you did yesterday. You speak softly and are super polite. You say things like 'Yes, please' and 'Thank you very much,' kinda like you're eighty or something. No swearing, no temper, no opinions, nothing. Oh, and only speak when they speak to you. If they think your memory is back, they might give you the berries again. And to me, too, if they find out I gave you the antidote."

Fear settled in Alfie's eyes and he sounded like a young child. "They'll find out. I know they will."

"Not if you're extra careful," Riley said. "It's just for a short time, until the *Moon Dancer* is ready."

"But you've really seen Mom?"

Riley nodded. She hadn't told him about the changes happening to Mary and her father. It couldn't help him to know. "Pea has a boat. When you're able to walk, we want to take it over there to see them."

"Let's go today," Alfie said. He threw back the covers. "Move, I'm getting up."

"No!" Riley cried. "That's exactly what I'm talking about! Alfie, you can't behave like that or they'll figure it out. You're going to have to be an actor and do the best job you can, or we'll never get away from here."

The sounds of the ship's outer doors being opened rose from below. "I had better get back to my cabin. They've moved me to the very top deck. I'm all alone up there. When you can walk, Bastian will bring you up to see me."

She stood up and reached for the bowl. When she did, Alfie caught hold of her hand. Tears sparkled in his eyes. "How can I do this, Riley? I'm scared."

"So am I," she said softly. "But you can do it, Alfie, I know you can. You're really smart—smarter than me. You got through your parents' divorce—if you can do that, you can do this."

"But that was different. Dad just left. I didn't have a choice."

"And you don't have a choice now," Riley said gently. "But Alfie, listen to me. You're not alone, not now. I'm here for you. I know that until we got here, you and I hated each other. But I don't hate you now, Alfie, I love you. And I'll do anything to protect you."

He looked up at her. "You mean that?"

"Of course I do. Don't you realize that? You're not my irritating cousin anymore, Alfie, you're my little brother."

"Even though I'm taller than you?" Alfie said as a weak smile rose on his face.

"Yep, even though you're taller."

Alfie sniffed and nodded. "Thank you, Shorty. Thank you for saving me."

"We're in this together, Creep. Just you and me."

"And Bastian," Alfie added.

Riley smiled. "And Miss Pigglesworth."

"And Pea," Alfie said.

"And Maggie."

"And Gideon," Alfie said.

"Exactly—just us."

Making it back to the top deck, Riley was too stressed to try to go to bed. She was relieved and grateful that Alfie was back. But now the real work for him was about to begin as he tried to hide his restored memories.

She stood out on the promenade until the meal bell chimed and then headed out to the dining area. From the moment she arrived for breakfast, she noticed a change. Lisette greeted her and said she could return to the children's table.

Riley looked over and saw Bastian was already there. Kerry was nowhere to be seen.

"Where's Kerry?" Riley asked.

"You won't see her for a few days—she is spending time alone to consider her actions," Lisette said. "I spoke with her and Bastian last evening, and it seems she has been causing a lot of trouble for you. I am also sorry that I didn't trust you. I was wrong. Today, after the sewing hut, you are free to do as you wish. If you want to join us in the orchard or vegetable gardens, you would be most welcome, and your help appreciated, but it is no longer required."

"Thank you. I'll be there," Riley said. She walked away from Lisette in a state of shock. She couldn't believe the woman would ever apologize. Part of her wondered if it was a trick.

As Riley took a seat at the table, she saw Shane talking to Beresford and her stomach tightened. Had they noticed the change in Alfie? Were they going to come after her? But at the end of the conversation, Shane was laughing and patted Beresford on the arm lightly.

"Are you all right?" Bastian asked softly when she sat down across from him.

Riley nodded as she picked up her spoon and started to eat. She wanted to tell him everything but couldn't let her emotions over Alfie show.

After the meal, Bastian and Riley left the table together. Bastian leaned closer. "I went up to see you last night, but you weren't in your cabin."

Riley looked around. "Gideon gave me the antidote, so I gave it to Alfie last night. He's back."

Bastian's face brightened. "It worked! That's fantastic."

"I know, but Alfie is scared that he won't be able to pretend to still be berried."

"He'll be fine," Bastian said. "Did you hear about Kerry?"

Riley nodded. "That's awesome. Now we can really get to work."

The day dragged for Riley. She was still tired from lack of sleep and anxious for Alfie.

Maggie noticed the change and asked her what was wrong. Once again, Riley pretended to show Maggie her work as she whispered the news.

Maggie patted her hand. "That's wonderful," she said, and Riley knew she wasn't talking about sewing.

At lunch she met up with Bastian, but they were careful to keep the conversation light. John, Ellis, and Vadin were close and adding to the discussion. The mood was definitely lighter and friendlier.

Ellis looked at Riley. "Do you want to play Ping-Pong tonight?"

Riley looked at him in surprise. This was the first time Ellis had invited her to do anything. It seemed with Kerry gone, the others at the table were completely different.

"Sure," Riley said. "But you know I'm not as good as you."

"I'll teach you to play better," Vadin offered.

Riley smiled at him. "Thanks, I'd like that."

After lunch Riley walked to the orchards. Lisette seemed pleased to see her there as a big smile crossed her face. "Welcome," she said. "Are you ready for some hard work?"

Riley nodded. Despite the work being heavy, she enjoyed it because she got to spend time with Kevin. The rhino grunted and snorted when she approached. He also did the cutest little dance of excitement.

"I'm glad to see you too," Riley said as she patted the rhino's head. "Let's do this."

Most of the fallen fruit had been gathered, but there were still trees that needed picking. Riley worked with the others to fill the baskets strapped to Kevin's side; then she would walk with him back to the *Queen* for it to be delivered to the ship's big kitchens.

As she worked, Riley would occasionally look up

to the sun, noting the time passage and worrying about her cousin. Was he all right? Had the others discovered the truth? Riley was still surprised how the relationship with her cousin had changed. From the anger and resentment she'd felt toward him for most of their lives, she now cared deeply and knew that even when they left Atlantis, it would last.

Before dinner, she walked up to Alfie's deck and knocked on his door.

"Come in," Alfie called softly.

Riley opened the door and saw Alfie sitting on the edge of his bed. His leg was still bandaged, and she could see the leaves poking out the top of the dressing.

"Are you all right?" Riley asked carefully.

"I'm still me, Shorty," Alfie said. "I don't know what's in these leaves the doc is using, but they're working fast. He changed the bandages today and the cuts are really healing. Would you help me stand?"

"Alfie, it's only been a few days."

"I know, but this stuff is magic." Alfie reached for her arm and pulled himself up onto his feet.

"It hurts a bit but isn't too bad. Would you help me down to dinner?"

"Are you sure?"

Alfie nodded. "The sooner I can show them I can walk, the sooner I can leave my cabin and we can get over to see Mom and Uncle Andrew."

Riley helped Alfie make it to the door.

"Well?" she asked. "Alfie, there are a lot of stairs. I don't think you're ready."

"Sure I am," he said with determination. "Let's just try it."

Once again everyone cheered and applauded when Alfie arrived at the dining area, supported by Riley. The boys from the table ran over and offered to help him the rest of the way.

When they sat, Riley was impressed with Alfie's acting. He was calm and unnaturally friendly. Just like he was under the effect of the Memory Berries. But there was a clarity in his eyes that had disappeared under the berries' effects.

Alfie stayed for the bonfire and singing and even managed to spend some time in the game room as Riley played Ping-Pong.

By the time Riley and Bastian helped him back to his cabin, Alfie was exhausted, but determined. "So can we take Pea's boat to the *Moon Dancer* tomorrow?"

"We have to check it out first," Riley said. "To see if it still floats."

"It does," Bastian said. "I visited Pea this afternoon and he took me to it. It has oars and is ready when we are."

"We're still going to need Galina's help," Riley said. "Pea told me he tried to leave a long time ago and the Leviathan stopped him. I'm hoping she'll sing to him."

"That's if she'll help us," Alfie said.

Riley nodded. "I'm sure she will. She helped with you."

"I don't remember," Alfie said.

"I'm not surprised; you were unconscious," Riley said.

"Is it a long walk?" Alfie asked Bastian.

"No, just past Pea's cottage. Actually, it's not that far from the slope we used but a lot easier to get to. If we help you, you'll be fine."

"Great!" Alfie said. "If you bring me down to lunch tomorrow, we can go right after."

"That's a plan!" Riley said.

After spending time with Alfie and Bastian, Riley returned to her deck. She walked out onto the promenade just as a couple appeared. They were holding hands and talking softly. They nodded to Riley as they strolled past, but then kept to themselves.

Sounds from below made Riley peer over the side. By the light of the torches outside the ship, she could see the workers closing the outer doors for the evening. Just a short while ago, the area was filled with people. Now it was eerily quiet.

After a while, the couple left the deck and disappeared into the ship. Alone on the promenade, Riley looked up at the stars, wondering, as always, how her mother and brother were doing.

31

RILEY WAS EXHAUSTED BY THE TIME SHE made it to bed and fell asleep immediately. She didn't wake up until the breakfast bell sounded. This was the latest she'd slept in since they arrived in Atlantis.

The morning dragged on as Riley worked on piece after piece of clothing that needed mending. But each time she finished one, she kept hoping that was the end. But there was always more work.

"You seem anxious today," Maggie said softly.

Riley nodded and quietly explained their plan to go to the *Moon Dancer*. "This will be the first time I see my dad in daylight. I'm frightened how much he might have changed."

Maggie patted her hand. "He is your father and you love him, and he loves you. The rest doesn't matter."

Riley grinned. Maggie always knew the right thing to say.

Riley and Bastian helped Alfie down to lunch. But he didn't need as much support. Watching him limp, she realized she might have been wrong about the doctor. It was not "modern" medicine, but whatever he was doing for Alfie, it was working.

After eating, Riley walked away from the table with Alfie and Bastian. She could feel Lisette's eyes on her, but she couldn't work in the orchards today. They needed to get supplies to the *Moon Dancer*.

Making sure everyone heard her, she said, "Alfie, you can't walk alone, not yet. Let us help you a little bit more."

Alfie nodded and opened his arms for Bastian and Riley to support him.

When they made it to Pea's house, they found the small koala standing in his blue cloak outside the gate. There was a large sack beside him.

"Alfie, my boy, look at you!" Pea cried as he trotted up to them. "How are you?"

"Much better," Alfie said.

"That was a harrowing experience for you."

"Which one," Alfie asked, "the alligator or the Memory Berries?"

Pea shrugged. "Both, I suppose." He rubbed his furry hands together. "Now, are we ready to go?"

"What's in the sack?" Riley asked.

"My tools," Pea said. He reached inside and pulled out a hammer and handed it to Riley. Then he gave a second hammer to Alfie and a machete to Bastian. "Just in case we meet some unfriendlies. Now, Bastian, if you don't mind, would you carry this sack for me? It's a touch heavy."

Bastian grunted when he picked up the heavy bag of tools. "What have you got in here?"

"Everything we might need," Pea said.

They walked through the jungle along a recently cleared path. When Alfie asked about it, Pea grinned. "I did this yesterday. I thought it might be easier for you, as the way is very overgrown."

"Thanks, Pea," Alfie said.

Riley smiled at the work the koala had done. Pea had tried his best, but he'd only managed to clear the branches and leaves up to their waists. They still had to fight their way through the top half.

Just before they reached the water, they heard a twig snap right behind them. Someone was following them.

Riley instantly held up the hammer. "Mada, if that's you, forget it. We've got weapons and we're not afraid to use them."

"It's me," Maggie called as she appeared behind them.

"Maggie, what are you doing here?" Riley asked.

Maggie pulled an edge of her cloak that snagged on a thorn. "I've—I've been keeping an eye on you for protection." She pushed back her hood and revealed her feline face. "I thought perhaps I could help you."

Riley looked from Alfie to Bastian. "I think it would be great if she came. We can both fix the sails."

"Absolutely," Maggie said.

"Then let's go," Pea said eagerly. "I'm anxious to see this sailboat."

They continued through the trees. Riley actually felt better having Maggie with them. She really liked her and knew she had the claws to take care of herself if Mada appeared.

They reached a point where the jungle ended

abruptly on a slight bank that led down to the ocean. A boat was lying upside down on the shore. It was covered in moss and looked like it hadn't been disturbed in years. But it was intact. To Riley, Pea's boat wasn't too different from the life rafts at the top of the *Queen*.

Riley and Bastian climbed down to the boat and tipped it over into the water.

"All aboard," Bastian called.

While Riley and Bastian held the boat steady, Pea climbed in and settled at the rear, followed by Maggie. Riley then climbed back up the bank to help Alfie down and into the boat.

Bastian picked up the oars and shoved the boat away from the shore and started to row.

Riley leaned over the side. "Galina? Galina, can you hear me?"

"Galina," Alfie added. "We need your help."

There was no sign of the mermaid as they paddled halfway across the channel.

"What is that?" Maggie said. She pointed to strange movement in the water. It looked as though there was a solid dark platform just beneath the surface. But the platform was moving.

"Uh-oh," Alfie called. "We've got company!"

"It's the Leviathan!" Bastian cried. He started to paddle back the way they came.

"Galina!" Riley cried. "Please help us!"

"Faster, Bastian," Alfie cried. "It's coming!"

The Leviathan's head rose out of the water and loomed above them. It opened its mouth, revealing all its sharp teeth, and started to roar.

32

"NO!" RILEY SCREAMED.

The Leviathan swam closer and rose higher out of the water and looked as though it might crush their boat. But then it slowed and lowered back down.

Galina surfaced and her enchanting song filled the air. She swam closer to the Leviathan, and everyone on the boat gasped as she stroked the massive sea serpent's head.

Finally, the Leviathan slipped beneath the surface and vanished.

Galina swam back to their rowboat and held on to the side as she pulled herself higher out of the water. There was a look of complete surprise on her face when she saw everyone. She looked at Maggie and tilted her head curiously.

"Well, hello there," Maggie called.

Galina looked at Riley.

"Maggie is our friend," Riley said to her. She reached out and squeezed Galina's hands as they held on to the side. "Thank you for stopping the Leviathan. We're trying to reach the *Moon Dancer* to see my dad."

Galina smiled and nodded. She held out her hand and Riley grasped it again. "We're so glad to see you too."

Galina smiled again, but shook her head. She held out her hand again and waved it a bit.

"I think you will find that she's asking for the towrope," Pea said softly.

Riley looked back at the mermaid and she nodded.

"Oh, sorry." Riley found the end of the towrope and handed it to Galina.

The mermaid nodded and vanished beneath the surface. Instantly the boat was propelled in the water much faster than Bastian could row.

"Wow, she's really fast!" Alfie said.

Riley watched the shore of the Forbidden Zone whish past as the mermaid towed them. They arrived at the ship's graveyard in a fraction of the time it would have taken without her. Before long, they were approaching the side of the *Moon Dancer*.

Galina surfaced and came up to the side of the boat. There was a big grin on her face.

Riley leaned over. "You are totally awesome, Galina, thank you!"

"You sure are," Alfie said. He looked over to the *Moon Dancer*. "Mom, Uncle Andrew, are you here?"

"Alfie . . . ," a voice called back. Soon Mary came out of the door to the cabins. "You're here! My baby is finally here!"

It had been some time since Riley had been here with Gideon. Then, it was night, and she hadn't been able to actually see her aunt or father. But now in the bright sunshine, she could see how much her aunt had changed. Despite wearing several layers of clothing scrounged from the yacht, Mary had a long black tail. Her exposed hands showed coarse black hair, and her head was changing shape as her eyes grew larger and her nose flattened and turned black. It didn't take much for them to see that Mary was transforming into a monkey.

When Mary saw Maggie in the rowboat, she screeched and jumped back.

"Mom, Mom, it's all right!" Alfie cried. "This is Maggie, she's with us. She's really cool!" Then he pointed to Pea. "And this is Pea. They're our friends."

Riley's dad burst onto the deck. "Mary, what is it? What's wrong?"

Riley was stunned by the changes in her father. His skin was pale and going gray. His hair and beard were gone, replaced by baby-smooth skin. His eyes had moved farther apart, and his mouth and nose seemed to be elongating. Gideon had said they were changing, but this was incredible.

"Dad, it's us!" Riley called.

Her father looked over the side of the yacht. "Riley!" He leaped excitedly into the water and was at their boat in seconds.

When he surfaced, Riley frowned at him. "Dad, are you all right?"

"Do I look all right?"

"Not really," Riley admitted. "I mean, you kinda look like . . ."

"A dolphin," he answered. "I know. There are mirrors on board the *Moon Dancer*. I'm turning into a dolphin and Mary is some kind of primate."

"No!" Alfie cried. "She's not. She's just . . ."

"It's all right, Alfie," his mother called. "We'll get out of here and everything will be fine."

Galina approached her father and sang softly.

"Hello, Galina. Thank you for bringing them here."

"You know Galina?" Riley asked.

"Of course. We're good friends, aren't we?" he said to the mermaid. When Galina smiled and nodded, he continued. "Gideon introduced us a while ago."

Galina nodded.

"Come aboard, all of you," Mary called, though she still watched Maggie nervously.

They moored the rowboat to the *Moon Dancer*. Riley and Bastian climbed aboard first and then reached down to help pull Alfie up.

When Mary saw the bandages on Alfie's leg, she squealed. "What happened to you? My baby is hurt. Who hurt my baby?"

"Mom, Mom, it's okay," Alfie said. "It was just a small accident with a tree. I'm fine, really." He looked at Riley and Bastian and nodded. "Aren't I? It was a small accident."

"Yeah, a very small accident," Riley added.

"With a tree," Bastian said.

"See? It's almost healed," Alfie finished.

"Oh, Andrew, we have to get them out of here," Mary cried, wringing her hands.

"We will," Riley's father agreed.

Maggie was next onto the *Moon Dancer*, followed by Pea. When Riley's father approached the side, he had difficulty using his legs. "It's getting harder and harder for me to walk." He looked back at Galina. "I wish I could spend more time in the water like you."

Galina smiled and nodded to him.

"You already do," Mary teased. She looked at Riley. "It's like trying to get you guys out of a pool. If he could, Andrew would spend all day in the water."

"Hey, I'm a dolphin," Andrew said. "Cut me some slack."

That comment chilled Riley to the bone. Her father was turning into a dolphin and didn't really seem to mind. Was the change magnifying his love of the ocean?

When they were all on board, Mary said, "We've made a start on the repairs, but need more tools."

Riley's father nodded. "There is a big hole at the bow. If we can't repair it, we're not going anywhere."

"Which is why I brought my tools with us," Pea said.

"Dad, Aunt Mary, Pea here is a carpenter," Riley said. "You should see the beautiful house he built."

"I *was* a carpenter," Pea corrected. "These days, I'm too small to use my tools. But I would love to help fix this lovely sailboat, if I may."

They headed below. Several lanterns had been mounted to the walls, showing them the way.

"There's still a lot of water down here," Andrew said. "But we can't do anything about that until we seal the hole. I think we should patch it on both sides just to be certain." He held a lantern close to the surface of the water. It showed a foot-wide hole in the yacht. Suddenly a hand poked through and everyone jumped. Then Galina's smiling face appeared. Riley caught hold of the mermaid's hand and tugged it playfully.

"All right," Andrew said. "Let's get those tools down here and get to work."

Within minutes of starting, Riley was aware of how much her father was changing. His fingers were becoming stiff and appeared to be fusing together. It was as difficult for him to hold the tools as it was for Pea.

Finally giving up, he handed a hammer to Bastian.

"Would you do this for me? I can't get my hands to cooperate anymore."

Bastian accepted the hammer and mounted the first board. While he worked with Pea and Andrew, Riley, Alfie, Mary, and Maggie went above to cut more planks of wood from two cabin doors. It was hard work and the area was tight. But by the time they had to return to Atlantis, there were two boards nailed into place.

As they made their way to the deck, Riley asked, "How long do you think it will take to fix?"

"I don't know," her father answered. "We have to seal the hole and drain the water from below deck. Gideon said he could bring us some tree sap that will work as a strong sealant, so it should make things watertight. After that, we need to wait for the next Red Moon."

"What?" Riley cried. "Why do we have to wait for the Red Moon?"

"I wanted to be gone before then," Alfie said.

"We can't," Andrew said. "We need the special high tide that only comes the morning after the Red Moon. It was Gideon who told us about the intricacies of it and he's right. Normal tides aren't enough to float us. It must be the tide of the Red Moon."

"But I hate the Red Moon," Riley said.

"So do we," Mary said. "Though we didn't know that's what it was called the first time. We saw the heavy fog and then things became surreal. We had to climb up a tree and hide in the canopy to stay safe."

"That's what I normally do," Pea said.

"Me too," Maggie agreed. "At least until the last one when Riley, Alfie, and Bastian smuggled us onto the *Queen* to keep us safe."

"It was the first Red Moon I've ever enjoyed," Pea said.

Her father sighed. "Well, we can't go anywhere until the next one. All we can do is fix the boat and wait."

"We must also make some sails," Maggie said, "or we won't be going anywhere."

"*We?*" Riley asked.

Maggie nodded. "I am not so far gone that I don't know the dangers of being seen in your world. But what you must realize are the dangers I face here. One of these days I will be killed during a Red Moon. Or worse, I may not be able to stop myself from becoming a deadly predator—I just don't know. But neither prospect holds any joy for me. I would rather risk my life in your world than face the uncertainty here. Please let me come along."

"That would be wonderful," Mary said. She had warmed up to Maggie as they'd spent the afternoon working together.

"Of course you can come with us," Andrew said. "We need to salvage the sails from the *Event Horizon* and get them to work here. We could use your help for that."

Maggie grinned, showing her long feline teeth. "And you shall have it!"

Miss Pigglesworth started to bark.

"We had better get going," Bastian said. "It will be dinner soon and we don't want to be missed over there."

"I don't want you to go," Mary squeaked as she held on to Alfie. "I need to take care of you."

"I don't want to go either," Alfie said, embracing his mother. "But we'll be back."

"Yes, we will," Riley agreed.

"Wait, before you go," her father called. He vanished inside for a moment, then returned holding a book.

"My diary!" Riley squealed as she took it from her father. "How?"

"You sealed it in the plastic bag," her father said. "I found it floating in your cabin when I was checking for things to salvage from the *Event Horizon*. I thought you might want it back."

Riley threw her arms around her father. "Thank you, Dad!"

Miss Pigglesworth barked again.

"We're coming," Riley called.

33

PEA REMAINED ON THE YACHT, SAYING he had no jobs in Atlantis and wouldn't be missed by anyone there. That comment made Riley realize how sad his and the other Cloaks' lives must be. If there was any way they could take Kevin with them, she knew she would. But hiding Pea and Maggie was one thing. Hiding a large rhino was something completely different.

Galina towed them back to where Pea kept the boat hidden. While they secured it and helped Alfie climb out, he said, "We have to work as fast as we can. Mom is turning into a monkey." He looked at Riley. "Did Gideon say the change would stop once we leave?"

Riley wanted to lie to him. To tell him that Gideon said absolutely. But she couldn't. "He said it *could* stop the change or even reverse it. But since no one has ever left, he doesn't know for sure."

"It will!" Alfie said forcefully. "It has to."

"Of course it will," Bastian agreed. He looked at Miss Pigglesworth. "Then you can turn back too!"

Miss Pigglesworth woofed and started to spin excitedly.

When they made it back to the Community, they saw everyone heading toward the dining area.

An Atlantean called Alfred approached. He smiled at Riley but gave Maggie just a passing glance. "Good evening, Riley. I'm sorry we didn't see you in the orchard today."

"She was helping me," Maggie said softly, with her head lowered and hood up.

Alfred barely acknowledged the comment. "Well, I hope I will see you tomorrow."

"You will," Riley said.

"That was so rude!" Alfie said. He looked at Maggie. "He didn't even look at you."

"Now do you understand?" Maggie asked. "Alfred and I used to be very close. He's started turning, too, but it's not noticeable yet, so he ignores me like the others do. When my hands change too much and I can't sew anymore, I will be completely ignored. If joining you risks my life, so be it. It's better than being invisible."

"I understand," Riley said.

Maggie turned and walked away. By the slump of her shoulders, Riley could see how much Alfred had hurt her. "Sometimes I really hate it here. The way they treat the Cloaks is disgusting."

"I just wish it could change," Bastian said.

Riley heard Gideon's voice echoing in her head about how it only takes one person to make a difference.

After dinner, the bonfire, and a few games on the *Queen*, Riley returned to her cabin. She sat at her desk, leafing through her diary. She'd laughed at her mother when she'd given it to Riley, but now it was her most treasured possession.

Reaching for the pencil that was supplied on the desk of her new cabin, she started to write, filling page after page with her experiences in Atlantis. Her hand was aching by the time she neared the end of her long entry.

Dad and Mary have changed so much. I'm scared that when we leave, they won't turn back. Gideon thinks they might. But he doesn't know for certain. He did say that if I spend too much time in the Forbidden Zone, I'll change too. Being young won't protect me.

Riley paused, thinking about her father and aunt. Would the change affect their personalities as well? Right now, they were mostly the same, though Mary was a lot more timid and her father kept looking at the water like he'd rather be there than anywhere. She picked up the pencil again.

I'm really scared about going back to the Forbidden Zone. I don't want to change. If we're lucky, we can repair the Moon Dancer *quickly and leave before it's too late for all of us.*

Riley closed the book. The entry was making her too sad to continue.

Not long after she hid her diary, there was a soft

knock on her outer door. She ran to it and was glad to see Gideon standing there. It had been a couple of days and she'd missed seeing him. She stepped outside and they walked along the deck.

"You went over to the Forbidden Zone today," he said. "I told you that was dangerous."

"I know, but your antidote worked, and Alfie really wanted to see his mother."

"So it was Alfie's fault?"

"Well, not completely. I needed to see Dad too. And we had to take Pea's tools over."

"You know I could have taken the tools," Gideon said. "And Pea." He stood at the railing and took a deep breath. Finally he turned to her. "Riley, the Forbidden Zone will change you. You have seen what it's done to your father and aunt. It will happen to you just as quickly, believe me. Please promise me you won't go back."

"But we have to help fix the boat."

"I have spoken with the other gargoyles about this. In exchange for you staying away, we will all work on the *Moon Dancer* to make it seaworthy. Then you may return to it on the next Red Moon and leave."

Riley gasped. "You would do that for us?"

Gideon nodded. "For me, it is what you want, so I will help. Though I will be desperately sad to see you leave."

"And for the other gargoyles?"

Gideon chuckled softly. "I told you, we gargoyles are a curious lot. They want to help to see what will happen with your father and aunt when they leave—if the effects reverse."

"How will they know after we've gone?" Riley asked.

Gideon didn't look at her. "We will know."

The days of waiting became a blur, and it was only keeping track through her diary that Riley knew two months had passed since her father had returned it to her. She had no idea, though, just how long they'd been on Atlantis.

Each new day became a replica of the one before. Riley rose early, had breakfast with everyone, and then went to the sewing hut to work with Maggie. After lunch, sometimes she would work in the orchard to spend time with Kevin. Other times, she would stay with Alfie and Bastian.

Everyone wanted to take the rowboat over to the

Forbidden Zone, but Riley had made the promise to Gideon, so they didn't. Instead they heard from the gargoyle on his regular evening visits how things were going.

Each time he visited, Riley and Alfie would ask how much their parents had changed, but the answer was always the same: "It is the Forbidden Zone, you must understand."

The answer scared her because she did understand.

With the long wait, Riley's friendship with Galina grew. They would often meet up near the rowboat and play in the water. Riley would always bring extra treats from lunch for her, and Galina would often give Riley pearls or treasures she found on the ocean floor.

Both girls knew they would miss each other badly when they finally left. But Galina understood and was helping her father and aunt as much as she could.

Gideon was also taking Maggie over in the evenings so she could work on the sails. Each morning in the sewing hut they would discuss what Maggie had done the previous night. But when the sails were ready, Maggie stopped going back. Just a few hours each night were accelerating the change in her.

Her fangs were longer and claws sharper. The feline

shape of her face was becoming more pronounced. Speaking was a bit more difficult, but Maggie remained as sweet and kind as always.

When Riley commented on the change, Maggie nodded. "I hope Gideon was right when he suggested this could be reversed when we leave."

"Me too," Riley said. "If it doesn't, how will you feel?"

"I will be fine," Maggie said. "Even if my time in your world is brief, it will have been worth it. These days spent with all of you have given me more joy than I have known in a very, very long time. You have become my family."

Riley saw the joy in Maggie's leopard eyes. She reached out and grasped her hand. "Yes, we are family."

34

RILEY CONTINUED TO WRITE IN HER DIARY as another month came and went with no sign of the Red Moon.

Pea also returned to Atlantis. The repairs on the *Moon Dancer* were complete, so he wasn't needed there anymore. Riley suspected there was more to it than the work. Pea was shorter than before, and his cloak was much looser. He could still speak, but his voice had grown higher. His change left her terrified for her father and aunt, who remained there.

Each day, Riley sat in the sewing hut with Maggie, hoping and praying for the Red Moon horn to blast. They had already prepared to go, and everything they wanted to take with them had been delivered to the *Moon Dancer*. She now kept her diary at Pea's cottage so she wouldn't have to return to the *Queen* to collect it.

Every few days they ran drills on getting to the rowboat and over the bridge before the tide went out too far. Galina was obviously sad at losing her friends, but she promised to help and enjoyed their practice drills.

There was nothing left to do but wait.

Another day dawned, and Riley rose and checked the sky. It was as beautiful and clear as always. Would today finally be the day? It was a question she asked herself each morning as she walked down the steps in the *Queen* to go to breakfast.

Making it to the sewing hut, she took her place beside Maggie. Kerry was working across from her and refused to even look at her. They had reached an unspoken truce and learned to ignore each other. It was the best solution to their problem and it was working.

Just as Riley finished with a shirt and was returning it to the repaired basket, the foghorn sounded. Riley gasped and looked back at Maggie. This was it.

The Red Moon.

35

JUST LIKE LAST TIME, EVERYONE PUT DOWN their work and headed toward the *Queen*. As they left the sewing hut, Riley reached for Maggie's hand. "I'll wait here for Alfie and Bastian. Go ahead, we'll meet you at Pea's house."

Maggie didn't say anything but nodded and then walked in the direction of Pea's cottage.

While waiting, Riley looked up to the sky. It was still clear with no sign of the fog. But then she noticed how quiet it was. There were none of the usual bird-songs or sounds of wildlife. Did they know what was happening? It was only then that she wondered how the Atlanteans knew when a Red Moon was coming.

Was there a lookout? Did they have weather charts? Did the gargoyles tell them? Or did they listen for the sounds of nature to tell them?

Bastian and Miss Pigglesworth arrived at the sewing hut first.

Alfie appeared moments later, running full speed. "Hurry," he panted. "The fog is coming in fast. It's like a living wall."

"It's early!" Riley cried.

"It does that when it's going to be a bad one," Bastian cried. "We have to move!" He caught Riley by the arm and started to run.

Long before they made it to Pea's house, the fog rolled in like a steamroller. At first it wasn't too thick, and they could still see where they were going. It tasted of the ocean and left salt on Riley's lips. But within seconds it became denser until they could barely see each other.

"How are we supposed to find Pea's house in this?" Alfie said.

Miss Pigglesworth barked, and Bastian said, "Miss Pigglesworth can lead us."

Following the dog was harder than they expected. They couldn't see her anymore, or where they were going, and had to follow her sounds.

As they moved, they started to hear other noises. At first very soft, a sound grew louder until they recognized it as a deep growl.

Miss Pigglesworth darted back to Bastian and answered the growl with one of her own.

"What is it?" Bastian asked.

Because of the fog, the growl seemed to come from all directions, but Riley didn't need to see to know who it was. "It's Mada."

36

"YES, IT'S ME," MADA HISSED. "DID YOU think I'd forget about you and what you did?"

"We haven't done anything," Riley said.

"Of course you have. You had the Leviathan eat my friend. Did you think I'd forgive that?"

"You were trying to kill us," Riley said.

"I won't fail this time." Mada paused. "Before you die, tell me, why aren't you on the *Queen* with all the other delicious little piggies?"

"Please, Mada," Riley said, taking a step back. "Please just let us go. We'll leave Atlantis and you'll never see us again."

"Oh no, Riley. You aren't going anywhere. The

Leviathan isn't here to save you. Gideon sleeps and the unicorns are busy at the bridge. It is just us now." Mada appeared out of the fog. He wasn't wearing his cloak, and his full tiger body was exposed.

"I know who you are," Riley said quickly. "You're Adam. Pea showed me the book you made. The pictures you painted were beautiful, especially of Susan."

"Don't say her name—you are not worthy!" Mada hissed. "Adam is gone. There is only Mada now."

"He doesn't have to be," Riley cried. "You can still be Adam. You can talk and think. There is still humanity in you. You don't have to be this ferocious killer."

Mada padded closer. "I like who I am. I celebrate the hunt—the kill. This is what I was always meant to be. . . ." His tail was a flash of color in the fog as his eyes focused intently on Riley.

Riley screamed as Mada leaped into the air and lunged at her.

"Children, run!" Maggie appeared out of the fog with her cloak off. A sleek leopard jumped onto Mada's back and knocked him away from Riley. "Go!"

Bastian caught hold of Riley's hand and started to pull. "Come on!"

"No!" Riley protested. "We have to help Maggie."

"Riley, go!" Maggie shouted. Any further words were lost as the two big cats started to fight. Their growling and snarling sent terrified shivers through Riley.

Blinded by the fog, they ran away from the terrible fight. Branches tore into their clothes and caught in Riley's hair as they tried to find their way to Pea's house.

"This way!" Pea called. "Can you hear me? Children, come this way!"

Pea's voice was like a beacon in a storm. Following it, they burst free of the trees and to the clearing outside his house.

"Pea, where are you?" Riley cried.

"Here," Pea called. "Follow my voice. Come, we must get to the boat."

They kept moving until Riley struck something and fell hard onto the ground.

"Ouch!" Pea called.

"Was that you?" Riley asked as she sat up.

"What's left of me," Pea said.

Riley saw his dark form in the fog. "Pea, Maggie's out there. She's fighting Mada!"

"We heard him stalking you," Pea said. "Maggie

said she wouldn't let anything happen to you and charged into the trees to save you."

"He'll kill her!" Riley cried. "We have to help her."

"How?" Pea said. "We have no weapons, and Mada is a powerful creature."

"We have to do something," Alfie said. "We can't just let him kill her!"

The fog deadened any sounds from the jungle. If Maggie was still fighting Mada, they couldn't hear it.

"Maggie knew the risk of fighting Mada. But her love for you was greater than the danger. You must not waste her precious gift. Please, we must get to the water before Mada comes after us again."

Tears came to Riley's eyes as she looked back into the jungle. But all she could see was fog. There were no sounds to be heard at all.

"Hurry!" Pea begged. "The tide will be going out. Soon the bridge will appear, and we won't be able to cross over it."

"Come on, Shorty," Alfie said. "Maggie gave her life for us; we have to go!"

Riley hesitated a moment longer, but then they started to follow Pea down to their small boat.

They could hear a soft voice singing and realized

that Galina was already at the boat and calling to them.

When they reached the water's edge, Bastian was first to climb down into the boat. He held it steady while Miss Pigglesworth and the others climbed in.

"Here's the rope, Galina," Bastian said. "We're ready."

The boat started to move as tears trailed down Riley's cheeks. Maggie should be here, but she wasn't because of Mada.

Nothing was said as Galina towed the boat through the water. Despite her grief, Riley could feel the water being drawn into the deeper ocean. It made towing the boat much easier as they moved with the tide. But then, when they rounded the top edge of the Forbidden Zone, they could feel Galina straining as she hauled their small boat against the direction of the water.

"Let me help," Riley's father said as he surfaced.

Riley couldn't see him because of the fog, but she could hear him moving with Galina. "Dad," Riley wept. "Dad, Mada just attacked Maggie."

"What?" he cried.

"Maggie saved the children," Pea called from the back of the boat. "Mada was stalking them and would have killed them if she hadn't sacrificed herself."

"Oh, baby, I'm so sorry," her father called.

The fog made it almost impossible to see her father in the water, but she did have the occasional glimpse of him, and what she could see didn't look like her father at all. His body was elongated, and his eyes were so far apart. His mouth was jutting out. Her father was more dolphin than man.

"Dad . . . you've . . . you've . . ."

"I know, sweetheart," he said. "But I'm still your dad and I still love you more than anything. Nothing will ever change that."

Her father and Galina fought the outgoing tide, and soon they made it to the ship's graveyard. The fog made the already-disturbing area even more eerie and frightening. The masts that rose out of the water looked like bones, or malevolent ghost ships.

"I don't like it here," Alfie said softly.

"It's just fog," Andrew said. "It makes everything look spooky."

They made it to the *Moon Dancer*. Because the tide had gone out, the large yacht was lying farther on its side. They had to struggle to climb on board, and when they did, they had to hold on to keep from sliding off it again.

Riley waited for her father to climb on board,

but he remained in the water. "Dad, aren't you coming up?"

"Sorry, kiddo, I can't make that climb. But I'll be right here with Galina. I'll come aboard when the *Moon Dancer* is righted."

"But it's not safe."

"We'll be fine where we are," he promised. "Just get inside. This is going to be a long night."

Riley was about to protest, but Mary called, "It's all right, Riley, you'll understand when you see him."

Her aunt was perched on the railing, helping Alfie on board. When Riley was close enough, she hardly recognized her. Mary wasn't a full spider monkey yet, but she was close. Her long red hair was now short black fur that covered her entire body. Her thumbs were missing, and her tail was even longer. From what Riley could see, she was also much shorter. But she could still talk and gave Riley a powerful hug when she was on board. "We've been so worried about you. If it weren't for Gideon keeping us updated, we would have gone mad. Come inside now, before we're heard."

Moving along the deck was like trying to walk

across a steep, slanted roof. Each step was difficult—especially with the fog making the surface wet and slippery. Eventually they all managed to get inside. But they stayed in the passageway, as it was safest.

"Where is Maggie?" Mary asked.

Tears returned to Riley's eyes as Pea explained what happened. "She defended us against Mada. With him being a large tiger, I fear he has killed her."

"I am so sorry," Mary said to Riley. "I know how you felt about her, and how she felt about you."

"She was so excited about leaving with us," Riley said.

"She will be with us, in spirit," Mary said.

The long night seemed endless as the sounds from outside grew louder, closer, and more intense. Alfie wanted to turn on a lantern, but that idea was quickly dismissed as the light would surely attract predators.

Outside the yacht there was a lot of roaring. It wasn't exactly like Mada, but it was loud and sounded like it came from something big. Riley was sure it was near the yacht.

"The lions are here," Mary whispered. "Everyone, stay quiet now."

Riley had to cover her mouth to keep from screaming when they heard at least two lions walking along the deck. Their heavy breathing was mixed with deep growls and clicking nails. Without speaking, Bastian slid over to the door and braced it with his back.

The lions must have heard or smelled him, as they started to scratch at the door to try to get in. The intensity of the roaring increased, and the tearing at the door worsened.

"Alfie, Riley, help me," Bastian whispered. "Brace the door."

Riley's heart was pounding as she slid along the floor and squeezed in between Bastian and Alfie, pushing against the door.

The pounding against the door and sounds of claws tearing into wood seemed to go on and on. The old door was solid oak, but it had been in the Forbidden Zone for many years and it was rotting and tearing easily for the lions.

Soon another roar sounded. It was deeper and louder. It was answered by the lions. But then there was a yelp and the sound of clicking nails on the deck again as the lions fled. Whatever made the deeper roar was large enough to terrify lions.

All around the yacht were sounds that Riley couldn't bear. Each one worse than the last.

Sometime during the endless night, they heard another loud thud coming from the deck. Then there was pressure on the door. Riley was about to scream when she heard Gideon's soft voice. "It is only me; do not fear. Open the door."

"It's Gideon," Riley cried as she moved away from the door. "Bastian, let him in." She struggled to stand on the slanted floor and strained to see the large gargoyle in the entrance. But with the fog and darkness, she couldn't. "I'm so glad you're here. Maggie fought Mada to save us. Please, can you go check on her?"

"I have her," Gideon said. "She is gravely wounded. I hope you can help her."

Riley felt Mary move, and then her aunt said, "We'll face whatever predators come. I need to see Maggie to help her." Moments later, a lantern was turned up. "Bring her in."

Gideon was standing at the entrance with Maggie in his arms. He tried to enter, but with the angle of the yacht, he couldn't get through.

"Boys," Mary called. "Help him."

Alfie and Bastian lifted Maggie gently from his arms. They lowered her to the floor. "She's still breathing," Bastian said. "But she's bleeding badly."

"I'll get something for that," Mary said. She vanished agilely into one of the cabins.

While she was gone, Riley slid over to Maggie and saw claw marks on her sides and deep punctures on her throat.

"Can you help her?" Gideon asked.

Riley nodded. "We'll do everything we can. I told you my mother is a doctor. She's always teaching me first aid because I want to be a surgeon. But this looks really bad." Riley was putting pressure on several of the deep punctures to stem the bleeding.

When Mary returned, they tore up the old bedsheets and made bandages for Maggie's wounds. They wrapped her up as best they could.

"Maybe you should take her to the *Queen*?" Alfie suggested. "The doctor's leaves work really well."

"They do," Gideon agreed. "But the doctor won't help Maggie. Remember, she's a Yellow Cloak. He only helped Miss Pigglesworth because of Bastian."

Riley nodded. "They want all the Cloaks to die."

"Precisely," Gideon agreed. "I know Maggie

wanted to go with you. Even if she passes this night, she can die in peace knowing she made it back to the *Moon Dancer*."

"She won't die," Riley said. "We won't let her."

"That is why I brought her to you." Gideon started to back out of the entrance. "Please take care of her. I will stand guard out here as long as I can."

The long night grew even longer as Riley stayed with Maggie, bandaging her wounds and then stroking her head and begging her not to die. After a while, they became aware of movement beneath the yacht.

"Something's happening," Alfie asked.

Gideon looked up. "The fog is fading, and the tide will soon turn. Dawn is approaching. I must go before the sun touches me."

Riley left Maggie and struggled to the entrance. She threw her arms around the large gargoyle. "Thank you so much for everything, Gideon. We couldn't have done it without you."

Gideon put his arms around her. "I shall miss you more than you will ever know. Please do one thing for me. Do not speak of Atlantis to others; it may bring them here. It is true that Atlantis has its problems, but we must protect it."

"We won't betray Atlantis—or you," Riley promised.

Gideon held her tight. "Have a safe journey home, Riley, and be happy."

"We will," Riley sniffed.

Pea walked forward and patted Gideon's thick leg. "Goodbye, my old friend. I will think of you often and always fondly."

"Be well, Pea," Gideon said. "Take care of Maggie."

Pea nodded. "Count on it."

Gideon nodded to them and then opened his leathery wings and took off over the Forbidden Zone.

As the moments ticked by, the heavy rain started. The *Moon Dancer* creaked and groaned as it moved in the rising tide. The slant grew less and less until it was upright and floating.

Bastian went below and checked the repair. When he came back, he nodded. "It's holding. No water is coming in!"

Riley's father called from the water, "Mary, everyone, come on, let's get this boat moving!"

Bastian and Alfie carried Maggie into Miss Pigglesworth's old cabin and settled her on the bunk. Riley wanted to stay with her, but she was needed on deck.

Outside, the rain was coming down in heavy

sheets, but the dull gray sky was getting lighter. Each moment, the boat swayed in the rushing tide.

"We have to hurry," Andrew called. "I can feel the tide slowing. We don't want to get stuck again!"

Mary was already at the helm, and her long primate arms held tight to the wheel. "Riley, set the mainsail! Alfie and Bastian, help her."

Riley's training on the *Event Horizon* kicked in as she went to the mainsail and started to work. But this yacht was much bigger than their small sailboat, and the sail only made it halfway up the tall mast.

From there, Riley went to the headsail and set that up. Again, the difference between the *Event Horizon* and *Moon Dancer* was obvious with the size of the small sails. Yet despite their size, they filled with wind and started to draw the old yacht forward.

Riley was too busy with the sails to notice that her father still wasn't on board. "Dad?" she called.

"Down here," he answered.

Riley finished with the sail and peered over the side. Her father was still in the water with Galina, and they were both holding on to a rope that led to the front of the yacht. In the dim rising light, she saw more of her father and gasped. He wasn't human anymore. His legs were gone, replaced by a long body that ended in a fluke.

"Dad—Dad?" Riley asked fearfully.

"It's all right, Riley. I'm fine. I know I might be hard to look at, but I'm still just me. Just like Mary is Mary."

"And I am me," Pea said. "Perhaps a bit smaller and furrier than before. But still the same."

Riley wanted to cry at the sight of her father gliding gracefully through the water. He had changed so much. Was it too late to save him? Would he or Mary be able to turn back once they left the influence of the Forbidden Zone?

"Uncle Andrew, are you and Galina pulling us?" Alfie called.

"Yep, we're just your personal tugboats."

With Mary and Pea at the helm, and Andrew and Galina straining to pull the front end around, the *Moon Dancer* finally caught the full wind and started to pick up speed.

"It's working!" Mary screeched as she jumped up and down like an excited chimp. "It's really working!" She held on to the wheel and turned it.

"We're coming about! Riley, boys, watch the sails!"

Riley had to shake herself to focus on the job at hand. The yacht was so much bigger than their old boat and needed more sails and space to move about. But with the wind and her father and Galina working with them, they pulled away from the boat's graveyard and glided smoothly along the coast of the Forbidden Zone.

Soon the open ocean spread out before them. "This is it," Andrew called from the water. "We're on our way. Boys, I need your help to bring me on board."

After Riley's father embraced Galina and said his goodbyes, he was hauled on board. It was then that Riley saw the full change in him. Her father had become a talking dolphin.

"Dad . . . ," Riley cried.

"Don't worry about me," he said. "Like Gideon says, when we leave Atlantis, the change may reverse. But until then, I wouldn't turn down a blanket soaked with salt water. This fresh rainwater is starting to sting."

While Alfie collected a blanket and wet it with ocean water, Riley knelt beside her father. "Dad, what if Gideon was wrong? What if you don't change back?"

Mary called, "Then we'll deal with it. Just as long as you're all safe."

That offered little comfort to Riley as she helped wrap the soaked blanket around her father the way people did with beached whales.

"We'll be fine," he said. "And if the worst case happens, we'll move to Florida and I'll live in the ocean. It will give my research a whole new perspective." He tried to smile, but his face wouldn't allow it.

From over the side of the boat, they heard Galina start to sing. But it was louder and more urgent than ever before.

Riley ran up to the side. "Galina, what's happening?"

Galina pointed to the open water. The gray, rainy skies were changing as black-and-red scudding clouds filled the horizon.

Riley turned back to her family. "It's the storm that brought us here! It's coming back to stop us!"

37

THE STORM CAME UPON THEM JUST AS quickly as it had when they were on the *Event Horizon*. No matter how much Mary turned the wheel, it was right behind them and gaining speed.

The water turned choppy and the winds rose. As they watched, the Leviathan started to bear down on the *Moon Dancer*.

"Galina," Riley cried. "Can you stop it?"

The mermaid shook her head and pointed. She started to sing.

Riley followed Galina's arm and saw the multiple heads at the surface. Some had arms raised in the air. These were the terrifying merfolk, the ones that

Riley first saw from the *Event Horizon* and the ones that brought them to Atlantis.

"Are they controlling the storm?" Riley called.

Galina nodded.

"And the Leviathan?"

Again the mermaid nodded.

The immense sea serpent glided up to the yacht and struck the front end. Not so hard as to damage it, but enough to knock it around like a toy boat in a bathtub.

"He wants us to go back," Andrew called.

"No!" Mary shouted. "We're getting these kids home!"

"Boys, help me," Riley's father called. "Hold me up at the side of the boat. I want to speak with them."

Bastian and Alfie lifted Andrew to the side of the yacht. He struggled to stand on his tail fluke. He flapped his front fins at the merfolk. "Let them go home," he cried. "Have you forgotten what it is to care for your children? These are mine, and I won't let you keep them here!"

As the storm descended on them, the waves grew higher and winds whipped faster. The Leviathan made another pass at the yacht. It raised itself high out of the water and came down on the front bow.

The boat's back end was lifted out of the water, throwing everyone down to the deck.

"Stop!" Andrew shouted at the Leviathan. He flapped along the deck, getting closer to the sea serpent's massive head. "Release them!"

The serpent slid back into the water, but kept bumping the yacht, driving it back toward Atlantis.

"Everyone, come here," Andrew called.

Riley ran up to her father.

"Listen to me now," Andrew said. "This will be the hardest thing I will ever ask of you, but you must do as I say."

By the look in his eyes, Riley already knew what he was going to say. "No, Dad, please . . ."

"Riley, I must go back in the water. I have to stop them. They can't keep you here."

"Daddy, no!" Riley cried. "Please, you can't."

"Uncle Andrew, the Leviathan will kill you," Alfie said.

"No, it won't. It's intelligent, I can feel it. So are the others out there. They used to be people; I have to talk to them, reason with them and explain why they must let you go. With Galina beside me, we can clear a path for you to go home."

"But you'll come back, right, Uncle Andrew?" Alfie said.

Andrew started to shake his head.

"No . . . ," Riley wept.

"Honey, I have to stay," he said. "Look at me, we both know the truth. I belong in the ocean now. Maybe I always have. I knew I could never make it home. Not looking like this."

"But Gideon said you could change back when we leave Atlantis, or—or we could live in Florida," Riley wept.

"This is going to be so hard for you to hear, but I don't want to change back. I love being what I am now. I belong to the ocean. I know it's selfish of me and you may hate me for it, but I need to stay. You know it, too, don't you?"

Riley sniffed. Finally she nodded.

"I love you more than anything, but you must let me go. The ocean has always been my second home. It calls to me every minute I'm on land, beckoning me back. I can't give it up now."

Riley could hardly see her father through her tears. "But, Daddy, I love you. . . ."

"And I love you too. Please tell your mother and

Danny that I will always love them, but I have to go."

He looked at Bastian and Alfie. "Please put me back in the water."

"Daddy, no."

"Please, Riley, try to understand. I belong here."

A million thoughts and memories flashed through Riley's head. Her father was right. He always preferred the ocean to being on land. On the rare occasions he was home, he would be planning his next trip, or listening to whales. It was always the ocean. . . . It called to him like a siren. Riley never doubted that he loved her, her mother, and Danny, but the ocean was always his first love.

Finally she nodded and helped Alfie and Bastian lift him in the air and carry him over to the railing.

Riley's father craned his head as much as he could to look at Mary. "Hold her steady, sis. Get these kids home!"

Mary was still at the wheel, squeaking and howling in sadness. She nodded. "I love you, Andrew."

"I love you too." He looked at Riley. "Now kiss me goodbye and let me go."

Riley threw her arms around her dolphin father

and held him tight. "I love you, Daddy. Go home and be free. . . ."

Riley, Alfie, and Bastian lifted him over the side of the yacht. He tumbled into the water and surfaced. With Galina at his side, the two of them swam at the merfolk.

Riley ran to the front of the yacht and peered down into the water. These would be the last moments with her father and they were too precious to miss. In the water, her father and Galina swam around the giant Leviathan.

"Please," Pea called, "I can't see. What is happening?"

Bastian bent down and picked him up. "Andrew and Galina are talking to the Leviathan and ocean people."

Pea looked back at Riley and said softly, "Your father is a great man."

Riley was unable to speak as she watched her father in the water. Soon the bumping of the Leviathan against the yacht stopped. The other merfolk sank beneath the surface and the sky started to clear, leaving only the post–Red Moon rain.

"Daddy!" Riley called.

Her father rose to the surface again. Then dove down. A moment later, he leaped out of the water and twirled joyously in the air and splashed down again.

"I love you, Riley!" he called. "Be happy!"

Riley nodded. Finally she called down to Galina, "Please take care of my dad!"

The mermaid nodded, waved a final time, and dove beneath the waves.

They did not surface again.

38

MARY STOOD AT THE HELM, STEERING the *Moon Dancer* smoothly over the water. During their time preparing the boat for departure, she and Riley's father had salvaged directional equipment, charts, and a compass from the *Event Horizon*. Settling on a course, she directed the yacht toward Miami.

During that time, Mary took Riley aside and handed a cell phone to her.

"Where did you get this?" Riley cried.

"We found the other emergency packs on the *Event Horizon*," Mary said. "Your dad left a message for you and your family on there. He said you were not to watch it until you got home with your mother and brother."

"But—"

"Riley, after he changed so much, Andrew knew he couldn't come with us. He said he belonged to the ocean. He was so torn between his love for you and the family, and the water. In the end, he knew he just couldn't leave it."

Riley took the phone and looked at it. For so long she'd resented her father's relationship with the ocean. She felt like he always chose it over the family. This time it was true, he had. But somehow, after everything they'd been through in Atlantis, losing him to the ocean didn't destroy her like she thought it would.

Happiness was so precious, and seeing her father in his true element, it was pure joy. He was gone. But it wasn't divorce; it wasn't death or abandonment. She had lost her father to a dream and she knew her family would be okay.

Three days passed and there was still no sign of change within her aunt, Miss Pigglesworth, Pea, or Maggie. Nothing was said about it, as everyone hoped they needed more time.

The sun was shining brightly overhead as Riley stood at the railing, watching the water. In the distance a humpback whale breached and landed with a big splash. Riley waved at it as fresh tears came to her eyes. "Say hello to my father. . . ."

It still felt like her heart had been torn from her chest even though she knew her dad would be happy in his new life. And Galina now had two devoted fathers.

Needing to be alone, Riley spent most of her time in Miss Pigglesworth's cabin with Maggie. The bleeding finally stopped, but Maggie remained unconscious. Riley prayed her mother would be able to save her.

It was during these quiet moments that the reality of the situation finally struck her.

She was going home.

But everything had changed. Her aunt Mary was now a talking spider monkey. Alfie loved her just the same, but what kind of life were they facing? If Mary didn't turn back, she would have to spend the rest of her life in hiding with Pea and Maggie. What was going to happen to them? Riley knew they would be welcome in her home. But would they be prisoners? What about Bastian and Miss Pigglesworth? Did they have family left? Would they leave or stay?

"Riley! Riley, come out on deck!" Alfie called excitedly.

Riley wiped away her tears and left Maggie settled in bed. She walked out onto the deck.

"Look!" Alfie said, pointing up.

"My oh my!" Pea cried, shielding his eyes with his hand. He was out of his cloak and enjoying the freedom from it. "What kind of bird is that?"

"It's not a bird," Alfie said. "It's an airplane."

"That's an airplane?" Bastian asked.

Alfie grinned. "It sure is." Alfie threw his arms around Riley and embraced her tightly. "Shorty, we did it! We got away from Atlantis!"

Riley reached into her pocket and pulled out the cell. Her hands were shaking as she dialed a number she thought she'd never dial again.

"Hello?"

Her mother's voice brought fresh tears to Riley's eyes. She sniffed and nodded to Alfie. "Mom . . . ?"

"Riley!" her mother cried. "Riley, is it really you?"

"Yes, Mom, it's me. I'm here with Alfie and Mary. We're on a sailboat called the *Moon Dancer*. Please, would you and Danny get to the port in Miami? We're finally coming home."

ACKNOWLEDGMENTS

What a strange and unpleasant time we've all been through. Since I first started writing this book, the world we all knew, just a short time ago, is gone. Now we need to get used to wearing masks all the time and washing our hands until they bleed, and are becoming far too comfortable with the term "social distancing."

If there is only one good thing to say about this "Covid" era, it's that we are all going through it together. No one is exempt from it, and this one virus binds us all together as human beings.

So if you are reading this book while you are in a "lockdown" (that's another word we're getting far too used to hearing), then please know that I am there with you. All writers and artists are.

To be honest, it's been difficult for me to write during this time. But it's knowing that you're out there that keeps me going.

So in these acknowledgments, I wish to acknowledge YOU. Yes, you, my dear readers, because if it weren't for you, I think this time of uncertainty and illness would have been so much worse for me.

Of course, I am still eternally grateful to my agent,

Veronique Baxter, and to my wonderful editor, Anna Parsons, and the team at Simon & Schuster that also keep me on the right track when it's so easy to be derailed.

But mainly, it's you.

I love you all and wish you a wonderful and safe tomorrow. We'll get there together . . . you and me. I know we will. And we'll all be stronger for it.

Stay safe and stay happy. . . .